July 18/2017

To Lilo &
Brenda

The
Road
That
Led
to
Somewhere

Wishing you
continued
Peace and
Harmony

Christine Moody, the wife of Dr. Charles D Moody
Founder of the National Alliance of Black
School Educators (NABSE), presenting the book
to former Prime Minister of South Africa Nelson Mandela

The Road That Led
to Somewhere

Tour group being guided through the Historic Site upon which the book is based.

Library of Congress Catalogue Number
    PS8595-A44R62   C813'-54   C80-094329-5   PR9199.3.W352R62

This book was manufactured by Olive Publishing Company Ltd., 932 Lakeshore Road 107 RR#3 Essex, Ontario Canada N8M 2X7

(519) 727-4866

ISBN: 978-0-919007-00-0

    7 8 9 10

Bryan Walls receives Chancellor's Award

The Iona College Chancellor's Award for 2002 was presented to Dr. Bryan Walls at a special gathering at the University of Windsor February 26.

The Award, which is a stained glass representation of a Cross of Iona, recognizes the outstanding achievements of an individual who has worked to promote social justice, to advance humanitarian causes and to exemplify the universal spirit of compassion.

Dr. Bryan Walls (right) accepts Iona College Chancellor's Award from Rev. Jurrien Camman

Dr. Walls filled these requirements admirably. He is the author of *"The Road that Led to Somewhere,"* which tells of the escape of slaves from the southern United States to Upper Canada and the development of their settlement in the area now known as Puce in Essex County.

Dr. Walls is also a founding member of the John Freeman Walls Underground Railroad Museum in Puce. He continues to find ways to serve not only the local community but the international one as well. He visits the local schools to tell the story of the Underground Railroad and the struggles of the former slaves as they settled in this new country. He also works with the Toronto Police Force to further their anti-racism initiatives.

In accepting the award, Dr. Walls recited poetry and told stories of a forgotten native people in the Caribbean Islands. "History is so valuable," he said. "When we understand that all people are capable of cruelty, we realize that all people are also able to love and respect their follow human beings."

We were pleased that our Chancellor, Rev. Jurrien Camman, was recovered sufficiently from heart surgery to present this award on behalf of the college.

THIS BOOK IS DEDICATED TO OLIVE MARIE GRAYER WALLS WHOSE INSPIRATION DURING AND AFTER LIFE HELPED IN THE WRITING OF THIS STORY. JUST AS SHE LIVED IN HARMONY AND PEACE WITH EVERYONE FORTUNATE ENOUGH TO BE TOUCHED BY HER, SO SHALL THIS BOOK ATTEST TO RACIAL HARMONY AND PEACE WORLD-WIDE.

ACKNOWLEDGEMENTS

The inspiration to write and preserve not only personal history, but also Canadian and American history began three years ago during the most trying of circumstances. The near selling of the family homestead to strangers was one of the circumstances. The deed went back to the hands of a fugitive slave. Mr. Robert Baksi, my lawyer friend, was the problem solver who, through brilliant legal manoeuvers, brought it back into my, and thus the family's, hands. I thank you, Bob.

The council of Maidstone Township and Mr. Leonard Phillips, a noted historian, are acknowledged for their assistance in designating the property an historical site.

On the same theme of history, the historian of the family, and a member of the Michigan Genealogical Society, Mr. Floyd B. Walls II, of Ypsilanti, Michigan, cannot go unnoticed. Floyd researched for four years in harmony with myself, and was tirelessly devoted to the project. He entered into the "King's Chamber", so to speak, and uncovered historical wealth for Canada and the United States. He unfolded academic wealth that would rival any precious chest filled with gold or diamonds. I thank you, Floyd. Floyd's documentation is a story in itself.

A whole list of acclamations would be needed to describe the professionalism of Nate and Phyllis, owners of ATTIC TYPESETTING in Toronto. Thank You, Nate and Phyllis.

Another list of acclamations would be need to describe the quality of advice of my editor, Edna Barker. Edna is a freelance editor in Toronto and in my opinion the best. Thank you, Edna.

For encouragement I was given, and friendly sharing of helpful information, I would like to thank Marty Gervais of Black Moss Press, Judy DePassio of DePassio Art and Design and Jean Scheifele of Choice Publications. Jean's book, *Live, Live, Live with Enthusiasm,* greatly helped reinforce my own. I thank you again.

I am grateful to Mrs. Bealey for allowing me to get to know her well enough to call her "Bahtsie." Your qualified opinions were more than just rewarding. Thank You.

Mr. Derek Patey is the creative quarterback behind this book. I respect his modesty enough to resist filling two pages of acclamations. Thank You, Derek.

My Aunt Lylia Walls Joyner gave me the title and the confidence to write in a "real life style" that has given me hours of pleasure. May your life be a happy one.

My brother, Bradley "Little Hawk" Walls, must be thanked for sharing in my triumphs and disasters, and as someone once said, "helping me treat the two imposters both the same."

My parents and grandparents, I love you, but you already both know that.

I wish to thank Tony Davis, my good friend in Nassau. I smile when I think of your hospitality.

Appreciation goes out to Tasker Kelsey for his understanding of the trials and tribulations of a dentist who loves his patients first and business second.

I thank my relatives and friends for being just that, especially John and Jane for living this story.

I would be remiss not to thank my kindred spirits and friends, Allen and Winston Walls for their tireless efforts in bringing history alive in the form of The John Freeman Walls Historic Site and Underground Railroad Museum. Esther Gordy Edwards, the director of our Sister Museum has given me great inspiration and encouragement. She is truly a source of good in the world. Paul Murray, one of the greatest painters of our time has given to me personally and the Historic Site a great gift, the compliment of saying that both I and the Historic Site gave him great inspiration to create.

So, as a final and loud expression of gratitude, I thank the readers of Maidstone township, the United States, Canada and the world for turning to Mile I of *The Road That Led To Somewhere.*

Dr. Bryan Walls and Esther Gordy Edwards

JOHN FREEMAN WALLS HISTORIC SITE

In 1846 John Freeman Walls, a fugitive slave from North Carolina, built this log cabin on land purchased from the Refugee Home Society. This organization was founded by the abolitionists Henry Bibb, publisher of the Voice of the Fugitive, and the famous Josiah Henson. The cabin, subsequently served as a terminal of the underground railroad and the first meeting place of the Puce Baptist Church. Although many former slaves returned to the United States following the American Civil War, Walls and his family chose to remain in Canada. The story of their struggles, forms the basis of the book "The Road That Led To Somewhere" by Dr. Bryan E. Walls.

Erected by Proverbs Heritage Foundation with the assistance of Maidstone Township and the Ministry of Culture and Recreation.

Contents

Part I   The Mystery of Freedom

Part II   1813–1845
Escape to Freedom

Part III   1845–1909
Life in Canada of fugitive slaves
through the eyes and hearts
of John and Jane Walls

Part IV   1845–1909
Life in Canada of John and Jane Walls

Part V   1945–1979
Freedom's Mile

Part VI   1979
Freedom's Hope
Clearwater, Florida

Royal Canadian Mounted Police in front of entrance to the twenty acre Historic Site in Canada.

Historic Site is Located 20 minutes from the Detroit - Windsor Border in Maidstone Twp. Highway 401, Exit Puce Road, North One Mile

To order "The Road That Led to Somewhere"
Contact Olive Publishing Company Ltd.
932 Lakeshore Road 107
RR# 3 Essex, Ontario Canada
N8M 2X7

Introduction

Present-day inhabitants of Canada and present-day descendants of American abolitionists have been given a legacy in the field of human rights, of which they can be justly proud, and which they must perpetuate in order to not betray the legacy of their forefathers.

This documented novel tells the reason, through the struggle of one family. Their's is a one-in-four million story. Nevertheless their story symbolizes the endeavors of all the families who specifically followed the side of the tree that the moss grows on and the light of the north star. Their story more generally expresses the desire of all families to remain free and live in peace and love and harmony.

This is not another ancestral research novel, but it takes a positive quality that such novels have to offer and uses it. This quality, the fitting together of the pieces of an interesting puzzle, enhances a great love story, an adventure story, a historical document and a sermon on the need for better understanding between people—now and in the future, based on the history of the past.

I thank you for taking the time to read this fictionalized biography and feel certain it will be time well spent. The time that I spent writing certainly gave me great pleasure. I decided to tell this incredible story through Earl Walls, a member of the Boxing Hall of Fame. Earl provides the framework for the plot. His mind's eye, which represents, in reality, his thoughts, peruses and reflects on research that took four years to collect and one hundred thirty-four years to create. He discovers a rich legacy for all peoples who desire to learn more about how to live in racial harmony and peace. He gives an incredible, extreme, a one-in-four-million story, and asks the reader to make his own decisions based on his own individual experiences. He makes the reader feel real, and happy.

Dr. Walls presenting his novel to Nobel Peace Prize Winner Bishop Desmond TuTu of South Africa on behalf of the Government of Canada.

Mrs. Rosa Parks and Pathways to Freedom students visiting the Walls Historic Site.

Everybody pay attention
Listen what I'm going to mention

PART I

The Mystery of Freedom

The Road that Led to Somewhere
Has brought us all the way to where we are
Follow the side of the tree that the moss grows on
And the light of the north star

MILE I

The cigarette smoke curled languidly towards the rafters, spurred on by the excitement of thousands of fight fans awaiting the scheduled contest. There would be twelve three-minute rounds; the victor would hold the Pacific Northwest heavyweight boxing title, the highest boxing honour leading to the World Title. Edmonton Arena had never known such knife-cutting tension. Olive Walls, dressed in her finest second-hand clothes, felt this tension. But she was helped by Frank, her husband, and five representatives of their ten children, to smile in such a way that a picture could not do justice. Her son Earl, third contender in the world and Canadian Champ, British Empire best,[1] was aspiring to represent Canada as the first Canadian black world heavyweight champion. He needed this win to further his climb.

The two boxers were the personification of sinew and muscle as they entered the arena. For what seemed like an eternity to Olive, they stood toe-to-toe in the ring. In her heart her son stood not in a ring but a cage, and she was afraid; a chill swept her spine and she wept. She heard from somewhere, "Earl Walls is coloured; I did not know there were any blacks in Canada."

"You must have heard of the underground railroad, you fool," Olive wanted to say, but instead she yelled, "That's my son!"

The bell rang. Earl thought, "No, no, not already, what am I doing here? Why? My family, yes, my family. I cannot let them down." His ear was red within seconds and he knew for certain why he was here—it was the need to survive and fight his way to the top, just as John Freeman Walls, his great grandfather, had fought his way to freedom.

A crushing blow missed his ribs but caught his stomach.

"Thank God for the hundreds of sit-up exercises I did," Earl thought. "This is the champion I am fighting; my God, relax, relax, think, think, don't cry, what cry, my mama didn't raise no cowards."

"Combination," he heard someone yell from somewhere; yes, the yell came from his corner. "Move, Earl, move, raise your gloves." The champ was confident; Earl was smart and hungry for success.

Two lightning lefts landed before the champ realized he had been hit. When he did realize it, a right was making him grimace and his mouthpiece was floating into the judges' seats. The bell rang; round one was over.

Earl went to his corner. He was the product of years of practice and training.

"Good, Earl, good, you have to move more, Earl, you are too flat-footed. It's round two, Earl." It's round three, four, five, six, seven, eight, nine.

"Earl, you are winning, I think, but he is the champ, Earl, and he is white; you have to win big, Earl!"

"Is a knock-out big enough?" Earl muttered.

"That's my boy, Earl, that's my boy. Earl, I know you are tired but keep your gloves high."

Round ten came. Earl was fighting by instinct, the champ by skill and experience. A right hook missed Earl's jaw, the career-fatal knock-out punch, but hit his throat instead. Earl did not realize its significance; he just felt pain and anger. He countered with a blow to the nose and an uppercut to the jaw. The champ's jaw joint moved backwards and the brain fluid was not cushion enough to keep his knees from buckling; he was down.

The count was ten; Earl's mind raced with excitement. "I did it, I love Canada, I love my family, I love. . . My God, I cannot speak, My God, I cannot talk." Earl's larynx had been busted. The happiness and tears in his mother's eyes were the only things that kept his own tears back.

In 1978 in Toronto, Earl sat at the head table in the banquet room, awaiting his induction into the Hall of Fame. He gently rubbed his throat and remembered the great contest which had occurred twenty-four years ago. He thought also of the months he had spent retraining his vocal chords to his even-now-limited articulation. He was worried that the effects of this battle scar might somehow muffle the words of his acceptance speech. As he lifted a glass of water to his lips, he thought also of his mother, whom he loved dearly, and that he would gladly erase all this glory to have her alive again.

Earl, you are a black, be proud and strong. This thought pushed back the nervousness he was falling into. The thought was his; the words were his mother's. *You are John, the slave's descendant, just as good as anyone.* These were the words that finished the motivational phrase uttered countless times during Olive's life. This phrase, and especially the words *the slave's descendant,* resounded in Earl's head and gave him the strength to rise from his chair and deliver an eloquent acceptance speech.

As Earl lay in bed that night, he reflected on this great moment in his life, this great moment in Canadian boxing history. "I was the first black from the Maidstone slave settlement to represent my whole country. I was third contender in the world when I retired, and rated the best in the British Empire."

You are the slave's descendant, just as good as anyone. The saying still crept into his mind. It annoyed him that this thought would somehow distract him from his happiness and excitement.

As Earl tossed in his king-size bed, he became even more pensive. "If racial harmony existed for my great grandpar-

13

ents, my God, why can't it be better today? I must, in some way, tell the world why they made their incredible journey, and I must somehow tell the world how it happened. And having told why, and how, I must ask the world to live in peace and love and harmony. They fought for freedom, they lived and died in freedom and, because of them I, my sister and my family travel the new miles of the road in honour of Canada, the United States and the world."

The portion of Earl's mind that controlled his fertile, subconscious thoughts was making preparation to unfold a mystery.

Christmas came, and with it the life-long tradition of a family reunion in Puce, Ontario, outside of Windsor. As many of his ten brothers and sisters as could, plus nieces, nephews and cousins, would be there. A house full, no less, would bring Christmas in the right way.

Frank Walls was playing euchre and fending off teams of his offspring who were trying to dethrone him. Rumour had it that Frank would, if necessary, signal his partner in crucial situations. However, in seventy-eight years he had never been caught—or at least he had such respect from his heirs that it was purposely overlooked.

Fun and frivolity were in the atmosphere, and relatives and friends from as far as Windsor and Ypsilanti looked forward to dropping in. Olive's famous hospitality lived on, continued largely by Freida, Lylia and Sandra, her protegées.

Earl sat majestically, his still-athletic frame attracting stares and pokes from young onlookers. "You mean he really was the Canadian heavyweight champion before Chuvalo?" Earl, however, was neither annoyed nor pleased by such attention, for his mind was deep in thought. A thought provoked by a haunting phrase, made even stronger by the physical surroundings of his mother's house.

Earl, you are a Walls, be proud, and the slave's descendant, just as good as anyone.

14

Earl, half asleep, smiled with contentment as if he had found the answer to some mystery; he knew what he had to do.

The next morning Earl walked from his father's farm, as if leaving the present and walking into the past. Earl Walls stood motionless in knee-deep snow; a piercing wind whipped at his pant legs. Frost clung to the aged cemetery stone at his feet.

He stopped and squinted, his eyes trying to peer through the tombstone and into the past. He ran thick, black hands over the smooth stone, as if trying to decipher the mystery, a message whose meaning had been buried as deeply as the two people resting beneath the stone. White woman and black man. He rose and a flock of pheasants suddenly flushed nearby, a rabbit ran towards a peaceful creek and the sounds of wings faded into the distance. His family's Canadian cemetery in Maidstone Township, on the Puce Road, how could it be the key to unlocking the mystery?

A chill ran up Earl's spine as he entered the house and realized he had returned to the beginning, some one hundred thirty-three years ago. The homestead, a lopsided, buckling log cabin, stood on four rocks, just across an open field from the serene gathering of family plots. Earl had visited here many times as a boy, but then it was just an unusual house with forgotten, yet somewhat beckoning, graves nearby. He felt an almost eerie feeling. The feeling grew stronger as he searched through the cabin's cramped, tiny rooms. It took time, but he understood the strange feeling that had started the night of his indoctrination into the Sports Hall of Fame. Bits and pieces were being recollected from boyhood, conversations with ninety-four-year-old Aunt Stella Butler. He wondered why they hadn't seemed important then, but now the pieces were being tied together.

The significance of the log cabin, the cemetery and, most of all, the people buried there to him, Canada and the world

15

was coming alive to the grown man. He lay on Aunt Stella's bed. At ninety-four she was still alive and going strong. The log cabin had undulating clay floors which, when she was around, were so clean you could almost eat from them. The cabin was a summer home for Stella and her seventy-year-old son Joey.

Earl fell asleep in the room of John Freeman Walls, the slave, and Jane, his wife. Earl's fertile, subconscious thoughts turned back through the pages of his family legend and Canadian and American history. His subconscious mind raced back to the nineteenth century, and finally slowed and focussed on a distant southern plantation, long since destroyed but never to be forgotten. The final mystery was unfolding.

PART II

1813–1845

Escape to Freedom

MILE II

Troublesome Creek wound through Rockingham County, North Carolina. The creek's main claim to fame was that it flowed in front of the governor's mansion.[1] But to two African slaves of Mr. Eli Walls on the morning in 1813, the winding creek's fame was enhanced by the fact that it flowed past the tiny cabin in which their son was being born. The Guinea woman's hips heaved, her widened legs straining under the pressure of childbirth. Her lips were dry, her eyes watery, but she would not cry—this was too momentous an occasion. She uttered words in her native tongue, which escaped the interpretation of her American-born midwives. The infant's head, already haired, was coming from her womb. The excitement in the log cabin at the fact that it was not a breech birth magnified the anticipation. They were not to be disappointed. The jet-black complexion of the infant shone through even the blood on its body. The midwife, Amanda, held the baby by his legs and slapped his buttocks, and he cried. John Walls was at the beginning of a long road.

The mother was referred to as the Guinea woman, indicating that she was brought from the Guinea coast. She was proud of her son's jet-black complexion. It would, at times, give him great pride and at others, great frustration. There are rusty black Africans but to the Guinea woman, her son's shiny black complexion set him above others. However, her son was not in Africa, her homeland, and parameters that would normally give status in Africa meant persecution here in North Carolina during slavery. Oh, how glad she was that her son could not compare the life he could have had to the one he would have.

The other, more experienced midwives were also busy on the night of John's birth, as the big house was bustling with excitement, too. The strain on the face of the master's wife came from the initial stages of the flux and childbirth. The room was mixed with the excitement of childbirth and the strange excitement that pending death can bring, before it turns into sadness and tears. As Daniel Walls was born, his mother died.

Eli Walls stood at the foot of the bed, his eyes watery and red. His lower lip quivered as he realized his wife would be a companion no longer. The small, pink child held in the black arms of the midwife only served to kindle the anger he felt inside. He yelled, "Why does my wife have to die and you nigger wenches live?" The fear in the midwife's face could not be duplicated in any period save slavery.

The disease of slavery had different stages, which eroded the physical and mental being of the victim. The slave master often became a victim with the symptoms of egotism, indifference, and finally inhumanity to other human beings, causing the death of his soul. Eli Walls was no exception, and the death of his wife set his disease at its final state—an incurable situation. He left the big house with whip in hand and, rather than release frustration on inanimate objects, went directly to the slave's quarters and relieved himself through their screams.

The first stage of the slave's disease was fear. The fervent desire to be free traversed through frustration and ended with freedom in the form of death or, to the very fortunate, the heaven named Canada that they sang about in their songs. However certain slaves had been torn from the wombs of their native Africa before they were truly ready to be born. For them, the fear stage of their disease, slavery, had mutated into anger more than frustration. Such was the case of Hannabal.

Hannabal stood outside the cabin he had built; inside was the newborn child he had fathered. He was in full smile when the screams of slaves being whipped reached his ear.

"Hannabal, Hannabal, Master Eli done gone crazy with grief and 'bout to kill all of us. What should we do?" The words came from the voice of a meeker slave as he ran into Hannabal's presence.

"Can I not even be happy at the birth of my first son? Do I have to be reminded that I am a slave even on this occasion?" Hannabal turned and walked away, knowing the concern of his fellow in chains was unfounded. Master Eli held too much esteem for material wealth to permanently damage his property.

The walk along Troublesome Creek was to the north. Hannabal eyed the north star and thought, "The side of the tree the moss grows on is the way to Canada and out of slavery. My newborn son must learn what I have learned about the road to freedom. I cannot run. I cannot run." With this Hannabal fell to his knees but was too proud to weep. "Allah be praised," was all that his thick, black lips could utter.

Thus into this world John Walls (black) and Daniel Walls (white) were born.

In the following months the Guinea woman suckled both John and Daniel, as her breasts were more than ample for two children. Her frame and breasts were even large enough to allow for simultaneous suckling and she would often smile at the sight of the two beautiful babies touching and playing. As far-fetched as it might seem, it was a foundation for an almost brotherly love. John and Daniel grew up together, rooted in the same life-giving milk but burdened by the social climate of slavery.

As one year blended into the next, the relationship born in infancy allowed John's and Daniel's boyhoods to continue in a manner unusual for the times—unusual because they were the best of friends. A smile would come to the face of many an adult on seeing the two boys at play. During certain games the boys would alternate playing slave master and slave, their young, innocent minds not knowing, or caring about, the true significance of each. They were merely mimicking their elders.

Troublesome Creek held a special attraction for the boys. Almost every morning, early, they could be seen running along it, jumping, laughing, turning cartwheels and doing handstands. Wrestling along the bank of Troublesome Creek until one or the other said, "Give?" was the limit of their aggression to each other. The two innocent boys were happy. On occasion Daniel would even teach John how to read, a definite taboo during slavery.

In John's fifteenth year, an incident occurred that caused his first psychological scar and was a continual reminder of his true plight. He and Daniel were playing master and slave and it was John's turn to be master. Unfortunately, the boys did not see Eli walking towards them, or perhaps they did not appreciate the significance of their mimicking and found no reason to care. John let out a blast of words he had often heard Eli use.

"You no-good nigger, Daniel, I am going to skin your black hide."

Daniel immediately replied, "No, master John, please." But before he could finish, his friend was being carried off towards a tree. Before his fifteen-year-old mind could realize what was happening Daniel saw his friend being tied to the tree and whipped to the limit of consciousness by his father.

"Don't you ever even pretend to be master on my plantation, you uppity little nigger." The words resounded in the boy's ears time after time. Daniel instinctively pulled his father's arm, trying to get him to stop. "We're sorry, we're sorry, Father," he said. The words tempered Eli's rage and possibly saved John's life. Eli half dragged Daniel along Troublesome Creek and back to the big house while John, Daniel's friend, lay on the ground, his young body branded with the beginnings of slavery's infectious disease.

John remained where he lay for several minutes—several minutes that seemed like an eternity, several minutes that allowed centuries of his people's persecution to pass before his eyes. When John rose he was not the same as before; he had been a young boy, oblivious to society's influence, protected to a large degree by his unprecedented friendship with Daniel. His heart had been pure. Now he knew he was a slave, a possession, a material object and for the first time he appreciated the words repeated many times by his father. *Remember, the north star and the side of the tree the moss grows on is the way to Canada.* John made a silent vow. Even though it was mandatory for slaves to take the last name of their slave master, he would one day be called John "Freeman" Walls. The cool water of the stream carried away some of the pain and blood that had crusted on John, the slave.

Daniel's face was red with anxiety and fear. The fear was for his friend with whom he had had an almost brotherly relationship these past fifteen years. The anxiety was because of his father's inhuman nature. His young mind was beginning, miraculously, to understand that Eli, his father, who stood looking out the window of the big house towards the slave quarters with a blank stare, was just as pained as John. Eli had inherited what his father and his father before him had acquired. Daniel was attempting, in his young mind, to explain why the illogical system of slavery was so destructive to the spiritual health of his race.

In the field of genetics one may not know when a mutant gene will express itself. Somewhere back in ancient history—the precise instant is unknown—the bad seed of inhumanity to less fortunate human beings had expressed itself. The powers of good and evil had somehow been mutated. From that point on certain men became the carriers of the mutation of man's proper treatment of fellow man.

Daniel could almost hear what had been said: "This new continent, Africa, has fellow human beings whom we can help, and they can help us to improve our souls and our capacity to love and do good." This was mutated into: "This new continent, Africa, has animals whom we can rape and pillage and turn into black gold for our greedy aspirations here on earth."

"How can they be so ungrateful?" Daniel heard his father say. "Just last Sunday in church the text was Servant, Obey Thy Master. In my father's church they preached servant, obey thy master, and in his father's church they preached servant, obey thy master."

Daniel's mind already resisted the effects of the distortion of good and evil that had so encompassed his forefathers. He thought to himself, "Does the sermon not mean that all men are servants and must obey God, not that men themselves become gods and masters of other of God's children, be they black, white or any nationality, race, creed or colour?"

The rationalization and distortion of the statement servant, obey thy master, had been occurring for centuries. It had spread its bad seed onto fertile ground, and made Eli, as he stood looking out the window of his plantation, but a victim. The distorted philosophy had, over the generations, been reinforced by the approval and encouragement of Church and state. Daniel felt sorrow and almost forgiveness for his father as he realized that Eli's wounds went deeper into his soul than the physical wounds on John's back.

As Eli looked out the window again towards the slave quarters, he could see a commotion taking place and could sense the reason for it. Hannabal was certainly not thinking of forgiveness as he ran along the creek, half stumbling over its thick foliage, to the cleared area where he knew his son and Daniel often played. Word had come to him from a sympathetic informant who knew Hannabal well enough to be almost reluctant to tell him of the incident. He knew the news would create unparalled rage in Hannabal's proud African heart.

Tears came to Hannabal's eyes as he saw John crawling from the creek; John's actions were instinctual. "John, John, my son," Hannabal cried. "Allah be merciful, Fa Toubob.'"

24

The African words, seldom used, were taboo, as their meaning—"kill white man"—would cause the greatest penalties to the individual user. Penalty was far from Hannabal's mind. He lifted John into his strong, black arms and cradled him with such an expression of love that there was no doubt in his mind that he would defend his son even if it meant giving up his own life. John had never seen tears in his father's eyes, but now they flowed like the running water of Troublesome Creek. The tears traversed Hannabal's cheeks, crossed thick, black, quivering lips and fell onto the forehead of his son, across his cheek and onto his mouth and lips, which were open. The sense and taste of his father's own tears intoxicated John's mind and set it reeling with a mixture of emotions: love, fear, hate, rage and the desire to be free.

Hannabal carried his son oh so gently back to the log cabin father and son had built together. The walk took more time than Hannabal wanted it to. Onlookers formed a simulated funeral procession, as if impending doom were walking with the father and son, who had been made to appear tragic by the chains of slavery.

When the cabin door closed and the other slaves watched the last crack of light being blocked out, they knew only too well that when it opened again all would not be as before. Things were far from being well, but would get worse. Hannabal had no need for their thoughts. He knew he must seek revenge; he knew he must give up his life; he knew he would soon be freed by death.

John and Jubil, Hannabal's wife, could sense the fire raging in their loved one's heart. They were afraid, but they knew words were necessary. John spoke first, knowing he must rise above the pain in his body to protect someone dearer than himself.

"Father, please remember what you taught me, to follow the north star and remember the side of the tree the moss grows on is the road to Canada and freedom. Once you are free one day, I will escape with mother and we will be together like a family again. Better than this, we will die as free men, not slaves. Father, if you are to die, die as a free man, run north, run north."

The expression on Hannabal's face changed from intense commitment to revenge—an endemic requirement of his African tribe whenever a relative was scarred by death—to careful rationalization of the alternative of freedom.

Jubil couldn't speak but she knew her son was right—that no matter what the cost, Hannabal must try to escape rather than seek revenge. Jubil also knew that for Hannabal to stay would be the worst punishment, a punishment that would erode his very nature and make him a personification of walking death.

"Yes, Hannabal, you must run," she said quiveringly.

Hannabal sat on the chair his son had so proudly made and given him for Christmas. He was torn between responsibility to his family, desire to kill and desire to escape. His mind was clouded; fear for his own life had become too unimportant a consideration. With his head held in the palms of his large, black hands, he reflected back over the fifteen years since John's birth and realized that only his great sense of responsibility had kept him from running. He put his son's freedom before his own. *If you remember nothing else I teach you, remember the side of the tree the moss grows on and the north star are the way to freedom. To the north there is a place called Canada, which is a heaven of freedom, John, like my native Africa.*

His words had not fallen on barren soil. John, never more than now, understood their true significance. Hannabal still sat silent in thought, watching a spider crawl over the wall that he and John had built. He remembered the great pride they had taken in their artistic ability. Carpentry, for them, was a source of rescue; work, for them, was a kind of freedom. They were proud to have the same profession as Joseph and another whom they praised during church services. Hannabal knew John now, and even further understood why carpentry made him so valuable to the slave master. The intensity with which he would work was unparalleled on the planation. The slave master was proud and attributed this to fear. Hannabal knew for certain that John was maturing; the son watched the father at work and saw that the father worked, not out of fear, but rather to occupy his mind, to avoid thinking about the terminal stage of slavery's disease, namely the desire to be free.

Hannabal raised his head; John's head and thoughts turned towards his father. As if a great weight of decision had been lifted from the cabin, Hannabal made up his mind: he wanted to be free. And he realized that John, his son, had been properly indoctrinated with the same compulsion. His work was completed; he decided to run north to Canada.

Eli Walls was still at the window, and he saw the procession to Hannabal's cabin. Because he was in the terminal stages of slavery, he could not realize that his life had been saved by John, the slave whom he had so viciously whipped not more than an hour before. He could not accept that his slaves were rational, emotional, caring human beings with hopes, aspirations and desires not unlike those of white folk. A strange apprehension did overpower him at one point; it was enough to prevent him from rushing out with whip in hand to disperse the crowd. He could even be heard muttering, "I wonder if the nigger is planning to kill me. No, no, that would be too intelligent a thought."

After he said this he turned from the window and swallowed a double shot of whiskey to help confuse any fear welling up inside of him. Eli's fit of temper caused what had happened; his arrogance protected him from assuming the blame.

MILE III

A shot was fired, but a loud scream drowned out the noise. John's mother ran out at 3:00 A.M. after Master Eli, begging him to let her husband escape. The horses and men were too frenzied to try to avoid knocking this crazed black woman down. She ran from rider to rider, pleading with unintelligible words.

"Get away, you black wench," they answered her. The men thought only that this was the greatest of all insults to the ego of slavery: a nigger was trying to escape.

Jubil realized her husband had not forewarned her of his escape only to protect her and John from the reprisals of Master Eli, should he, in his rage, insist that they had helped. Ten days had passed since John's beating. The time had almost healed John's physical wounds, but not the wounds in his heart. He knew his father was making preparations to escape but, like Jubil, he did not know when.

The joint carpentry work was suffering. Hannabal would often look at his son, who could not see how to work for the tears in his eyes. "If you cry, John, you will cause suspicion," Hannabal said curtly, but John knew only too well that this display of indifference was only to hold his own tears back. They loved each other.

Jubil almost sensed, as Hannabal made love to her that evening, that it was for the last time. Her arm fell over to the opposite side of the bed where her husband had been each night for the past fifteen years to cushion its fall. His absence made her wake with a start, her heart pounding as if threatened by death.

"Hannabal, Hannabal," she cried. "John, your father."

28

Her own cries were not heard: the horses and men outside the big house were too much competition.

The sound of the rifle made her run from the cabin as if hoping to sacrifice her own life for her husband's. John ran from the slave quarters and Daniel from the big house at approximately the same time. They both picked up the Guinea woman, John's mother and Daniel's mammy, from the ground and half carried her back to her cabin. A river of tears crossed her dust-covered face, as if etching a map which pointed towards her breaking heart.

John and Daniel looked at each other with eyes that finally told and comprehended all. They might never live to see a society of peace and love and harmony in this lifetime. Both simultaneously yelled, "Why, John? Why, Daniel? Why . . ."

After five days the fear on the Guinea woman's face turned to relaxation and excitement. Could her husband have outrun the hounds, staved off wolves and bears, found the moss, followed the north star? My God, he was free!

Ten evenings later her excitement—and part of her sanity—left her. Her husband had outwitted, outrun, outfought all save one. Eli was a man possesed. His companions had wanted to return to their comfortable homes after eight days.

"He has escaped, let's leave it to the bounty hunters up north." But they could not dissuade Eli.

His dogs would find the scent then lose the scent. No one had received sufficient sleep in the past five days and half of the sleep they did get was on horseback; one unfortunate individual had even fallen off and broken his wrist. Eli would not give up.

Hannabal could not believe he had actually endured for so long; his panting was as much a part of him as his accelerated heartbeat. His feet were bloody and his head was light from lack of oxygen. But he ran on. The north star and the moss on the trees were his only interest. Food was a luxury—a raw squirrel had to suffice; drink was more of a necessity, but still less important than running. He could not count the number of streams he had crossed; he was grateful that they confused the hounds enough to keep him out of reach, ungrateful because they sapped his strength. Nevertheless, he would hear the hounds again and again. On the fourteenth day, Hannabal could hardly concentrate on his goal. He ran as if in a trance; the pain in his body, the lack of sleep and sustenance were too overpowering. Then he heard the dogs and Eli's shout: "Do not shoot him. I am going to sell the nigger south and get some of my money back after I skin his black hide."

He could only hope for a second wind, a second wind that had long before been used up. As he reached a clearing, he knew he could not outrun the hounds and horses, but knew he must try. The hunters were laughing and shouting, making jokes of his futile attempt yet angered enough to kill him for the inconvenience he had put them through.

Hannabal was a hundred yards ahead when he felt the pain; his feet were pistons of pain and speed. He felt with the pain a sort of euphoria as a smile crossed his face and a hand went to his chest. The words, "I am free," came from his mouth as he fell.

Eli knew he had seen a slave determined like no other in his lifetime, or in the vicinity of North Carolina's tobacco fields.

"Get up, you no-good nigger." The words were almost a display of kindness and respect that hunters have for a worthy prey.

"Get up, get up." The words were spoken without the usual whip, and brought questioning stares from Eli's companions.

But Hannabal did not move; his heart had burst and he was free.

Jubil beat at Eli's pant legs and clawed at the rope leading to the horse that Hannabal's body was draped over. Eli's greed was the only thing that saved her life. He made preparations to sell the Guinea woman south within a week and would have sold John, too, had not Daniel's quick mind pointed out the need for a good carpenter.

John's black hands trembled as he held his mother on the day of her departure. Her voice and actions displayed a childlike quality he had never seen before. He knew she loved her husband, who was now gone. John knew he loved, but had lost, both of them.

He walked tearfully back to his cabin. At age fifteen, not yet man and not quite boy, he was confused. "Should I seek revenge now or should I wait until I grow older and stronger?" This thought walked with John. As he entered the cabin and sat down on the bed, the sense of confusion left him; lying on the bed was a Bible, opened to Proverbs. He read:

"My son, forget not my laws; but let thine heart keep my commandments: For length of days, and long life, and peace, shall they add to thee." John read this passage and understood. He realized that Daniel was the only one who could have placed the Bible there.

Often in the years that followed, John would read this, his favourite passage, and others to the congregation of church-goers. His loud masculine voice would inspire the followers. "Revenge is mine, sayeth the Lord," one member would say, and another would yell, "Preach the Good Word, John. Hallelujah."

John's unique, though limited, reading ability gave him status during church services. He would joyfully accept invitations to read and preach, and all would be pleased.

"Swing low sweet chariot, coming for to carry me home," the congregation would sing at the end of the service, indicating their longing to be free.

MILE IV

One year of drudgery blended into another, and another, but time and Christianity were having a soothing effect on John's heart. But he needed more. He found it one warm August day when some two hundred slaves had gathered on the bank of Troublesome Creek. The negro spiritual could be heard for miles, sung by some of the best voices of the time. Goose pimples were all over John's body as he was caught in the powerfully emotional atmosphere of Negro revival and baptism ceremonies.

John stepped down the side of the bank, ushered by friends' arms on either side, into the warm water. This place where the creek widened offered excellent advantages for baptism, as at its deepest spot it was only waist deep.

John's shroud clung to his black skin where it had been wetted, perspiration broke out on his forehead and he knew no sensation as overpowering and exciting.

The honours of baptism were performed by Reverend Melvin, a learned slave, a good man and so filled with the Holy Spirit that Eli himself dared not criticize his baptismal ceremonies. Baptism by him meant membership in God's Church, a coveted honour that John was about to experience.

Reverend Melvin held the back of John's head and, with one hand over John's mouth, said, "I baptize thee in the name of the Father, the name of the Son, and the name of the Holy Ghost."

With this he pushed John's limp body under the water of Troublesome Creek. John could feel the surge of energy over his face, as if his troubles were being washed away. He could, for a brief instant, almost see the faces of his father and mother, smiling in delight at their son's accomplishment.

What was no more than fifteen seconds seemed like an eternity, an eternity that John wished would not end.

Reverend Melvin pulled John from the water and could see in his eyes and face, and from the strange tongue that John was speaking, that he was not the same as before. John was a born-again Christian, pure of heart and confident that he could face the trials and tribulations he was destined for in the many scores of years that he struggled to endure.

John almost ran from the water, shouting, laughing and embracing those close by who could not help but feel and share in his happiness. Another was sharing in his happiness also, but from a distance. His searching eyes scanned the crowd as if saying, "You must be, if you haven't already been, baptized also, and feel this great feeling." John saw Daniel, who was standing off some one hundred yards, his presence representing an unheard of precedent for the times. Equally unprecedented was John running to him, his wet shroud still clinging to his jet-black body. His arms, made strong from years of carpentry, were thrown around his white brother, who could not help but reciprocate his black brother's happiness. The slaves who looked on could not understand this strange scene, but knew they were privileged to witness an occasion of racial harmony, a harbinger of a time when racial harmony would be the rule rather than the exception.

MILE V

In the next year, the leading proponent of racial unrest on the plantation fell sick with age and neglect of body. The night Eli died Daniel walked, as if in a trance, from the big house and along Troublesome Creek. "What a fitting name," he thought, "for what is in store for me and the plantation." The tobacco fields were ready for harvesting and the smell choked his already congested sinuses. He stopped long enough to cry and hold his father's watch close to his heart.

"I loved him but I did not know him," he thought. "I have inherited Troublesome Creek and the burdens of a slave master. Damn my father, and damn slavery. Why am I so bitter? Maybe it's because I am not strong enough for the burden, or else the burden is too heavy for anyone."

Daniel walked into the woods to collect his thoughts, to face the real challenge ahead. "What am I to do, what am I to do? Lord, please give me the answer."

Daniel walked and walked along Troublesome Creek again. The instant he reached the spot where the baptism had been held one year ago to the day, he remembered his mammy and how pleasant it had been to be comforted by her big, strong black arms and how rewarding it was to play with John.

"Yes, John," he thought. "How could I have forgotten? John will help me make the living. I don't need to worry about how to run the plantation." A great burden had been lifted from his heart on the very spot where he had embraced John during his baptism.

Daniel's walk back to the big house was one of resolution and contentment. The sadness felt as he entered his father's bedroom and the weeping of slaves made him realize that the greatest of all tragedies was not death, but the fact that man's inhumanity is always rewarded by tears.

"I will not be like my father; my God, no, I cannot. John will help make the living. Yes, John will not let me down.'

John could not know what had taken place because, at that instant, he was in the caring arms of Sarah, a house slave from a neighbouring plantation. The physical pleasure that he was deriving was small reward for the stigma of slavery, attached to his being forced to jump the broom and marry. Master Eli had made arrangements for his marriage; the arrangements were founded upon greed, and were but another example of slavery's inhumanities.

John's father had indelibly scripted his impressionable mind with the desire to be free. He respected Sarah, but resented their slave's marriage. To be forced to wed someone not of his own choosing kindled no love, but made him cry in his heart, "Why can I not even be free enough to choose my own wife?"

John's mind raced back and remembered that the side of the tree the moss grows on and the north star were the way to freedom; but at the same time, he remembered his father's limp body draped over the horse, arms tied and feet dangling with crusted blood and bone sticking through, and sleep was long in coming.

Daybreak came and Sarah knew she had had a man but not a husband. She could not question this, only accept and survive. John left before the cock crowed, with social courtesies and promises that he would fulfill his commitment to her as soon as his master would allow it, and thanked her with a smile.

The wagon creaked as it went along Troublesome Creek toward Master Walls's plantation. John thought, "What a fitting name for this corner of the world. Can the Africa of my mother be similar to the Canada of my father's dream? Either would have to be better than Troublesome Creek. I want to be free!" His words echoed loudly through the morning fog, as if in hopes that the wind currents would carry the sound and himself into some promised land.

In the days following the death of the old slave master, John's desire to be free reached a fever pitch, contained only by the medicine of carpentry, his salvation from the severe frustration of slavery. The slave quarters were refreshed with new structures and old structures were given new strappings. John's skill as a carpenter was admired by all; he was not much liked by less ambitious victims in misery, but he was respected.

John cared more for respect than for admiration. And Daniel had verbally entrusted him with the running of the plantation, within the limits of his own decisions. So hard work was merely his duty, not meant to show up others who were less ambitious or capable. John was an exceptional friend but he was still a possession of Daniel's; neither of the two, at that point in time, knew how to remain friends without frustrations.

MILE VI

One of Daniel's hoped-for possessions was the Irish and Scottish Jane King. Daniel met Jane at the King plantation annual barbecue, one of North Carolina's society gala events. Daniel was more than ten years older than Jane, who had still not fully matured. Her potential suitors could fill the guest roll.

David King[2], Jane's father, was heir to one of the wealthiest plantations in Rockingham County, and he took great pride in pointing to the mountain that had been named after his grandfather. The Kings, one of the first families from Scotland to emigrate, had settled when North Carolina was mere woodland. They had cleared the land and established a foundation rivalled by none other in the vicinity. Stories were told about how Indians would travel many extra miles to avoid the King land and Edmund King's fiery temper. The story of Edmund single-handedly killing a grizzly bear was, however, too much for even the most naive of imaginations.

One fact was undisputed: the Kings were very proud, strong-willed people who demanded and received the respect of all their neighbours. The annual picnic was a demonstration of hospitality, not pretentiousness. David King was a somewhat reluctant successor to all the tradition attached to his family; he would have been quite content to manage the affairs of his plantation and sit in his favourite chair and read. Although he held his distinguished forefathers in high regard he felt no need to compete with their accomplishments and feats.

To David, self-respect was as important as the respect of others. Jane was his only daughter and his pride and joy. Her mother, the wife of his youth, had died with the flux when Jane was only an infant. David knew he would have to marry again someday, to father a son who would carry on the King tradition.

Jane had grown up under the guidance of one parent and a loving mammy, which had helped her to form unprejudiced, true feelings. Her father's wealth, and his predelection towards academic goals rather than material ones, gave Jane an independence of thought; her ideas did not need to conform to those of her times. The love of her mammy gave Jane the ability to return affection without caring what the colour of one's skin might be.

Her inner beauty and intelligence were not freely shared; they were reserved for those whom she determined were deserving enough to be graced. And others, the majority, could only observe, at arm's length, the one-hundred-ten pound beauty by whose wealth and intelligence they were intimidated.

Jane cared little for the fact that she did not sound like her more popular eye-batting, dim-witted peers who knew what to do to catch a husband. In her earlier years she had contemplated the convent, but realized it might confine her inquisitive mind and desire to travel. She would have been quite content never to marry—until she met Daniel.

Jane was placing an apple in the mouth of a pig when someone asked if she needed any help. She was ready to answer the question with her usual friendly indifference, but the smiling face of Daniel Walls made her smile back. They often said jokingly in later years that, had it not been for hunger pains, they might never have met.

Jane, who was a talker, found in Daniel an intelligent listener. His silence meant that he cared enough for her to subordinate his own self to the enjoyment of listening to her. Jane, who had recently come back from a two-year vacation in Europe, was bubbling to talk to someone who could truly appreciate what she had seen and heard. In the course of an afternoon and an evening, Daniel almost felt he had been to Europe himself. He could see himself walking down the streets of London mimicking, out of respect, the proud English walk. He could almost see the green hills of Ireland and the mountains of Scotland. Jane's description of the Scottish folk dances and games brought a smile to his face. The streets of Paris were also made vivid by Jane's almost photographic descriptions; he wished he could buy her a painting from one of the artists who lined the streets across from the River Seine. Daniel was hard-pressed to maintain a measure of control as he listened to Jane's description of the romantic French coastline. He was falling in love.

They talked also of England's anti-slavery movements, and of the court cases for equality and black freedom, which were setting precedents for the whole world. Daniel could not help but be amazed at Jane's knowledge of such matters, a knowledge unheard of in any woman in these parts. Her approval of Governor Graves Simcoe and the First Legislative Assembly of Upper Canada, which abolished slavery in Canada in 1793, left Daniel almost jealous; he wished he knew as much as she did. Little did he know that Jane was destined, with his help, to write a page in history herself which, though unpublished in her lifetime, would endure and stand beside other great events which would further racial harmony and justice.

The courtship lasted for three years, because Jane's education took precedence over her emotions. She travelled to Europe again, and back to Ireland and Scotland, the land of her forebears. She was gone for a year and a half. As soon as the ship landed Daniel made a marriage proposal—a matter of urgency rather than romance. To his great pleasure Jane accepted, with the condition that she be free, not another of the master's chattels. Daniel accepted, not fully knowing what she meant. Jane talked again of the things she had seen in Europe, the attitudes, the dress and the civility of the continent.

"Why, Daniel, do we have slaves?" Her question rang in his mind. He saw an image of John who, Daniel knew, longed to be freed.

MILE VII

As John rode along Troublesome Creek, he could not understand why, but was somehow pleased that a hawk accompanied his journey. The spring surroundings in North Carolina were beautiful but charged with tragedy. As a boy, John had befriended people on the basis of what they were rather than what they possessed; he had retained this philosophy in his manhood. One of his friends was Peter Redmon. Peter was ahead of his times in terms of attitude. He could out-talk anyone, including his master. There had been stories of how he had, on occasion, even taken liberties with his overseer's wife in the form of whistles and winks, and certainly no slave wench was safe.

Peter's high yellow complexion helped him, and was even considered to stem from possible genetic ties with his master. It helped make his actions, and his ability to get away with uppityness, more understandable to his fellow "Les Miserables." He had a carefree personality. He was a free spirit who made everyone smile. This morning John was smiling as he rode and thought of visiting Peter. These visits gave John some of his rare moments of happiness.

John had met Peter through Sarah, who was best friends with Peter's wife, Mary. John and Peter were natural comrades: Peter was a talker and John a listener. They had friendly disagreements on a lot of topics except one: the need to escape. On that topic they agreed completely. They would discuss escape plans often, in the cabin or the woods. John would share with Peter his father's information: *Remember, the side of the tree the moss grows on and following the north star is the way to Canada and freedom.*

Peter could not understand the significance of the moss and John explained that it always grew on the north side of the tree. He chided Peter for being a dumb nigger but laughed at him in a loving manner. He looked forward to his intermittent visits to Sarah's and Peter's plantation whenever Master Daniel would allow them.

On this beautiful spring morning in North Carolina these thoughts were greeted by Sarah's tears.

"Sarah, what is it?" John cried.

"John, Peter has run, Peter has run."

John immediately remembered his father's bloodied body and he asked, "Is he dead, Sarah, is he dead?"

"I don't know," Sarah reported. "He has been gone five days and we've heard nothing."

A strange happiness came over John as he thought, "My God, he is free, he is in Canada!" This feeling shocked him for an instant, and he felt as though he, and not Peter, had escaped. But, before he could express this to Sarah, she added, "John, that is not all; Master is going to sell Mary and me and the kids down south as he is in a fit of temper and thinks we are all in cahoots and plan to do the same thing. He...he...he threatens to kill 'that nigger John' for corrupting Peter's feeble mind. John, you must not come closer to the plantation, you must return and let Master Daniel protect you. John...John, what are we to do, what are we to do?"

John was numb with grief, anger and fear. He stared with wrinkled brow and squinting eyes that pointed north and as he did, he could almost see Peter, his skinny legs black from wallowing through the swamp, crawling over trees, fighting off wolves, bears and wildcats, as he hid himself by day and travelled by night. He could see the strain on Peter's face as he drank water from the hoof prints of cattle. He could see Peter crossing a river in Ohio to what is now Toledo. He could see Peter free, and he smiled.

"Why are you smiling John, why are you smiling? You can't be happy?" Sarah's voice brought him back to a reality so overpowering that he could not answer her. His eyes told all; they were blinking and Sarah saw his tears for the first time.

John silently led the horse and buggy in the woods outside the plantation and waited with Sarah for nightfall along Troublesome Creek. While he waited, he looked into Sarah's beautiful black face; he kissed her eyes and moved lovingly to her nose, neck, ears and lips. They held tightly as if death, at any moment, would cruelly and savagely pluck them from the earth and from each other. They escaped physical death but not the psychological death caused by slavery. In analogy, life really was but death.

John resented the fact that others had made decisions for him, even to the choosing of his wife. They had had two children in five years, but there had been a psychological barrier between them. Now that barrier as they lay on the bank of Troublesome Creek, Rockingham County, North Carolina, floated down the winding stream, past the Walls's Plantation, past the Governor's mansion and into the sea of eternity. John knew he loved Sarah, and that he was to lose her.

Nightfall came and with it the perils of what he was about to do. During the day, he had quizzed Sarah on the possibility of escaping north. She had answered, "Master is fearful of Peter returning with you, John, to run off with us and the kids, so he locked the children in the shed to discourage us."

John decided to escort Sarah home stealthily and to make an attempt to look at his two children. Slavery had prevented him from ever knowing them, and he knew this might be the last time he would see them.

"Our daddy deserted us." That is all that this page of unfair history might have revealed to future generations. Oh, how

41

he longed to be free. As he stared at his small children through the cracks of the shed, his heart was full of hatred for all the ills of society which had allowed such an injustice as this to happen. Slowly the hatred was tempered and replaced by an old Negro spiritual, "Swing low sweet chariot, coming for to carry me home."

He wondered why he had thought of this song, but the reason didn't matter. He loved, he lost, and a part of him died that night. The portion of him that remained was strengthened and would help him to clear the hurdles that fate placed before him many times during the remainder of his days.

The trip back to the plantation was made better by the cool night air. John was intoxicated by sorrow, grief and the futility of his circumstances. Sleep was long in coming, but when it came it was welcomed. John, the slave, ravished with sadness, was continuing his long road.

Daniel and Jane felt the repercussions of Peter's escape. The wrath of neighbouring plantation owners focussed on any owner who was too liberal with his slaves, thereby encouraging uppityness and rebellion. Ironically, however, because of the escape and the brotherly relationship started in childhood, an even greater closeness was to develop between John and Daniel. This bond was cemented even further through Jane's predilection for racial harmony.

The event which precipitated this type of communication was John's visit to the big house. Daniel had requested his presence: he wanted to discuss the affairs of the plantation. Nevertheless John thought it was a ploy, and that Daniel would try to ascertain what part he may have played in Peter's escape.

John entered the big house with fear, but he was resolved to face any repercussions like a man.

"I make the living," he thought, "they need me." This gave him a sense of pseudo-confidence. Daniel and Jane were sitting in the parlour as he was escorted in. For the first time he felt anger at Peter for leaving him behind.

"Damn Peter, but I love him," he thought, as Jane began to speak. It was not so much what she said but rather how she said it that led John to feel that peace and harmony were in the room. He answered her in low tones, an indication that he felt relaxed. The clock on the wall kept time with the beat of his heart.

"How is the work coming, John?" Daniel asked.

"Where are the reprimands for being Peter's friend?" John thought. "Oh, fine," John said out loud.

The room was filled with peace, tranquility and, even stranger, a type of harmony between three people; not two whites and one black, but three people. John's jet-black complexion seemed to almost glow from the reflections of the oil lamps.

"Sit down, John, and make yourself comfortable." The invitation contained more than mere words to John. A discussion took place between the three. John explained how the tobacco crop was coming along, and how he had heard that more and more demand would be placed on the tobacco plantations of North Carolina because of the popularity of smoking. He knew everything there was to know at that time about the planting, harvesting and curing of tobacco. Daniel and Jane looked at each other in amazement at the comprehension of this usually quiet man.

John's freedom of speech motivated the others to add conversation. Daniel, who was very dependent on others to make the living, talked about the rumours of unrest in northern and southern states. The unrest was caused by a difference of opinion on many topics, especially slavery. Daniel was not patronizing John when he said that he wished slavery would end, and that he felt something else could be done without the importing of slaves.

John practically jumped from his seat with approval, and again showed his intelligence by relating his father's stories of how they had handled prisoners of war in Africa. To be conquered and lose their family identity was more punishment to the prisoners than anything their captors could do to them. Ancestor worship was important; to be unable to physically participate in these ceremonies was a living death.

John went on to explain how Hannabal and Jubil had told him about puberty and death ceremonies, where great wooden masks would be used by the African dancers. The dancers believed the spirits of their ancestors dwelt within the inert objects.

Jane could not help but discard the womanly role of letting only the men carry the conversation; much travelled herself, she wanted to learn even more about John's native Africa. John, who was complimented by being asked questions, discussed things which he had been told by his parents, that he himself had almost forgotten he had known.

He remembered the great African nation of Timbuktu, the elephants that would be ridden by soldiers, the pomp and ceremony of the great dynasties and Queen Nefrititi, who was one of the most beautiful black queens of all time. John related Hannabal's vivid description so accurately that the three felt as if they had been there.

Jane spoke. "This is what I was discussing with you, Daniel. These are not slaves, animals of some lower order, but proud human beings, who have created empires and nations long before our forefathers were aware there was a North American continent. Reforms are taking place all over Europe. When will civilization truly reach North Carolina?"

"Not in our lifetime, I am afraid," Daniel answered pensively, "but if I have anything to say about it, civilization will reach the Walls plantation here in North Carolina."

Jane never had more love for Daniel than she did at that very moment. As John walked to the fireplace to warm himself on this chilly spring night, she knew that John was not just a slave, but a man whom she could respect.

Midnight came too quickly. The three shared thoughts and ideas that, quite possibly, had never been spoken between black and white during slavery. But when mixed races talk they learn; when they do not, they remain opinionated and prejudiced.

44

The words "Good night," meant more than good night for Jane, Daniel and especially John. John walked home that night by way of Troublesome Creek. He felt like doing somersaults and handstands again, as he had as a child, but contented himself with running home. He was happier than he had been in years, without really knowing why. He was unused to being treated like a man, an equal human being. He was respected for his carpentry and his work organization; but to be appreciated as a person brought more happiness than he could contain. He laughed, he ran, he cried.

But, as if a spike had been driven through the happiness in his heart, he stumbled and fell at the foot of a tree, the very tree to which he had been bound and where he had been whipped at age fifteen. His father and mother came into his mind.

Remember, John, the side of the tree the moss grows on and the north star are the way to freedom and Canada.

John's joy turned to sadness and he achingly yelled as loud as he could, "I will never be truly happy until I am free in Canada." His cry knifed through the silence of the night and the slave quarters were shaken, causing many to awaken in fright. They feared a lash would break open their backs as the scream had broken their sleep. The sound that did reach the big house caused Jane to ask, "What was that noise, Daniel, so late at night?"

Daniel replied, "Don't worry, Jane, it is probably just some unfortunate animal caught in a trap." Daniel did not realize how true his statement had been.

From then on the three worked in harmony tempered with respect. They worked for their mutual best interest. However, Daniel could not fully understand why the new John he had witnessed opening up, apparently happier with his station in life, had so quickly become objective, indifferent and businesslike.

"He has to be one of the best-treated slaves in Rockingham County. I can't understand, Jane."

Jane's experiences at home and abroad allowed her to understand and she replied, "He is treated well because he makes the living for us, but he is still not a free man, Daniel; only an appreciated slave. He is too proud and intelligent a man to accept anything less than full equality; John will never be truly happy while in North Carolina."

Daniel stared at Jane, astonished at the profound words she had spoken. Even though Daniel felt a brotherly love for John, he did not know his inner feelings as well as Jane did although she had only known him for a short time. Daniel turned and walked away, through the living room and into the parlour, absorbed in his own thoughts. He sat down on a velvet chair and wished he did not have to carry the burden of being a slave master, and the burden of a man in the early stages of an incurable disease. His eyes shut and he fell asleep.

MILE VIII

The years that followed were becoming less and less endurable for John; although social conditions were more pleasant for him and other slaves, this taste of freedom was almost worse than no freedom at all.

The institute of slavery had forbidden learning, as the nourishment of independent thought, which it created, brought more discontent. So, too, was the freedom of expression and self-worth, causing more discontent within John. John felt no malice towards Daniel; he loved Daniel, and had supressed his desire to escape because Daniel needed him to make the living. He could not let his boyhood friend suffer. Daniel's failing health made John's emotion even stronger, and created even more discontent and conflict in his role as a slave.

"Can slavery be so distorting me that I am actually resigning myself to live like this and even accept this lowly life?" John thought. He already knew his immediate answer.

He was torn, but could not leave this friend of his youth, who had shared his mother's breasts, his benevolent slave master full grown. John's Christian duty would not allow him any other course of action.

The sun was rising over the tobacco plantations of North Carolina. John watched as it rose red and orange; he thought: "Thank you, Jesus, for the beginning of a beautiful day." To him the sun's rising signalled not just the dawning of a new day, but the dawning of a new era, a new generation, the continuation of his, the slave's, journey. This feeling of happiness was unusual as there were many hurdles placed before him by the burden of slavery. John walked towards the tobacco field with hoe over shoulder, as if captain of an army about to make an assault upon deadly weeds. The other slaves followed almost in unison with John, singing with half-asleep voices:

Swing low, sweet chariot, coming for to carry me home,
Swing low, sweet chariot, coming for to carry me home.
Looked over yonder, and what did I see? Coming for to
   carry me home,
A band of angels coming after me, coming for to carry
   me home.
If you get there before I do, coming for to carry me
   home,
Tell them all, I'm a'coming too, coming for to carry me
   home.

John's loud voice would often carry the tune but today he could only smile at little Sammy. His five-year-old frame tried to mimic his elders' walk and he sang words he could hardly pronounce. "Chariot" was transformed into "carrot," and the rest could hardly be made out. But it was obvious that Sam was proud of his first hoeing expedition. John's smile was touched with sadness as he thought of his own children, whom slavery had taken from him. "Where down south are they? God bless them, wherever they are. May they die free."

This was his only answer to the emotional dilemma he was facing. Slavery had a way of creating a very rationalizing mind. As Jane came into his vision, he remembered a comment she had made which had given him some solace. "John," she would say, "God grant me the strength to change the things I can, accept the things I cannot change and the wisdom to know the difference."

Jane was a great woman in John's eyes, and well loved and respected by the other slaves. Her servants called her "Missie Jane," a loving familiarity, which was a manifestation of her bond with them. Jane would talk to them as equals and ask about their feelings and desires. The common desire among those old enough to realize their true station in life was to be free. At first they were reluctant to be open and honest with her, because they had learned through experience that to survive meant to create few waves. The slaves who pretended to be dumb and happy found that their masters and mistresses carried the whip less.

At first they would only say, "We's happy niggers." Over the months this changed. "Missie Jane, we's want to go to Canada; tell us 'bout Canada." Jane felt tears coming to her eyes the day little Sammy jumped into her lap and said, "Missie Jane, I's going to Kanadia when I grow up." His smile was overpowering; she could not give the slightest reply or hint of his true destiny.

"Maybe I can help you someday," she answered with the most sincere words she could.

She walked into the tobacco field searching for John on this particularly cloudy day. He could see that her face showed her fatigue, but he also saw concern and sadness. She was the first to speak. "Will there ever be a life of happiness for any of us? Daniel is dying, John!"

Jane's tears were flowing freely on John's shoulder before he felt the impact of her words. He held her in his strong arms; over the years, his care had evolved into liking, and respect. The other slaves kept hoeing, but they cast sad, knowing glances at their "Missie Jane," whom they liked and respected as well as John did.

John looked over her head and into the morning sun, just born, and prayed silently that his friend would be cured or would not be made to suffer much longer. They both walked towards the big house in silence, John trying to convey some of his own masked strength to Jane. The children had come to love and respect "fixer" John, as he was called, and Mary, his favourite, would always jump into his arms. The four children were seated in the kitchen, too sad to want to greet "Fixer John," and too confused to appreciate the implications of death. John and Jane entered as Corliss placed biscuits on the table to help distract and make the children happy. Her own tears could be seen falling onto the hot dough.

John and Jane entered Daniel's room with reverence and emotional pain. John felt tears on his cheeks and remembered how he had peeked through the shed at his own soon-to-be fatherless children. Then he had cried with hatred; now he cried with love. His hands went quickly to his eyes; he was concerned by Jane's response to his tears, and knew that he, the man, must be strong. John's tears did not go unnoticed by Daniel, but Daniel could only muster the strength to blink the tears from his own eyes.

John and Jane listened as Daniel spoke in a quivering voice not far removed from death. He gave to them his verbal last will and testament; it was to be the seed of a family legend, which would pass down through generations.

"John, you have been with me on all great events in my life. We were born on the same day; you were present at the marriage of Jane and I. It is only fitting you should be here now. I have had time to think and reflect on the life we have had and you have had." Daniel stopped for a few seconds to breathe in more air and then continued to utter words that had been well thought out. "I cannot answer the question adequately—why should you, just because you were born in slave quarters, and born black, have suffered so. Fate is too unjust. I mean to right fate, and am only sorry that you have been penalized for thirty some years. I hope you remember the Commandments and the words I have, with my own ears, heard you recite on Sundays. I hope the good Lord allows you to live well past one hundred years as a free man. John, you are John Freeman Walls; the manumission papers are signed and at the foot of my bed. I am too weak to reach them."

The words 'free man' clouded John's senses for a few minutes; as he came to himself he dropped on his knees beside Daniel's bed, words not needed to express his gratitude. As his head bent and his hand clutched his dying friend's hand, his tears fell on first, his black, and then Daniel's white fingers. Before he could regain his composure, he heard even stranger words, that even overshadowed the first.

"John, I will you³ Jane and my four children, as no man on earth could be kinder and more loving to them than you."

These words left John reeling with a feeling of astonishment and confusion.

But he then realized Jane would soon be widowed. His friend, who loved her very much, wanted the assurance that his family, of which John had become a part, would be cared for in his absence. The knowledge that John would be looking after Jane and the children would allow him to die with peace of mind. John raised his head and looked into Jane's eyes almost instinctively. Jane also felt the full impact of Daniel's words; her eyes answered that she would obey her husband whom she loved, and who was dying. She nodded at John, whom she knew she could learn to love. John Freeman and Jane King were continuing along the long, and now even more perilous, Road to Somewhere.

Three months had passed since Daniel's death; John and Jane had wrestled with their true feelings for one another. The parlour was the scene for many monumentous occasions, and this night was no exception. John was standing by the fireplace; Jane sat in a handsome, green velvet chair the texture of which complemented her own soft skin. John was nervously rubbing his hands together and talking about tobacco, and other topics of little interest to either at this time. Their main interest was each other. Jane was the first to speak.

"John, we are too intelligent to believe that, even though legally free, this apartheid society would accept our marriage and our living as normal man and wife; yet we must, as Christians, be married."

John grunted, a nod registering his agreement.

"You know, John, Daniel's funeral brought relatives from all over the county. Even though they only get together on such occasions, they still have strong family ties. Their prejudiced emotions are so strong that they won't allow a black man and white woman to marry and inherit the plantation—especially if the white woman is their relative. The penalty would be death. The scandal to their family name would be reason enough." Racial harmony between Daniel, John and Jane was the exception to the rule; having tasted it, their hearts were intoxicated with peace and happiness. That harmony had caused Daniel to make his supreme gesture of love; it was causing John and Jane to contemplate braving all consequences or hurdles to live in Christian harmony and love as man and wife.

"Jane, you are a well-travelled, educated, sophisticated lady whom I could not woo by mere physical attraction. With your personality and inheritance, you could find many a willing husband. Why would you even consider me, and the problems I would bring you?"

"John, let me answer by asking you—you are a handsome, Christian, baptized black man, proud and manly, free now to choose any wife you want, to even go north and choose a white or black woman without four children. Why would you consider me?"

John moved from the fireplace; his shiny black complexion had a sort of aura around it. A black hand touched her shoulder, and before she realized it a white hand went to his neck. Jane continued, "People do not marry because they meet someone who is different; they marry because they love each other. We are all members of the family of mankind, not different races. Your difference of skin colour, John, does not add to or cancel out the more important qualities of your personality."

John kissed her nose and lips for the first time, a kiss that would definitely not be the last as their love would endure for many years and through many more hardships.

This night convinced them once and for all that Daniel had been right in his sincere last request. Daniel was greatly ahead of his time.

MILE IX

The sun rose on another North Carolina spring day; the air was charged with anticipation. John's and Jane's decision was like a double-edged sword. In order to avoid certain death if they stayed in North Carolina, they faced possible death if they tried to reach Canada with four young children. Jane had learned the skills of travel and she was forced to put them into practice.

"God's eye is on the sparrow, so I know he watches me." John quoted from an old Negro spiritual to comfort his mind. They made their preparation to head north as quietly as they could in order not to arouse suspicion. Even the slaves were not informed, for fear a Judas might appear in their midst.

Jane visited her father, David, to collect some of her inheritance and to say a goodbye that both knew might be their last goodbye. David was, as usual, reading a book; his mind could almost sense that his daughter was about to embark on a journey far more dangerous than a sea voyage to the old country. He hugged her, not asking many details about her destination or her reasons for going. As a final request he said only, "Please write me, daughter, or visit, if I can be of help." From these words and by the look in his tear-filled aging eyes she knew how fortunate she was to have been born his daughter.

Jane drove the buggy home with her four children, who asked many unanswered questions. She arrived at the Walls plantation after nightfall, knowing only too well that this was the night.

The bags were carefully and quietly loaded into the buggy by John, who was waiting with perspiration on his brow. "Jane, will your father see to the affairs of the plantation until Daniel's folk hear and take over?"

"Yes," she replied.

John could only half look at the slave quarters; he knew any remorse he might feel about leaving would be but short-lived, because the desire to be with Jane and his new family in free Canada was stronger. The horse pulled tiredly; his already long journey had lathered him far beyond normal. John, Jane, the four children and Corliss, the house servant and mammy to the children, were beginning the physical journey to freedom. Corliss had learned from the children that something very strange and exciting was to take place. She did not know what, as the children had not been informed of the precise plans. She waited in her kitchen until the buggy arrived; she put the pieces together as she watched the loading of the buggy.

"Can I go? Can I go, Missie Jane?" That was all she could utter. Jane looked at John for approval. He was reluctant at first but, having wished he could safely take all his old friends in misery, smilingly nodded his head with satisfaction.

The buggy, filled to capacity, creaked a melody that made all feel almost like singing, but they dared not.

"Troublesome Creek, you old devil," John said, "I don't want to see you no more." Then he uttered the prophetic words: "Maybe one of my descendants of another time can come back to you and appreciate what I have done." The moon that night was a beacon of light, which the six sojourners rode under thankfully. One traveller looked at another landmark in the sky.

"We will follow the north star, Jane, and remember the side of the tree the moss grows on is the way to true freedom in Canada, hallelujah!"

Two days had passed before word of the escape reached Jed Walls's plantation. The shocked look on his face was replaced by anger, which turned his cheeks brick red. The anger he felt would not allow him to say anything other than, "You mean that black nigger? Get my gun." Fourteen men were summoned within a matter of a few hours. Spring planting made more men unavailable.

"We got to catch the no-goods, or we can't rest in peace," they said; it became their battle cry.

"Remember Eli." Some of the men, the older ones, had actually been on the hunt for John's father.

"Remember Eli running Hannabal to death? We will have no trouble catching a black with women and children, and when we do, we will kill them all as an example."

The dust of the horses was symbolic of the futility of man's inhumanity. Dust to dust was inevitable; why not let the living be happy, John thought. Mankind's thinking had changed over the generations; but to John and Jane, as they fled guided by the light of the north star, the importance of peace and harmony could never change.

The two-day head start with horse and buggy was perhaps the only salvation for the unlikely freedom runners. They would camp in the woods by day and travel by night to avoid any form of suspicion. During one of the daily forages for food, John heard his name called from almost a quarter of a mile away.

"John, help! Please, John, help."

John ran with strength of years of hard physical labour, his black muscles rippling under the strained overalls. This call had not been in vain, for there before his wife and family-to-be was a pack of wolves made brave by their hunger. The women and children were in their wagon, which the wolves would have to leap at in order to catch their seemingly easy prey. Jane was bloodied from one bite; but the strength afforded a mother protecting her children helped her fend off their passing attacks with but a piece of wood. John at first felt fear, but that emotion was quickly replaced by courage upon seeing Jane's beautiful body bleeding and the children huddled in Corliss's shaking arms in the corner of the wagon. Surprise and the desire to survive, especially after all he had been through, inspired his actions.

John stopped his run only long enough to pick up an axe he had fortunately laid by some kindling wood he was preparing. He yelled like a madman in a voice that could be heard for—fortunately earless—miles and ran into the pack of wolves swinging his axe, uncaring for his own safety.

Jane stood up in disbelief. Her husband-to-be was attacking a pack of wild animals single-handedly. Blood splattered into her face as one wolf, his head half severed, was thrown through the air and landed on the ground at the foot of the buggy wheel.

John, Hannabal's son, was standing in one spot, uttering words unknown even to himself, as if some ancient warrior from Africa had possessed his body and he was fending off lions on some great veldt. John wielded his axe, screaming all the time in a strange African tongue. Three wolves made a simultaneous charge, knocking him down, but not before another had found the blade of his axe in its head. But John was quick and strong and eluded the two wolves that were going for his throat.

Jane jumped from the wagon and picked up the axe, which lay seemingly endless feet from John. The axe was raised over her head and, with all the strength her slight body could muster, she generated enough downward thrust to break the wolf's neck in one blow.

The last wolf had found John's hands which were placed

around its jaws. In shock and disbelief, Jane witnessed the strength of muscles built up by years of carpentry. John's bleeding fingers were as powerful as a steel trap and in no more than a few seconds his arms pulled apart and opened the wolf's jaws wider and wider. Its tongue protruded from its mouth and its eyes bulged from its head, and Jane heard a final snap as its jaws were physically torn apart by John Freeman Walls. He was a man determined to fight for freedom; nothing short of death would prevent him from continuing along the perilous road to somewhere.

Corliss dressed their wounds, which were miraculously superficial, a blessing considering their wild surroundings. John and Jane lay in each others' arms that night, realizing that any question or doubt about their love for each other was washed away by the fact that they had, but a few hours before, offered their lives for each other.

The road to freedom was so important to John that its length and hardships had no significance—they were just necessary hurdles. He found himself, at one point, pulling a child out of quicksand; at another, he limped for miles on a sprained ankle in order to save the horse for the women and children. The six drank water from cows' hoof marks and ate berries as their only sustenance.

The days turned into weeks and the weeks into more weeks. They knew they had eluded Daniel's relatives, but they also knew that slave patrols would be licking their lips at the bounty reward offered for such a conspicuous group of travellers.

Daylight caught them in open terrain and their apprehensiveness was not unfounded. Three riders approached them; the freedom seekers knew when they heard the Kentucky accent that the riders were to be feared.

"What you all doing?" the riders asked. The question sent shivers up Jane's spine. She had to make a drastic, quick decision.

"Am I ever glad you gentlemen passed by. I am on my way to Indiana and this nigger slave, who my husband assured me

56

was worth something, is lazier than all get-out and becoming quite insolent. If you gentlemen would just lend me your whip—I want to be the one to have the pleasure of tanning a little of his black hide off."

These words shocked the slave patrollers but they could not resist the implications of fun and frivolity, and forgot about any more of their usual questions. John was also in a state of shock, but knew his life was being saved at the expense of his black hide. "This could be worse than the wolves," he thought as he was dragged out of the wagon. The laughing Kentuckians tied him to the wagon wheel as one held the horse. Jane, with all the theatrics she could muster, pretended she enjoyed whipping his black hide and swung with controlled anger, using her small frame as excuse for not being able to hit harder. One patroller said, "Miss, let me show you how to do it."

He received a soft blow on his head and heard Jane say, "I ain't no frail southern belle; I whips my own niggers." John's cries were a mixture of real hurt and misplaced laughter. The five minutes seemed like fifty but the curiosity and appetite of the slave patrollers had been satisfied, and they felt certain that their job of harassing niggers had been adequately and amusingly done on this day.

The Kentukians were to talk about this day for many years. John and Jane were to laugh about this day. In years to come, John would only need to say, "Jane, I'd rather fight a wild wolf than face your whip," and a burst of laughter would leave many an uninformed spectator wondering about the sanity of the strange twosome.

The road John, Jane and family continued along was, fortunately, made shorter by the positive effects of Christianity, a Christianity somewhat foreign to the twentieth-century mind.

"Servants, obey thy masters"; the text formed a cornerstone of the mid-nineteenth-century mind. The slave bore the mental and physical burden imposed by such "Christian" thinking; he also became more religious himself. Heaven, God, Africa, drums, Negro spirituals...all were woven together to clothe him in the only security that his life of drudgery would allow. A sensitive Quaker Christianity fought against such drudgery, and responded to the slave's spirutal and physical desire to be free. Thus the first anti-slavery society was formed.

This anti-slavery society became a necessary link in the underground railroad, a railroad that did not necessarily travel in a logical straight line to Canada, but rather was, at times, as illogical as the social climate that permitted slavery. Fortunately for John and Jane that foggy night in 1842, its form of Christianity had reached Indianapolis, Indiana and, more specifically, the home of Ephraim and Mary Stout.

Mary Stout was busy at her favourite pastime, cooking and frequently sampling her own food, when the news came. Ephraim was breathless as he ran into the kitchen. "Mary, Mary, the most unusual thing, Mary. There are seven fugitives from North Carolina, but they aren't all black."

Mary turned almost full circle, her plump fingers dripping with still-to-be-jelled grape jelly. "Not all black. I hope they're not white criminals."

"No, Mary, the lady and four children are white and far from criminals, but Christians."

Mary's face lit up with an aura of impending fear and love for the unseen pioneers in harmonious race relations.

"Where are they, Ephraim?"

"Mary, they are in Isaac's barn and I would hardly believe their story, were it not for their honest appearance. The woman, Jane, was willed, with her four children, to a trusted slave, John, by her husband on his death bed. And, in order to escape life-threatening persecution of his relatives they had to flee north in the night. Can you believe it, Mary, can you believe it?" Ephraim's question resounded through the ample clapboard house. His words were confident and seemed to mock anyone, past, present or future, who would judge only the colour of skin.

"They are positive the relatives are still trying to find out their whereabouts, and even have a poster taken from a tree some hundred miles back stating, 'Hear ye, hear ye, reward for John Walls; black as ace of spades, hide and soul; for kidnapping one Mrs. Jane Walls and four children viciously, maybe with black girl named Corliss. Reward assured on capture of slave, John, dead or alive."

John had pulled this notice from a tree; Jane had become so angered that only her tears kept her from uttering unladylike comments. Only after a few minutes could she say, "John, how could they be so cruel? I love you." John smiled. Until that point Jane had never stated her feelings for him. Her words made the poster seem almost like an ironical blessing.

Ephraim was still telling his wife of his discovery. "They are in Isaac's barn," he told her as he recovered from his run.

Ephraim was born a Quaker and knew no other life. His had been a good life but as always, not without its share of trials and tribulations. He was now in his sixtieth year—he had been widowed twice and was now married for the third time. Although his wife was some twenty years younger, she was his equal in terms of mutual sharing of love and respect.

59

In his boyhood he had received rigorous religious discipline; it had taught him to help people without regard for superficial characteristics. As he drove back to Isaac's barn he remembered a scene from his boyhood which had left a psychological scar. A black man in his community had been hanged for knocking a white woman down in broad daylight and falling upon her in an uncontrollable seizure. The early inhabitants' ignorance of the slave's brain damage, which had occurred after a cruel whipping, left all to misinterpret his action. They deemed it worthy of death. The sympathy Ephraim felt for the poor unfortunate motivated him to become a leader in more Christian and liberal endeavours; thus he helped to free slaves from bondage, in keeping with the Quaker philosophy.

Mary's plump body undulated from the bumpy buggy ride. As she crossed her arms in order to keep her upper and lower body in control, Ephraim remarked, "Things are even worse for John and Jane now."

Mary could only look at her husband in a trusting manner, knowing that whatever had prompted this prophetic statement had been well thought out in his mind.

They reached Isaac's barn and found that other Quakers had also heard of the strange circumstances of the sojourners, and were extending the hands of friendship.

The women had already let their maternal instincts loose on the children who, though debilitated by their rigorous journey, were able to respond to the love they were being shown with laughter and hugs. John and Jane stood together as if defying any and all to question their right to live one of the most beautiful love stories of all time—especially during the period of slavery.

Jane spoke articulately, not trying to be pretentious but merely relating to equally well-educated peers. John's words were fewer but they showed that he was a proud, free man with a self-taught, fertile mind.

The crowd gave way only when Mary and Ephraim arrived. These two were experienced and respected abolitionist practitioners; they would know what to do. The look on Jane's and Mary's faces when they met, bespoke the possible influence of Karma; they both knew they were at the beginning of a lifelong friendship. And John's smile made both Mary and Ephraim realize that this was no broken black, but a free person who happened to have black skin.

The buggy was loaded and Ephraim and Mary took the seven fugitives back to the house. They knew they must help to further the fugitives in the direction of the north star.

As they rode in the buggy, the fugitives remembered Mary's words upon meeting John and Jane: "You are all safe with us; we are Quakers and must love thee first." John felt the presence of good. His soul and body had many times been confronted with its opposite, so he knew the difference.

Ephraim and Mary smiled as they escorted the group to the attic. "Thee must not chide me for being rude, but safety for thine person is my only concern." Mary's over-protective, sincere displays of concern were rewarded by silent appreciation; she could not help but feel thanked. Her plump arms went around Jane's slight body. She planted a kiss on John's cheek and teased him that his jet-black complexion had turned red, which left all in laughter. John followed in the fun by showing the palms of his hands as jovial proof. You could almost reach out and touch the vibrations of love for fellowman, which cemented a lasting friendship between the Walls and the Stouts.

The Stouts fed their guests and provided clothes and other physical necessities. The children were happy, and played. Corliss was learning to read; her mind was almost bursting in her enthusiasm to fill it with more and more knowledge. Mary could scarcely believe how quickly this love- and knowledge-starved traveller from oppression learned. She had seen the same enthusiasm in others she had helped along the road to freedom, but Corliss was more enthusiastic than anyone.

Mary marvelled also at Jane's origins; a family of wealth and substance, a mother who died before she could be remembered, an intelligent father and a grandfather who had a mountain named after him. "My word," Mary thought, "how could a woman, in these times of organized bigotry, be so soft, so pure in heart, so down to earth?" Mary Stout had heard of the lust between certain white women and black men. But Jane was different: she was a lady of breeding, who could have married a governor or perhaps even a president. And she was in love with, and loved in return by, a former slave.

Mary would listen night after night to Jane's stories of her trips to Europe, of the streets of England, France, Ireland and Scotland. She could almost see the kilts flashing to the bagpipe music, the green pastures of Ireland, the mountainous coasts along Scotland. Mary's sensitive nature would even cause her to cry with happiness on occasion.

Jane had found a friend; Mary had found a treasure. Long hours were shared in mutual interests, and time was shared taking care of the children, a task Mary loved, being both stepmother and mother herself. Lucinda and her favourite, "little Mary," the youngest, would take turns sitting on her knees competing with each other for expressions of endearment. They would both laugh at Mary's laughter, which sent her pleasingly plump body into comical contortions.*

Mary got up from the long table and smiled. "Little people, I think we must go to bed now!" That meant cookies and milk, and made even the most wide awake pretend they were sleepy. Jane looked at Mary with a smile that needed no explanation.

---

*The fact that Mary loved children could be attributed to the fact that being the third wife of Ephraim, she was stepmother and mother.

Quaker records show that Ruth Howel, Ephraim's first wife, had several children before her untimely death: first Jane born January 29, 1816, Charles 11/11/1817, Robert 2/7/1820, Elias, 4/17/1822, Enoch 2/17/1824, Anner 1/12/1825, Ruth 1/14/1827, Ephraim Junior 6/3/1829.

John was in the other room, quiet for reasons known only to himself and Jane. When he did speak it was almost silently, under his breath, for fear his words would sound rude. "I want to be mentally free, I want to follow the moss and the north star to Canada." John also wanted to communicate his appreciation to the Stouts, whose underground railroad ties, he knew, would eventually help him to true freedom. He expressed his gratitude through ability to build. The whole Quaker community could feel his great worth as a man. Ephraim would often be amazed by John's endeavours. John would take a block of wood and create a bowl; another block would become an axe handle.

The intensity with which he worked showed that he was troubled. Freedom desire, while he was in Indianapolis, was subordinate to physical desire. He was frustrated, and his frustration was a form of psychological slavery. Corliss, young but mature, represented John's wife publicly and they both acted the part of Jane's bidders. Their actions were governed by prudence; although they were in the north and supposedly free, they did not want to challenge the accepted behaviour of the populace. A white woman married to a black man could irritate the most liberal of minds.

The Stouts understood the necessity of prudence, but they were saddened by it. They knew that the love shared by John and Jane was real and—even more important—Christian. It was an ideal relationship and should have been applauded as such; instead, it had to be hidden, to avoid harrassment.

John and Jane would often take leisurely Sunday-afternoon walks through the wood paths. They felt secure physically,

---

Quaker records further tell us that Mary Stout, formerly Mary Shoredar was born February 19, 1800, Chatham County North Carolina. Mary Shoredar's marriage to Ephraim was witnessed by Mary Doran, and John—no last name given. The offspring of Mary Shoredar and Ephraim were respectively, Berroni 2/5/1831, died same day in Spiceland, Therres 10/27/1832, Mary 12/4/1833, died 1/21/1834, buried in Spiceland. Thus, Mary knew the joys and sorrows of motherhood.

but they were uncertain about their personal relationship while in Indiana. Jane would talk about the abolitionist meetings she would attend with Mary, and the wonderful network of good people forming the underground railroad. "John, I must go back to North Carolina and help some others to freedom." These words were just disregarded notes, for John was not paying attention; he did not hear her words. He looked around at the trees and heard the hundreds of birds chirping and said, "Jane, we must jump the broom." These words Jane did hear, but before she could respond, John had taken her into his strong black arms. With only her toes touching the ground, they answered each other with a kiss.

MILE XI

The ceremony was brief and the wedding party small. Safety was paramount, commonsense prevailed. The children, Corliss, Ephraim and Mary were the only guests present. An atmosphere of love prevailed. Ephraim, being an elder in the church, performed the services and all smiled when John insisted upon physically jumping the broom, leaving no room for doubt about what was happening.

The broom was held by Corliss and little Mary. There was a pause, which seemed endless, before John and Jane approached the broom. They looked at each other, not needing to smile to communicate their true feelings. They jumped as they approached the broom. The height they achieved was adequate to clear the broom, but as they reached the highest arc of their flight, they seemed to freeze in time and motion. In that instant one could see a white woman and black man, their heads turned towards each other, their eyes focussed on each other's now smiling faces; they were oblivious to everything except their love for one another.

64

They were oblivious to the happenings of the past and present which so affected their destiny.

The seed was planted by the screams of slaves carried in chains from the jungles of Africa and thrown into the ships' dungeon, pits of disease and pestilence; the countless slaves jumping overboard still in chains somewhere in the vast Atlantic; the virgin princesses' descendants, perhaps descendants of Queen Nefrititi herself, being subjected to rape and defilement; the ships that had landed with only a third of the original cargo, the majority infested with maggots and fed to the sharks; the ungodly slave blocks where mothers pleaded in vain for their doomed off-spring; the cotton and tobacco fields where slaves sang songs about freedom in the form of escape to Canada or death.... The seed was nurtured by the look on Hannabal's face when his heart burst under the strain of going beyond the limits of human endurance; Daniels' act of supreme love for two people on his death bed; the hardships in the woods, the wolves, the slave patrollers, the lack of food and sustenance; Daniel's relatives, who were in another county in Indiana, fervently searching to retrieve Jane and kill John.... They were not mindful of future hardships, their life in Canada, their descendants' struggle to remain free; they were not mindful of their descendants' appreciation for them, some one hundred thirty years later.... A future world beyond their century where racial harmony would be the rule, rather than the exception, where white and black need not marry in order to understand and communicate higher human principles, where black and white could own land in Florida, break bread together, live, love and die as free spirits, free of the bondage of bigotry and inhumanity to man.

When John and Jane landed on the other side of the broom they had made a giant leap, from the ills of mankind's past into the present and future of mankind's struggle for racial harmony and love, where man is not judged by the colour of his skin but rather by the content of his spirit. A time when

65

one of their descendants could represent the whole nation of Canada and the British Empire as the heavyweight boxing best; where another of their descendents could further the work of an organization of brotherhood. A time when many others like John and his father before him, like Joseph, the father of Jesus of Nazareth, could become carpenters, and teachers of this worthy profession, construction supervisors and writers. And still others could reach professional heights and make the best of their talents, as people first, black men and black women second.

The days and months that followed gave John and Jane enough confidence and peace of mind to deal with life on a new level; no longer were they fugitives first and people second. Jane's aspirations toward abolition became stronger and stronger as her association with Ephraim and Mary taught her more about the underground railroad.

The culmination of her studies came while John and Jane were seated on the porch after a hard day of work, free-lance carpentry for one, tending to children for the other. Jane turned towards John and in a voice quivering with anticipation said, "John, I must go back to North Carolina."

John knew her purpose without having to ask, and thought, "Is it right for me, who was a slave, to enslave Jane's abolitionist ambitions and, by so doing, give my brethren no chance of escaping slavery?"

John clenched his fist at the mere thought of his wife's being hurt, but he spoke his true feelings. "Jane, I only wish I could go with you to protect you." Both knew they had tested and concretely expressed the respect that their new marriage, in order to endure, had to have as its foundation.

MILE XII

Proper preparation and enthusiasm allowed Jane and Corliss to head their rumbling buggy down a more hospitable road than their flight had taken on their journey north. As the wagon wheels came closer to the state of North Carolina and the cloud of slavery that hovered over it, Jane and Corliss could almost feel the changing atmosphere.

By nightfall Jane and Corliss were at an underground station—Mary had very carefully mapped the stations out for them. The abolitionists were more than pleased to spend an evening with Jane: they enjoyed her interesting conversation, and even more interesting personal story. Jane and Corliss awoke the next day, gave thanks to their friends in the common cause of freedom and, after complimenting their hosts for the fresh eggs and bacon, continued into the heart of oppression. Several days of the same underground experiences made both of them realize how valuable it would have been to have travelled the total underground route on the trip north. They could not help but feel appreciation for the help the Stouts had given them.

The North Carolina sun shone like a beacon warming their bodies and their hearts. They could see it rising in the east, surrounded by an aura of white and a platform of red. Jane turned to Corliss with a smile and said, "Corliss, we will achieve our goal and here is how. You will be less conspicuous than I, so you will enter the slave quarters. First, when you reach the quarters, seek out any you know well enough and warn them to create no fanfare over your arrival, for whatever relative is minding the plantation will surely kill you if he finds out."

The word "kill" rang in Corliss's head like a thousand

drum beats; she envisioned impending peril. Jane had to gently shake her so that she could pay attention to Jane's critical instructions. All that day Jane repeated the instructions. By the third time she repeated them Corliss was so frightened that she ran through the woods outside the plantation. She ran along Troublesome Creek not caring where she was going or why; she could only cry hysterically.

Jane ran after her, knowing that the instructions and threats had been necessary. She calmed Corliss's hysterics with an embrace. Jane's tears were a reminder and a reassurance to Corliss, who knew that Jane also risked peril, especially because of the circumstances of her departure. The thoughtless severing of Jane's life thread would have been its own reward; questions would be asked only later. Even a sheriff could have been persuaded to look the other way; her conduct was too outrageous for their prejudiced minds to accept.

Jane and Corliss sat by Troublesome Creek and gained strength for the body upon eating the basket lunch prepared at their last underground station; they gained mental strength by telling each other the good that would come out of their deed. Corliss could remember the scars of slavery; they were even more vivid than the indirect scars Jane had felt. When Corliss was only fourteen something had occurred that she had never told anyone about.

While walking along Troublesome Creek, on an errand for Master Daniel, she had heard noises in the distance, which aroused her curiosity. She walked in the direction of the sounds and, much to her shock and disbelief, saw what appeared to be a human figure dangling from a rope. A thin pole had been driven into the ground just under the heel of his left shoe. This shaking pole was all that supported his life. Corliss saw horses moving away in a southerly direction; their riders were laughing and holding up a long branch that had been torn from a tree while still green with sap. She wondered why the branch was being waved like a flag of victory but dismissed the thought and returned her attention to the pitiful sight at the end of the rope. She summoned all the courage in her fourteen-year-old body. She knew she must somehow save the man's life; she did not ask why. As she came closer she saw blood dripping onto the ground; she screamed upon seeing a sight that made a horrible scar on her young mind. Corliss stared in horror at a tree. The tree bore not only its natural fruit, but also an unnatural fruit—an earless fugitive. Blood dripped from the sides of the tragic victim's head; where his ears had been, only bloody holes remained.

The slave was still alive and labouring for his very life, trying to balance on the thin pole stuck in the ground. Corliss mustered all her strength and managed to place a bigger block of wood under the man's feet. This gave her time to climb the tree and, with much difficulty, her young, weak fingers untied the rope.

Slave patrollers had found the man, an unfortunate soul without travelling papers, and discovered he had escaped and was running from the Scott plantation in Kentucky. They left him tied to the tree, confident that he was too weak to live. This cockiness on their part saved the man's life. The slave patrollers had rewarded themselves with the man's ears; and Corliss had rewarded the slave with his life.

The slave patrollers had had their sport; they also had their hanged nigger's ears. Their bounty would be assured, especially since one ear had been tattooed, and would leave no doubt in the master's mind that his slave had met a fatal and justified end.

Corliss, remembering what she had seen her grandmother do to stop uncontrolled bleeding, placed mustard leaves over the two holes on either side of the man's head. Corliss related to a shocked listener how she had, in the days that followed, nursed the fugitive until he was healthy enough to express his thanks. Soon he felt able to continue his escape; the assumption that he had been killed afforded almost certain safety. His final words to her impressed on her mind the importance of freedom to her partners in misery. "Corliss,"

69

he said, "the loss of my ears is but a small price to pay. I hope you are free someday and can help others as you have helped me. You will be a great lady, you have a good heart. God bless." She listened, speechless but filled with thoughts too powerful for her mind to appreciate until now. And now, under the clouded sky and the cloud of slavery hanging over North Carolina, she said with firm resolution, "Jane, we will and must help."

By nightfall the two sojourners, one white, one black, were crawling or running in a crouched position through the familiar tobacco field towards the slave quarters. Jane was thinking, "I hope I fed the horse adequately; I hope I programmed Corliss properly." She realized it was now or never; it was too late to turn back, review plans and check preparations. Three hundred yards from the log cabins, which her husband and Hannabal had built, she stopped; she knew Corliss was the only one who could go the last, but most perilous, little way.

As Corliss crawled, she could not hear the dried branches breaking under palms and knees for the pounding of her own heart. A field mouse ran over her hand and, for a brief second, she could hardly control her emotions. She almost screamed; that would have meant certain death. Instead she transformed her fear into the words, "Jesus, help me and Jane," and ended the prayer with tears.

She crawled on, knowing that the point of no return had been passed. She knew she must forget her fear, which could only hinder success and threaten their lives. In a few more minutes, she was looking into the window of the nearest slave cabin, and into the eyes of young Sammy; he was a few years older but no less talkative. Sammy was startled and turned to his mother, yelling, "A boogie man, a boogie man!" Corliss was paralyzed. She didn't know what to do, only wishing that someone else were in her place.

She felt herself being carried into the cabin by strong arms, one on either side of her body. As she gradually regained her faculties, after a half hour or so, she stared in the eyes of a roomful of puzzled black people. However, they had sense enough to feel the presence of something good. The good they were to learn of, the escape to Canada, caused an overpowering need for spontaneous praise to God. Although only an hour elapsed, a new lease on life was begun for the seven present in the room, plus little Sammy.

Jane's thoughts for her own safety were subordinated to her thoughts for the safety of the nine people crawling back across the plantation fields. She could scarcely believe the sight of little Sammy riding on Caesar's back, pretending his father was a beast of burden—at this point in history the analogy was not far from the truth. Jane smiled and shook her head; she thought to herself, "Sammy's free spirit must not grow up in slavery. I am more determined than at any other time—I'm determined to free these slaves and others for future Sammys of the world."

With the strength of commitment that Jane had drawn from her past experiences and what she had just seen, the task of following the north star and moss became but a mere formality to the determined freedom seekers.

Jane knew from her own experience that they must hide by day and travel by night as she and John had done. What she did not know was that she and John had been lucky.

On the fifth day of their journey they heard the familiar baying of hounds in the distance. The sound was too close to allow thoughts of safety. The three men made long wooden spears; their action was instinctive, and governed by knowledge inherited from ancestors who had done the same for many generations. Caesar, knowing he must take the initiative for the women and his son Sammy, gave them instructions for them to take charge of the wagon. Even though it was not quite dark, he told them to run the horse as quickly as endurance would allow north and towards the safety of another nightfall. "We will catch up," he said; Jane reluctantly accepted his words as motivation to leave. The women and children embraced the men, knowing full well that their husbands' freedom could possibly come in the form of death.

The three men ran in another direction than the people they loved. The women appreciated the bravery of the men for the opportunity it gave them to possibly taste freedom. "The hounds will follow us, hopefully," Caesar reminded them. He was soon to find he was right. And he was helped by the coming of nightfall. The forest at night, without a full moon, gave the three African descendants an advantage, enhanced even further by their dark skin.

When the first dog attacked he could only see their white eyes and grimacing teeth before he felt the spear impaling him in the throat. The other two dogs, as if realizing they were not dealing with ordinary prey, hesitated in their attack after seeing the fallen victim. It almost looked as if they were wishing they had not charged ahead of the other dogs on leashes by a mile or more—but it was too late.

Caesar, who had been trained in his teens as an Ashanti warrior, was too experienced with his makeshift spear to give the hounds any advantage. The spear whistled through the air and the target he had chosen blinked for the last time. The hound's eye was pierced and its brain permanently pithed; it was dead. The third dog found the other warriors no less skillful adversaries; two spears quelled its howls and left the main party of men and hounds, who were moving inexorably closer, wondering about the strange and sudden silence.

The hunted warriors now, slaves before, ran on through the night with their heads looking up continually through the thick forest and leaves, searching frantically for that beacon of hope in the vast expanse of sky and space, the north star.

When the slave patrollers discovered the dead carcases of their hounds their faces grew red with anger; their rage was the personification of death. "Those are some dead niggers," they all agreed, and they forged on.

Caesar realized that the three warriors were running out of time. He gave them Jane's instructions on the location of the nearest underground railroad station, and they made a decision to split up. This would confuse the hounds and give the warriors a chance to find the Quaker farm and safety. "It is but a day from here, according to Jane's map of landmarks. If, after three days, we are not all joined, fear the worst, look to your own safety and continue north to Canada." As Caesar said these words, he felt an emotional impact, as if he were giving his final will and testament. The friends hugged each other as potentially free men and departed.

Caesar's route was the one chosen by the slave patrollers; it seemed as if fate was dealing him a bitter blow. But he also had the chance to give the highest gift a human being is capable of giving: his own life.

A day and a half passed by and with each passing hour Caesar's chance of escaping diminished. From the sounds of the approaching slave patrollers, and from a reconnoitre on the last evening, Caesar knew he was dealing with insurmountable odds. He made a decision: if he was to die, he would die as a warrior. On the evening of the second day he was still, miraculously, eluding the jaws of death, but he knew it was a mere matter of time. That warm summer evening, one could only see the silhouette of his kneeling body, his hands in a position of prayer. He prayed for himself, his wife and little Sammy and others. He smiled at the thought of them being safe and free. He removed his clothes, as if driven by some force beyond his control. His black skin was shimmering in the moonlit night; he tied his shirt around his private parts as if it were a loin cloth, reminiscent of his native attire in Africa. He praised Allah and God, respecting both his father's religion and his own, and proceeded to carry out his own form of last rites.

Caesar crept like an African hunter with the skill and cunning of a jungle cat. His will and determination were no match for any moving thing in the dark blanket of the forest.

When Caesar reached the patrollers' camp, he could only see the fire and the human bodies lying near by. "Where are the dogs?" he thought; but he did not care.

Surprise and ancestral instinct as a warrior were on his side; he wished he were at home in Africa, not placed in this incongruent climate. "Why can't my ancestors see that I am still one of them, a man, a free man, not a slave?"

Caesar ran into the camp of sleeping men. The patrollers had been so confident that they hadn't felt the need for sentries; they were soon to realize their error. The first to realize found a spear entering his chest and piercing his heart. The cry of the dying and Caesar's own warrior scream woke the others, giving Caesar only time enough to throw his spear through the neck of another patroller, who was going for his gun. The other three ran into the woods with Caesar after them, his hands the only weapon he had left. The three, he realized, were running towards the dogs tied but a hundred yards away. The dogs were yelping viciously, annoyed that their sleep was disturbed by this crazed human warrior. Caesar had caught one patroller, whose body went limp and lifeless from Caesar's stranglehold; the warrior felt teeth entering his heel, and the feeling continued into his arms and back. The nine hounds were crazed and as canine teeth found Caesar's throat, he could see the eyes of death that were glimmering as if on fire. As blood gushed from his jugular vein his last thought was, "Little Sammy, my son, is going to be free in Canada."

Caesar's fellow warriors had reached the underground railroad station, and informed the others of Caesar's plan for splitting up. The group waited in vain for five days for Caesar to arrive. The tears of Caesar's wife and Sammy were a combination of sadness and the hysterics of those used to tragedy, yet not willing to accept it. Sammy cried because his mother cried; he didn't fully realize that his father would not be able to join them in Canada.

The freedom runners ran on and on until they reached the

Indiana border and safety at Ephraim and Mary Stout's. Jane knew she had accomplished the near impossible, but she could not enjoy her achievement. Any contact with little Sammy made her remember the fate of his father. Upon hearing how Caesar had given his life to help save the others, the Stouts insisted upon a prayer service with other members of the Quaker community. Sacrifices like Caesar's made the Quakers even stronger in their commitment to continue their abolitionist ambitions. "These people surely are not beasts of burden," they repeated time and time again, until tears would fill the eyes of less stalwart souls.

The small group of sojourners, having received their first taste of freedom, were anxious to continue to the ultimate freedom of Canada. The appropriate underground terminals were mapped out and John and Jane stood with the Stouts, waving their arms like Moses, as if imploring the heavens to part the waters and let their people go.

MILE XIII

Although John was rejoicing for his friends who were escaping, his heart was heavy. He turned to Jane as they entered their room. "Jane, I will not be truly happy and free until we also go to Canada."

"John, I know, but I am going to have a baby." Jane's words rang in his ears and made all else seem unimportant. His deep inner happiness turned, in only six months, into a deeper outer sadness. Because of her small frame, and because she had endured psychological and physical hardships without knowing she was pregnant, Jane could not carry her child full term.

John stood outside the room as Mary and Corliss took on the duties of the midwife. They left no doubt in John's mind that Jane would be well looked after. The slap on the buttocks of the newborn infant made his mind race back to thoughts of his own father. The thought of Hannabal's oft-repeated instructions: *John, as soon as you are old enough to understand, remember the side of the tree the moss grows on and the north star are the way to freedom and Canada. Freedom, John, like my native Africa.* The fifth slap without a response from his infant made John realize that all was not well. He froze, as if in a state of psychological paralysis.

The door opened and someone asked him to come into the room, but John was oblivious to his surroundings. Mary tapped him on the shoulder and the tap was enough to bring John into reality. He responded with the natural reaction of a husband who cares deeply for his wife.

He walked into the room and looked into Jane's eyes. They were still watery from the strain of childbirth and the realization that the child had been stillborn. John instinctively realized he must be strong but he was too human to hold back his own tears.

Ironically the room was charged with harmony, the harmony which comes with an event congruent with God's divine will for mankind, tears that fell because his wife had been forced to crawl on her stomach with slavery's victims behind her. Her followers were eager, and thankful to this beautiful person who was leading them to the promised land. They did not know—and Jane herself did not know—that she was risking two lives; her own, and the life that was growing inside her. The insidious disease of slavery was still hounding them.

A dove flew by the window ledge, and hit the window with enough force to attract attention. Mary was the first to notice, and she said, "Look, the white dove of peace." All eyes turned to the window except John's. He said in anger, "How can it be peace, when I, a free man, cannot father a child without the effect of slavery? Jane's and my first child—and we are forced to hide even its innocent dead body from the outside world, here in Indiana. I feel like running, and shouting at the top of my lungs, 'Why? Why, world, what could this tiny infant do to hurt you; it just wanted to be free.'

With these words he left the room, after first gently placing the dead infant in his arms. The others looked at each other, too shocked to speak out. The power of this man's pride, and his sensitivity of character, lingered on in the room. John walked down the stairs; he saw the people gathered downstairs but walked through the door, off the porch and into the woods. With head uplifted and eyes towards the north star, he yelled at the top of his lungs, "Hannabal, Hannabal, Canada, Canada, Canada." Those in the house could not make out his words, but Jane knew that she must, as soon as possible, make an attempt to flee farther north, if for no other reason than her husband's physical health. "John will not much longer be willing to hide the fact that he is my husband," she said to Mary and Corliss. "When that happens, he will have signed his own death warrant knowingly. Mary, we must map out an underground route to Canada."

Mary understood, but could only nod her approval. She and Ephraim had grown to love John and Jane as close friends, and now her friend was in a condition almost too weak to talk.

John walked deep into the woods, hoping he had hidden his emotions enough not to upset Jane whom he loved, but knowing he hadn't. "I will make it up to her; I will make her happy," he thought. The thought tempered his frustration and made him think about the reality of their situation. John made a resolution then and there, and spoke it out loud in the silence of the forest. "Jane and I will conceive more children in Canada, and if it be too wild for her fragile body, I will send her back to Indiana and into the care of these good Quaker people to birth our child. I will remain in Canada until she returns, and trick the serpent of slavery." As John spoke and walked randomly he unwittingly disturbed a pheasant's nest. The sounds of their wings in the night made John smile and say, "Maybe I will see you again in Canada." With these words he kissed the top of his infant's head, the half-smile left his face and tears filled his eyes.

In next months John used his work as medicine to help contain his freedom desire. The neat Quaker settlement looked in even better repair as a result. John's propensity for goodness, which the hearts of the community could readily ascertain, gave him status; his reputation as a carpenter was adding to that status. Those few of these good people who had thought his intermarriage too liberal were made to realize that racial harmony begins when people become able to know each other better.

Jane, with much consultation and limited approval from John, was making preparation for one last abolitionist movement back to North Carolina. She also wanted to visit her father, David King; it might be their last visit. She was also determined to seek, out of necessity, enough inheritance to further them along the perilous and winding road to freedom.

John's jobs, though gaining in number, were still too intermittent and low paying to pay their way. Outside of the Quaker community, which didn't need many repairs, he received only left-over jobs and token pay. Necessity was the mother of Jane's courage. As she and Corliss waved back at her caring family and John, her husband, she felt for the first time that she and John were not ordinary humans. They had had to endure many physical and psychological hardships. Corliss even heard her say, "Why couldn't John and I have been born at a later date in mankind's history? When will racial harmony lift the burdens of racial bigotry? Is there a place where only normal human burdens need be suffered? To add the pressures of racial bigotry is too much—it breeds discontent and riot."

The Irish and Scottish Jane King moved cautiously along the road leading to her father's plantation. Dust filled her nostrils and the sun scorched her bright red hair.

David met her at the wagon. He lifted his daughter's light frame to the ground. They embraced as more than father and

78

daughter; it was the embrace of two people who knew they were seeing each other for the last time. They walked slowly into the plantation house arm in arm, they broke bread together and talked with a passion to share information and thoughts. Jane did not hide any facts.

Any emotions other than love and concern were all foreign to David where his daughter was concerned. David was an intelligent person; he loved his daughter's mind and knew he must mind his own business. Jane talked also of necessities of life, and money was given without question. She also gathered personal belongings and pictures to remind her, in the new world, of some of the good she left behind. "Provided," she thought, "we make it to the new world of Canada."

She slept that night in her father's house, and made a vow that someday, in a world of less racial bigotry, she would return again. Tears filled her eyes as she realized she might not be given the chance to fulfill her vow. The cloud of bigotry hung over her head.

Jane awoke the next day yawning and stretching—the aftermath of her tiring journey and much-needed sleep. She looked out the window; the sight of the plantation was almost breathtaking. The sun was rising in the eastern sky. A slight fog was lifting from the tobacco plants, simulating smoke, but to her early morning eyes it was a refreshing and inviting sight. Jane knew for certain she loved North Carolina. Then she witnessed the procession of slaves heading towards the fields; the slaves carried the burden of slavery. Even here, under the benevolent hand of her father, these people could not see the world as Jane had; to them the rising sun meant toil and drudgery. Their days were void of positive feedback, reward and feelings of self-worth. "Work is necessary," Jane thought, "but under the physical or psychological chains of slavery, without freedom, it is a high form of punishment." Jane could hardly comprehend why she was so pensive this morning. But she seemed to gain strength in her conviction that flight to Canada, no matter how physically beautiful she found North Carolina, was a necessary peril. She loved John more than a sunrise, and she hated human suffering in any form.

As she walked down the winding stairs and into the breakfast room, she knew that her reflections of early morning were like blessings from above, allowing her to cope with the tears in her beloved father's eyes. "Do not cry, Father," she said.

"Daughter, I would not, if I did not miss you and fear for your safety. My influence cannot adequately protect you; even though you have been here only a day and your journey was carefully planned, word has come to me that slave patrollers have caught word of it and are heading this way right now."

Jane's practical mind was busy thinking; she had a good mind for commonsense details. "Father, I must purchase a gun."

David nodded and the two left their breakfast and went in horse and buggy to a trusted gunsmith. They purchased, as the bill of sale indicated, "one rifle gun for which I have paid George Lamworth [sixteen or eighteen dollars]. Witness A. T. Woodburn, M. S. Peggott."[4]

The gun would be used to save her life if it was threatened. Jane realized she placed more confidence in the weapon itself than she did in her ability to use it. John would later comment, "Jane, you couldn't hit the broad side of a barn."

Jane would laugh and say, "But the angle of the ricochet might."

David and Jane sped hastily back to the King plantation to pick up Corliss and be on their way; their farewells were foreshortened due to fear. The two abolitionists and freedom runners headed north. Jane even commented as nightfall came, "Corliss, keep your eye on the north star, and the moss on the side of the tree, that is the way to Canada and freedom."

Corliss did not realize the significance of the words, not

knowing their origin. She only thought, "Is Jane losing her senses? I can't see the moss on the trees on this dark night, but I can see the north star."

The north star, the underground railroad and a Divine Hand rewarding good brought the two safely back to Indiana. But the safety of the Stouts was not security enough.

The wagon wheels had not cooled before John had loaded the children and bare necessities into the wagon. "Jane, we have had to hide in the attic the past three nights; we are certain the bounty hunters are after us. Mary even had to mislead an informant. He came visiting, on the pretence of giving me jobs, just to find out if we were here. Mary told him we had left for North Carolina some months ago."

Mary and Jane exchanged loving courtesies and promised to write. Directions were given on the underground railroad stations between Indiana and Toledo. Thus the underground railroad, a secret, complex network of free blacks, former slaves and white American and Canadian abolitionists, helped John Freeman Walls and his family to continue along their still winding road.

MILE XIV

Again it was spring. The snow was melting and thousands of migrating birds were heading north. Corliss would look up at them passing overhead and remark, "I wonder if they're trying to reach Canada, too?" John and Jane would only smile; their smiles contained worry, anticipation and fears. The wagon creaked along the dirt roads, which were often avoided by regular travellers. Woods were all around them, which gave John some sense of security about travelling a bit by day. He was anxious and knew he could make better time in daylight. The perils awaiting them in the woods were constantly in his thoughts; he need only look down to see the scars left by the wolves.

Corliss was falling ill with something which John and Jane hoped would pass. At times they would have to stop, and she would run off into the woods to relieve herself through vomiting. This illness forced them to do most of their travelling by night to avoid lengthy delays in relatively open terrain. As they travelled most everyone was absorbed in his own thoughts, as if realizing this was not an ordinary trip, certainly not a trip that was conducive to children's laughter and play. These were disciplined children, mindful of the need for safety; they could even be heard talking in whispers.

The freedom runners had more than they could handle—sickness, small children on one hand and slave patrollers on the other. John's and Jane's love was being tested. Yet Jane and John Freeman forged on, guided by Hannabal's words: *Remember, the side of the tree the moss grows on and the north star, is the way to freedom and Canada, like my native Africa.*

Fortunately, the spring nights were bright and afforded visibility. However, one night they regretted the spring brightness. "What is that, John?" Jane cried. But before they could react the horse had reared up; it took all of John's strength and horsemanship to control it. When John gained control they were within ten feet of the decomposing body of a young man.

John approached, hindered only by the stench and the thought that the perpetrators of the deed might still be around waiting to claim more victims for this undignified end. Closer inspection revealed a bullet hole in the man's back. The bullet would not have killed the man immediately; like some wounded animal he had run to some secluded portion of the earth to die a slave's death. The burial was swift and funeral services were held to a minimum. John's and Jane's Christian roots gave them strength to bear what they had seen and to explain to the children, who were almost in a state of shock, that this was God's plan; death was a normal thing. But they did not wish to reveal that there were individuals out there who ignored the commandment, "Thou shalt not kill." This would only serve to make the children more afraid.

John repeated his favorite passage from the Bible. "My son, forget not my laws, but let thine heart keep my commandments for length of day and long life shall they bring to thee.[5] Then he cried, "Why could not the slave patrollers keep your commandments? Why?" His final words were for the poor victim of slavery, who had lost his life too young to know life and too old to endure the disease of slavery. "God bless this man," John said. "He is finally free."

The freedom runners continued on their long road, wishing desperately for the end. The next underground station they reached was more than a haven of safety; it was also a surprise. They were on the inner boundaries of Ohio, in a town later to be called Toledo. The outskirts of Toledo were much the same as the outskirts of any city of that time, surrounded by woodland. The cabin in the woods, built but a few years before and reminiscent of the style used in North Carolina, reminded John, as he and his family walked towards it, of the familiar surroundings along Troublesome Creek.

Then he saw a figure coming towards him and he stopped—the others did not know why. The look on John's face made Jane feel frightened rather than secure. Her thought was, "Is this the station in the woods with abolitionist sympathizers that Mary and Ephraim had mapped out? Why is John so hesitant?" Before she could speak, she witnessed the reunion of two friends; the two men greeted each other as if each were Lazarus, newly resurrected from the dead. "John, John," the unknown man said, and John replied, "Peter!" Their arms folded around one another, to the happy accompaniment of smiles and laughter.

The days that followed were filled with more liveliness and fun than the Walls family had known since its conception as a family. Even though they had enjoyed the hospitality of the Stouts, the shadow of fear was too great to allow much happiness. Nearby Toledo and John's friend of old permitted a kind of freedom of expression—perhaps because they were so close to their ultimate destination.

Peter had aged considerably, and his receding hairline had altered his appearance. But in spite of the pressures he had endured and the physical changes they had produced, he had an attitude of carefreeness and niceness, which made others respect and like him.

John asked Peter about his escape. He learned that the information Hannabal had passed down to him, regarding the north star and the side of the tree the moss grew on, had literally saved Peter's life and led him to freedom. They both were careful to avoid much conversation about the slave families they had been forced to leave behind. "John," Peter said, "the underground railroad and you helped me to freedom. I met at least fifteen sympathizers; they took such good care of me that I, too, have become an abolitionist and will remain so for as long as slavery and freedom runners exist."

Peter told of how he would use his almost white complexion to advantage. At one station he was given the clothes of a Quaker, and with these, a Bible and a beard he had grown just for the purpose, he walked through the streets of many a town, "big as cuffie," defying any man, black or white, to call him a nigger again. "I was sharp," Peter remarked.

John could only laugh and say, "Peter, you haven't changed a bit."

The discussion of Peter passing for white led into a more serious conversation regarding the safety of John's and Jane's situation. Jane could, with her white children, easily enter the town for provisions; this she did. John, however, was not safe with or without his family; he knew a bounty had been placed on him, and his jet-black complexion was easily identifiable. It angered him that he was still not totally free. In Indiana he had occasionally pretended that Corliss was his wife and travelled more freely. But here, on the last leg of his journey, he could not risk any exposure in broad daylight. Peter was sensitive and sensed John's dilemma. Although he had to leave on abolitionist business, he prompted John to go to a place called Shanty Town. Ironic as it may seem, John's visit was the unlocking of his final barrier to freedom.

John wandered through the streets, not believing what he was seeing and not necessarily caring to see it again. "This cannot be freedom," John thought. "This is not much better than the slave quarters in North Carolina."

"Who pretends to be the carpenter, as certainly there was none." The quotation ran through his head. "At least there are no slave masters," he thought; that brought him some consolation.

A stranger came up and asked if he could borrow some money. Instinct kept John wary. "No," he said, certainly not wishing to flash the two dollars he had in his pocket. John turned and walked away but realized that he was being followed. His pace increased, but he was too proud to run. Possible African traits, suppressed by long years of slavery, had come to the surface.

He was in a big jungle, surrounded by darkness. He was being stalked by the most intelligent of all animals, a wild animal made crazy not by wounds inflicted physically, but by wounds inflicted psychologically. The wounds went so deep that this sorry victim looked to his fellow sufferers to relieve his frustration. He attacked John Freeman Walls from the rear.

John curled on the ground as the knife stabbed into his shoulder, his body was ravished with pain. He looked into the eyes of not just a crazy black man who had lost his mind, but the personification of years and years of racial persecution and its ugly byproducts.

John was strong and, more important, smart. He defended his life instinctively. Like a panther, he leaped from the ground and, before a sound could be made, he seized the crazy animal by the throat. He watched his own strong, black fingers manipulate the man's neck, watched the man's knees give way and his eyes bulge. Just before death occurred, John released the man and let him fall to the ground, gasping for breath.

John was a man of few words. All he said that night was, "When will I ever be free, when will I ever be free, when will I reach Canada?"

The blood on John's shoulder coagulated and the healing process began, as if prompted by his need to fulfill his destiny and perpetuate his name by attempting to continue along his long road to somewhere.

John slept, but not before worrying about the safety of Jane and the kids. "I know they will be worried about me," he thought, "but I must rest for strength. My Jane is a strong woman. I love my Jane."

A tap on John's shoulder shocked him into consciousness; he immediately crouched in a defensive position. John learned that there was good and bad in all races; in the space of a few hours, he was able to survive to see both. Charley Stewart was the name of the man who stood beside him now, and to John he would prove a needed friend. Charley was strong in stature, much like John, but certain characteristics set him apart from the average man. Charley's head was most noticeable— it was devoid of hair, a fact that contributed to his masculinity. His prowess as a boxer set him apart, too; Charley was a man who commanded respect.

John learned that Charley was a professional boxer on a plantation in Virginia. The plantation bred slaves for just that purpose. He had fought in bouts of forty rounds or more and up to the point of his escape had experienced no defeats. His prowess and success in the ring helped him to escape, he told John.

A month before his escape, he was scheduled to fight a champion by the name of Sid. Sid had the distinction of competing abroad; he won fame and fortune for his master in foreign lands.

86

Charley told John he was certain he could win, as age and quickness were on his side. Sid was old but, to his master, still potentially profitable. Charley asked his master, prior to heavy training, if he could visit his loved one on the neighbouring plantation. He wanted, he said, to rid himself of any further physical desires, to ensure his master an opportunity to make big profits.

"Well, John," Charley said with a laugh, "I did my duty, ridding myself of my physical desires, and then proceeded to rid myself of my masters. They even put the hounds on me John, and I outran the beasts." John realized that Charley's head start must have provided some advantage; even though he felt Charley's story was farfetched, he was not prepared to challenge his statement. He liked and respected Charley.

John told Charley his own story, emphasizing how Daniel had willed him his wife, Jane. He also stressed their escape proceedings. Charley could not believe until later, when he actually saw Jane, that John's incredible story was actually true. For a fleeting moment, he fantasized a future time when social harmony was an accepted fact.

Charley was thankful he had met a good friend—so thankful that he insisted upon including John and Jane in his final plans to escape. He had been in Toledo some two months and by listening and talking when appropriate, he had prudently learned the whereabouts of an abolitionist captain by the name of Mr. Sloan. John and Jane smiled as they looked at each other with a nod. This was the name given to them by Ephraim and Mary Stout. Mr. Sloan was to transport Charley to Canada in a fortnight. "I am certain he will take you also," Charley said.

John and Charley walked along the waterfront in an almost prance-like manner, and they talked of sharing a common reward which was Canada. "What do you think it will be like?" Charley would ask.

John replied, "My mother would sing spirituals and refer to it as the heaven that we sing about in our songs."

On hearing the word heaven, Charley yelled, "Let the foul wind of Virginia stop at the border of Canada and leave black Charley alone, for here we come, John." As Charley spoke John's name, he realized he desired to learn more about this quiet man, much blacker than himself, who had come this far with his master's wife. He asked, "John, how did you earn Jane, you old devil? Niggers always be wanting a white woman, ha, ha."

The look in John's eyes answered his question. For the first time in many a year, Charley felt a chill. John's piercing stare contained the anger of one willing to risk life and limb to defend the honour of his woman. "John, John," he said, "don't take me wrong. . .ah. . .ah." He stopped and John spoke, realizing that under Charley's rough, pugilistic exterior lay a sensitive, caring nature that deserved understanding.

"Charley, Jane is my wife first, Christian lady second, the mother of my children third, white lady fourth. It is not the advantage or disadvantage of any one attribute she possesses, but rather the combination of all of the traits of her external and internal character.

"The fact that she is white is just one of the reasons I love her, not the whole reason. Color was not then and is not now a serious consideration between us. It was only serious to the racially ignorant."

"Who is this stranger?" Charley thought. He was puzzled. This man who did not speak much, who had not had the advantage of an academic education, had issued a soliloquy on race relations that even Charley's more physical mind could understand. For the remainder of his life, Charley never touched on the subject again.

As if trying to make amends by sharing something enjoyable with John, Charley said, "Hey, I have something for you to see; come and watch your old buddy parlay three dollars into thirty." John did not understand what he meant, but was soon enlightened.

The smoke and stench of a poorly ventilated room choked

their senses. When the smoke cleared John could see six burly black men playing something they called poker. The feeling of fun led John to feel there was nothing more serious happening. In the corner of the room was a man that John had to take a double look at, as his eyes could not believe what they had seen the first time. Standing in the corner was a human specimen some seven feet tall. He looked so ominous and forbidding that the gun he held in his arms seemed almost comical and unnecessary. His eyes met John's and John nodded. It was the greeting of one who would rather be friends than enemies. The stare he received in return made John realize that there was obviously more serious business being transacted here than he thought. He thought the tall man must be a descendant of the Watusi tribe his father had spoken of, the giants of his native continent of Africa. Before John could continue his train of thought, Charley announced his arrival.

"I'm going to down you niggers here this evening; might as well give up your money now, cause Lady Luck sleeps with me. And you, Goliath, you mess with old Charley and I'll chop you down to five feet, ha, ha." John felt a chill as he heard Charley's disrespect and lack of fear of the giant of a guard standing in the corner. Out of instinct, he turned and looked at the man they called Goliath to detect his reactions, expecting the worst. What he saw made him realize how his new friend's prowess as a boxer was respected for, with a smile on his face and his hand outstretched to shake Charley's, Goliath said, "You the onlies nigger I wouldn't mess with, ceptum with this gun, ha, ha."

All laughed at Goliath's words and the tension—felt only by John—was relieved when someone said, "Nigger, you's crazy, sit down and let us whip your black ass out of some money." Someone patted Charley's back. John was sort of confused and awed by all of this, yet slightly caught up by it.

"Does your friend want to play?" someone else asked. All eyes turned towards John, and he could not hide the confusion on his face. He was torn between fear of

89

embarrassment and prudence. And he heard something in his mind say, "I'd rather be respected and liked," and with this thought came the encouragement to say, "No, thanks." Realizing they had lost a potential pigeon, the players blocked him out of their eyes and thoughts.

John was half asleep when he felt his heart speed up. "Black Joe, you crazy, get your hands off that money, my mama didn't raise no fools." He opened his eyes, anticipating what he thought was almost certainly a fight. "Oh, my shoulder is still sore from the knife wound, but I must help defend Charley," he thought. "What am I doing here?" To his amazement, the tension cleared almost as quickly as it had arrived, and smiles and laughs replaced it. Numerous times during the night, tension rose but was dispelled by lighthearted personal remarks. At one point, he even observed a player rolling on the floor with laughter. He came to the conclusion that what appeared to non-players as madness was, to these comrades, part of the game. He smiled to himself.

A pensive mood hit him as he sat on the straight-backed chair, head bowed, chin resting on his chest. He made a personal observation that could explain why white folks found black people confusing and boisterous at times. He went on to think that the exaggeration of emotions by his brothers, in relaxation or play among themselves, served as a necessary psychological release of the pressures and frustrations built up inside by the direct and indirect effects of slavery. A free spirit who feels physical and psychological oppression will shout his thanks for being free again at the first opportunity. With this thought, John fell asleep.

He felt a pain in his healing shoulder as Charley, forgetting his friend's recent misfortune, shook it to wake him up. The grimace on John's jet-black complexion made him stop shaking and with no apology needed, John woke up and smiled. He saw Charley's grin and the thirty-five dollars he was waving in John's face. "I am quitting." Coarse and lighthearted social courtesies were extended, in keeping with the remarks John had heard before he slept, and he and Charley left through the back door.

John spoke first, but he knew that whatever he said could not do justice to what he felt. His Christian upbringing had always taught him to be in the world, but not of the world; until tonight, he had not fully appreciated what Jubil had taught him. He was proud of himself, but too respectful of Charley to pass judgment.

He knew that his naive, innocent questions as to why Charley gambled would distract from Charley's happiness and John, as a friend, would not let this happen. Besides, anyone who could successfully risk his life in a ring could handle about anything. This gave him peace of mind about his friend's life style.

"Pressures of society," John further thought, "forced people to do things that, to others less pressured, appeared perilous." John could scarcely believe the seriousness of his thoughts, especially after the frivolous experience he had just had, but he was forced to continue his thoughts. Charley represented the risk-loving type. One certain conclusion could be drawn: no matter what you see a person do superficially, do not judge a whole person or, for that matter, a whole race, on the actions of a few. And even in those few, there might be good and admirable qualities. "Walk a mile in my shoes before you judge," John thought. These thoughts for a moment left John almost numb. "I can't be justifying slavery. I must be meaning that blacks and whites will realize human frailties possessed by all and be more forgiving in a future time; yes, yes, that is what I mean."

Two happy individuals walked back to Peter's cabin. One was happy because of thoughts of future goals, the other because of thoughts of immediate ones.

Charley and John reached the cabin and were greeted with a warm welcome and warm biscuits. Jane's independence as a person made her respect John and she greeted him intimately rather than harrassing him for staying out all night, a response common to couples secure and respectful of each

91

other. She could also sense a good in Charley that would protect John, if necessary.

"Where is Peter?" John asked. "I want to introduce him to Charley."

"When you didn't arrive home last night, he went looking for you."

"That's my Peter," John thought. "And, knowing Peter, he made the best of a bad situation," John remarked to Charley with a wink.

"I like Peter already," Charley answered.

Peter had come to Toledo and found a niche for his talents. His role was unique and almost remarkable for the times; with the advantage given by his light complexion, he comfortably traversed white and black cultures and had overcome his own humble beginnings. He had become an orator for the abolitionist movement. John and Charley went out to find Peter; in the centre of the humble buildings, many recently built—or thrown together—stood a platform. On it stood a man whom John knew but had not really fully appreciated.

Peter had a crowd of some one hundred or more and was using his silver tongue to fullest advantage for the cause of freedom. The words which greeted John's and Charley's ears were as music.

> Free, free, we must be free. I cannot emphasize this enough. Vote, vote, we must have a vote. I came here to Toledo running, but I won't run no more; I came here to Toledo crying, but I won't cry no more; I came here to Toledo a slave, but I won't slave no more.
>
> We must achieve racial harmony now. We must not let others, as did I, have to forsake their beloved families in futile hope of returning to free all. I know we can overcome. Look, we can make it. We must. Since I have been here, I have seen what the rewards of free expression and making the best of your talents can do. Look in the front row, you all know him, he fixed many of your toothaches. Hosiah, your dentist, not schooled in white schools, but having a much harder way to go. Why? Because he was black.

Hosiah was shocked by such attention but smiled a humble smile, reinforced with pride. John and Charley looked at

Hosiah but, before they could be amazed at his unique achievement, Peter's words had captivated them again.

I ran through the swamps of North Carolina to be free. I crawled along the banks of the rivers and streams. I fought animals and man. I followed the north star, remembered the side of the tree the moss grows on.

These words brought a chill to John's spine; he realized he had given Peter the clues, handed to him by his beloved father, and he was proud.

I will not again run through the swamp of bigotry, crawl through the banks of oppression, kill my fellow man to be free.

At this point, Peter became prophetic.

We will plant the seed here in the north for oportunities, training centres, somewhere, Toledo, Detroit, New York, Philadelphia; an organization will be founded, which will move with quiet power and have a calming influence on racial tension and frustration and serve to foster racial harmony, not only in this potentially great country, but worldwide, to the melting sun of the Caribbean, to the vast plains of northern and southern Africa. True racial harmony will result.

John and Charley listened intently for another hour; the crowd of people was as enthusiastic as they were. By the end, Peter had tears in his eyes and the listeners had hope in their hearts.

Peter's skinny legs were shaking, his brow sweating profusely, his hands limp on tired arms—but he smiled. The smile was even greater as he was helped off the podium by his friends, John and Hosiah. Introductions and courtesies were extended and the four new and old friends walked along the river bank, sharing thoughts and teasing each other. More importantly, they revelled in the eloquent words of Peter who had, in an impromptu speech, woven the thoughts of his less-gifted brethren into a concrete expression of mankind's need for harmonious relations, past, present and future. Even the littlest child could appreciate and act upon his words.

The walk back through the woods and to the cabin gave all

time to unwind before nightfall came. The dinner Jane prepared was interrupted with final escape plans, which brought back the perilous reality of John's and Jane's circumstances. Comment was made on the fact that slave patrollers were watching every boat leaving for Canada. Further to this, Peter and Hosiah were certain that John's and Jane's unique situation was infuriating the bigots and motivating them to seek with a passion their return to North Carolina. Hosiah mentioned that slave patrollers would even frequently break the law and pretend to recognize a black as one of their runaway slaves. "There is even talk of a type of law, in the white man's government, to allow the carrying back into slavery of anyone found in northern free states if a witness is found—which you know, John, would be no problem."

"We have to get to Canada," John yelled. "For no one would be safe below heaven's border, especially us. Just to tear Jane and I apart, they would uncover thousands of false witnesses. This is why we could not enter a town in Indiana or here. I have even had to pretend to be Corliss's husband, for fear of suspicion or harrassment. This is no way to live."

As Charley sat, the firelight flickered on his bald head and a rare, serious thought overcame him. He knew what he had gone through mentally and physically to escape and, more than ever before, he respected John and his wife, for he knew they had reached the highest limits of personal pain. "They must be devoted to each other," Charley thought, and he was almost overcome with human envy. But before he allowed jealousy into his mind, the pride of knowing them and the additional realization that he could help them, made him nod his still-bowed head with contentment.

Daniel Junior, as he was affectionately called by his stepfather, came and sat on John's knee. John looked at him, as if gaining the inner strength to be free himself, and to have his family free. As if to reinforce this feeling, which needed no more reinforcement, the other three children were pulling on his neck and competed for his other knee. Jane and the others smiled as they watched this unique black man being wrestled to the ground playfully, by children who were too innocent and pure of heart to let their love be affected by John's shiny black complexion. This was their new father whom they loved, and he loved them.

The adults looked at each other as if to say, "Canada must be reached at any cost. The seed of this type of racial harmony must not fall onto barren soil, or drown in the waters of the Great Lakes."

Hosiah broke the silence as he saw that John was grinning and bearing the pain in his shoulder in order not to distract the children from their happiness and fun. "Let me see your father's shoulder, children. It is too sore for play." With this, Hosiah looked at John's wound. It needed but a few of his learned remedies to make it healthy again. John thought, "A black dentist, now my people will be free! We can do more than pick tobacco. My father was right."

They were all tired, both physically and mentally, and they slept under the stars that night. As John lay on his back with his wife's head resting on his good shoulder, he felt a tear coming to his eye. He looked up and, in the vast expanse of the clear summer sky, he saw the north star and the way to freedom. He closed his eyes and slept.

The peacefulness of their sleep was perpetuated by the pleasant atmosphere of the Sunday morning Church service. Charley, Hosiah and Peter could only sit and watch, wondering what was about to happen, which because of slavery's shackles, had so seldom happened before. Jane started by reading from the Bible and followed her reading with a sermon. John was called upon to read his favorite passage from the Bible. "My son, forget not my law; but let thine heart keep my commandments: For length of days, and long life, and peace, shall they add to thee."

Emotion often overcame him during the reading, and he suppressed the tears that tried to come to his eyes. The show of emotion on John's face confused Charley; he was certain John must have read or heard something in the sermon that he had missed. Charley had not yet been baptized, nor had he felt the power of the Holy Ghost. What did move him somewhat was the children's singing, led by Corliss's strong voice. She sang as if her words could be heard by her Mama and other displaced parents of children victimized and torn apart by slavery, wherever they might be. The service ended with applause and amens from all.

MILE XV

They all moved as a unit towards the dock, their plan polished after days of preparation. Their hearts were pounding and the adrenalin released in the flight-or-fight response was uncontrollable. The sweat on John's and Charley's foreheads was not put there solely by the heat of the sun. As John walked along the pier he was perspiring not only for himself and family but also for Peter, whom he could almost visualize standing on the podium and silver-tonguing the populace of New Vistula. He could see a frenzy of emotions and desires on their faces, for betterment and advancement, which comes hand in hand with a taste of freedom. He could also see Hosiah standing beside Peter, using his doctor image to add more credibility and influence to Peter's already powerful words. He could also see the anti-abolitionist informants in the crowd, infuriated to the point of wishing and planning to perpetrate bodily harm on the ringleaders of a rally they had publicly discouraged, but which had taken place anyway.

John said the last three words of his thoughts out loud. Charley thinking John was talking to him, asked, "What is it, John?"

"Oh, nothing," John replied, not wishing to confuse his friend with thoughts not related to their immediate purpose, thoughts that would only serve to burden Charley's heart. He also realized that the mass rally and demonstration had been organized by Peter and Hosiah, who were overlooking the threats to their own lives. They were hoping to help camouflage their friends' escape to Canada. If John and Charley knew what was taking place, they might have postponed their historical trip to Canada. At the precise moment that John's thoughts had been spoken out loud, a rock was catapulting through the air and was stopped in midflight by the cheekbone of Peter, abolitionist and former slave. Hosiah heard the bone fracture and his friend groan as his hand clutched his face and he fell off the platform to the ground. Hosiah's instincts and skills were invaluable as he went to the aid of his friend, whose blood had already mixed with the dust on the ground. "Thank God it missed his temple," Hosiah thought, knowing Peter had escaped death. He knew that Peter, who could always make the best of a bad situation, would use this incident as flag and battle scar to heighten his determination to end racial disharmony—the disharmony that made the sympathetic onlookers frenzied and mad by the near assassination of their leader. The crowd looked for a release of their frustration and anger, and seized the unwary anti-abolitionists before they could flee to safety. The crowd was ready to take their lives as payment for their actions until Peter spoke, under pain and duress: "Let the law punish them, for as long as the law is just and fair, we will not riot. If it becomes unjust, we will take whatever steps necessary, even if it means giving up our own, or taking others lives. If true freedom and equality doesn't come in our lifetime, we will have at least laid a solid foundation so our future generations will not need to hold mass rallies and will not need to riot in order to live in harmony."

Hosiah marvelled at how Peter had fought back the pain, which was even causing his eye to twitch, to speak these meaningful words. Peter represented the many unsung and less famous links in the underground railroad network to freedom. John Freeman Walls and family, as they continued their perilous walk, did not care that they were lesser known passengers on the underground railroad; they were concerned with making a meaningful contribution to the history of a new country called Canada, and with paving the way for the achievements of their future generations.

In their other plan to escape to the Canadian border, Jane was cast as a mistress who, with her children and slaves, was going to visit relatives in Canada. If anyone asked, these relatives were her father's family; Jane hoped her story would be believed. Her farsighted mind had even produced a letter from David to his phantom brother, filled with social niceties and personal family affairs.

The ramp leading to *The Pearl* seemed endless feet away, and Canada even further. The first person they saw coming from the ship and onto the dock was Mr. Sloan[6], the abolitionist captain who ran cargo and fleeing slaves from Toledo to Windsor and Amherstburg in Canada. Sloan would often say ironically, "Just as a ship brought you into slavery, my ship will take you out." After the signing of the fugitive slave law of 1850, his words would ring even truer.

As Sloan read Mary Stout's letter of introduction and pleas for help, he could hardly believe the words. "White woman, black man, how could it be?" His philosophical mind realized the uniqueness of these passengers. He looked at Jane and said, "Never will I have such a group again. I must try at all costs to get your group of sojourners to safety for the significance you hold for Canada and a future world."

Jane stared in shock and disbelief at these words, so prophetic in nature; even Mr. Sloan did not realize why they had come from his lips. Jane blushed with humility.

On that warm, sunny summer day in Toledo, the northern portion of the continent called Canada was the only concern of the people nervously entering the boat. No salutations or other expressions of emotion were given except when necessary, as informers were everywhere. For tobacco money, they would cast a traveller back into the hands of oppression.

Wayman Scott was the first to see the gun, and anger crossed his face. John was the first to feel the barrel as it touched the side of his head, and to smell the sulphur, which indicated that the gun had been recently fired. John knew by the look on the face of the owner—not unlike a smirk—that the gun, at the slightest provocation, would be fired again.

"Where you think you goin', nigger? I know all you niggers think Canada is a heaven, but I sure 'nuff can send you to the real hell."

John could hardly speak as fear, anger and sorrow clouded his senses. He could only think in sad refrain, "Lord, not now, not when we are so close."

Jane spoke with a quivering voice; her timidity was interpreted by the owner of the gun to be anger rather than fear. "Leave my nigger alone," she commanded, words which shocked even John, and made his mind travel back to the slave partrollers and the fake whipping on the first portion of the road.

Once the initial phase of shock subsided, John could appreciate his wife's shrewdness and he loved her even more.

"I will not have you or anyone else harass my slaves," she said with more confidence than she thought she was capable of.

The children, schooled in necessary silence, were exemplary students, except for little Daniel Junior. When he saw the gun at his father's temple, he could sense a potential loss of someone he loved and cried, "Daddy, Daddy, don't hurt my Daddy."

The slave patroller looked at the crying youth and thought, not of Daniel's tears, but of the complexion of the face that the tears were falling on. He could only mutter, "My God," as he remembered the poster he had seen months before, describing a white woman and a black man wanted—black man need not be brought back alive. "I am rich," he said.

Sweat rolled from the brow of Mr. Sloan, but he did not buckle under the pressure: he made way for premature sailing. No allowance had been made for such an interruption; every action was spontaneous; they were burdened with the knowledge that any miscalculation meant certain death.

Charley saw the approach of additional slave patrollers and knew they would not escape without paying a price. His thirty dollars, which was all he had to his name, was far too little a bribe for those in the terminal stages of slavery's disease. His immense frame, toned by years of preparation for self-defence, reacted on instinct rather than common sense.

Before the owner of the gun could be allied with the six approaching figures Charley, like a panther, travelled from his seat with the acceleration that only a trained athlete could command. He seized the gun, which was discharged only a foot from the ear of John Freeman Walls. Charley's strength was so great that, before the hunter could react, he felt the butt end of the gun hit his ear. He fell off the boat and into the water with a splash that sprayed the faces of the people on the boat, who sat paralyzed with fear. The shock of the water brought consciousness back to the patroller, who swam away wishing he had not crossed the path of John and Jane Walls.

John and Charley leaped from the boat, beseeching Mr. Sloan to weigh anchor. The command was unnecessary, as Sloan was schooled in the perils and hardships of being an abolitionist captain—he knew what he had to do.

John and Charley covered the fifty feet to the oncoming patrollers, who were crazed with anger and had already raised and fired two of their six guns. Courage and surprise attack saved the lives of the two freedom seekers; before another shot could be fired, a physical confrontation was in progress.

The fight was ferocious in intensity. John and Charley were fighting not only for their own lives, but for the lives of those who were yelling hysterically from the boat. Wayman Scott had to hold Jane in his arms to keep her from rushing overboard in a futile attempt to help her husband. Corliss could not keep the children from screaming, and finally gave in and screamed herself.

Charley had knocked one patroller to the ground; before he could take care of another, he felt the pain of a board breaking over his shoulder and turned. The patroller, realizing he had not permanently incapacitated the steel-like shoulders of the fighter, looked into the eyes of a crazed animal. Charley's smile was more frightening than any sight he had ever before seen. Charley lifted him over his head and threw him, and his cries for help faded into the Blue Water, along with his body. John had been ravaged by kicks and butts of gun handles, to the point where the knife wound Hosiah had managed to set right was bleeding again, becoming as painful as newer wounds.

Once Wayman had insured himself that Jane would not rush overboard, he dove into the water from the boat, which was now more than a few yards from the shore. He swam as quickly as possible to help the lady's husband, the man who had helped him escape slavery. Like a man about to release his built-up frustration and anger, he climbed quickly to the dock. He knocked one slave patroller down, then went after a second who was coming at him with a gun barrel swinging in the air.

John's jet-black complexion was wet with blood, his own and his opponents'. A man who had staved off an attack by wolves was not about to allow mere men to keep him from continuing along his road to somewhere. John struck out and, while one of his arms stopped the gun barrel, the other crushed the nose and cheek of his foe, bringing John a little closer to freedom.

The anti-abolitionists had been distracted to Shanty Town by Peter's courageous camouflage attempt; that attempt had quickly had near-tragic consequences, and Peter's ruse was not successful. The anti-abolitionists were even now heading for the dock, and John, Wayman and Charley could hear them shouting and running to help their friends. The three freedom runners were sensible: they decided to save their remaining strength for swimming, instead of confronting the victims of slavery's disease who had been made crazy and bold by informants' descriptions of what was taking place. The three black brothers ran and jumped into the Maumee River, swimming for their lives towards *The Pearl*. As they hit the water, Jane lifted a gun from the deck of the boat, the gun she had bought in North Carolina and first fired on the Ohio waters. A shot rang out like a cannon, her body recoiled and she landed unceremoniously on the deck of *The Pearl*. The frightened anti-abolitionists could not know how unskilled the lady, who was now sprawled upon the deck, was; they prudently sought shelter, giving John, Wayman and Charley time to reach the freedom ship.

John regained his composure and breath inside the boat. Then he said laughingly, "Jane, I thought you could not hit the broad side of a barn, but you were right on target that time." His face was covered with kisses from Jane and his thankful family.

The boat ride to Canada was a great occasion for the freedom seekers: liberty and justice prevailed. Songs were sung praising God and laughter was heard; and the people wept the tears that come when words fail and a soul who has been asked to meet the greatest of challenges has succeeded.

John's thankful prayer was echoed by the great twentieth-century liberator, Martin Luther King:

Free at last, safe at last, thank God almighty, we're free at last.[7]

The joyful people on the boat sighted Amherstburg, Ontario, Canada on that summer morning in 1845 through an early morning fog, which made it appear almost unreal and certainly too good to be true. As *The Pearl* cut its way through the waters of Lake Erie the shoreline, almost cliff-like at points, appeared breathtakingly beautiful to the passengers on the boat. As they stared at the green foliage, the clean, unpolluted air filled their nostrils; the beauty they saw was like an intoxicant of freedom. "Canada is Heaven," John said as the fog lifted, gradually revealing more and more of the land four million slaves wished for but only forty thousand reached. John thought of his father, and was proud that he was now living out his father's dream.

At this point in their journey, Corliss led the fugitives in a song, which Mr. Sloan had especially rehearsed with them. The song would give them something to think about, and quell their nervousness.

Song of the Fugitive

I'm on my way to Canada a freeman's rights to share;
The cruel wrongs of slavery I can no longer bear;
My heart is crushed within me, so while I remain a slave
I am resolved to strike the blow for freedom or the grave.

O Great Father, do thou pity me,
And help me on to Canada
Where panting slave is free.

I've served my Master all my days without the least reward;
And now I'm forced to flee away to shun the lash abhorred.
The hounds are baying on my tracks; my Master's just behind,
Resolved that he will bring me back and fast his fetters bind.

I heard that Queen Victoria has pledged us all a home
Beyond the reach of slavery, if we will only come,
So I have fled this weary way, my guide the bright North Star.
And now, thank God, I speed the day in the underground railcar.

O, Old Master, why come after me?
I'm whizzing fast to Canada
Where the panting slave is freed.

I now embark for yonder shore, sweet land of liberty;
Our vessel soon will bear me o'er, and I shall then be free.
No more I'll dread the auctioneer, nor fear the Master's frowns;
No more I'll tremble lest I hear the baying of the hounds.

O, Old Master, 'tis vain to follow me;
I'm just in sight of Canada
Where the panting slave is free.

Yes! I am safe in Canada—my soul and body free,
My blood and tears no more shall drench thy soil, O Carolina,
Yet how can I suppress the tear that's starting from my eyes
To think my friends and kindred dear as slaves must live and die.

O dear friends, haste and follow me.
For I am safe in Canada
Where the panting slave is free.[8]

The freedom seekers sang the song twice; by then Fort Malden could be seen and everyone was asking questions of the smiling Mr. Sloan. He explained that Fort Malden had represented a line of defence during the war of 1812. However he realized that the facts he was spouting, this morning at least, were overshadowed by the significance of the fort to John Freeman Walls and Jane King Walls. To them, Fort Malden was a fortress against the injustices of persecution and racial bigotry, the things they had to escape to live as normal human beings not chattels, and to love and live as true husband and wife, not as black and white.

The passengers could not show enough appreciation verbally; through tears of joy and invitations to visit them later, Mr. Sloan was rewarded.

He could not bring *The Pearl* up to the dock, as the water was too low, but he instructed his grateful passengers to walk on a rock below the surface of the water. The water would be only waist deep as the freedom seekers stood on the rock. The rock supported a parade of adults in single file, holding children in their arms and on their shoulders, and teetering back and forth, oblivious to the perils of drowning. They reached the shore and followed a sort of underground tunnel, which led from low land to high land. The tunnel was the last obstacle between the people and their long-sought freedom.

That night they all sat on the banks of the lake, praising God for delivering them out of the land of bondage as he had delivered Moses and his people long ago. Corliss's voice echoed through the starlit sky, causing people a mile away to wonder and listen, straining for more of her beautiful notes. The torch lights from Fort Malden glistened against the black background of the night, as if candles had been lit to give thanks for their deliverance.

Morning came and with it the dawn of more than a new day. John's eyes were already open and looking to the east as the sun ascended into the Canadian sky and shed its light over the land of freedom and opportunity. He blinked, not because of the sun's harsh rays, but because of his tears of happiness, which fell from his eyes and onto his jet-black cheeks. The happiness he was feeling was tempered by the psychological scars of the hardships he had become accustomed to and almost expected as part and parcel of life. He could not fully appreciate that he was nearing the end of his long road.

John had much to learn about his new country. Jane had begun to tell him about those who had forged a legacy of human rights for this country. This legacy was forged as far back as 1793, when Governor John Graves Simcoe and the first legislative assembly of Upper Canada (as Ontario was called) passed Canada's first anti-slavery law. This legislation did not outlaw slavery, but harnessed it: it outlawed the buying of new slaves, and immediate freedom was granted to those slaves who outlived their masters.

All slavery was abolished in the British Empire by Imperial Order in the year 1833. Canada became, in the eyes and hearts of thousands of courageous slaves, the heaven that they sang about in their songs.

The signing of the Fugitive Slave Law in the United States on 18 September 1850 made escape to Canada the only sure way to freedom. The new law allowed for the return into slavery of any escaped slave unfortunate enough to be caught outside Canada.

The Fugitive Slave Law inspired the creation of the underground railroad, a secret, complex network of free blacks, former slaves and white American and Canadian abolitionists. The railroad helped to bring more than forty thousand slaves to southern Ontario communities.*

Historians estimate that, of the forty thousand former slaves who found refuge in Canada, twenty thousand returned to the United States and their families after the Civil War.[9]

Before the Civil War, there were more than four million slaves in the United States. Of these four million, forty thousand would escape to Canada; of these forty thousand only half would remain in the north. And of the twenty thousand free Canadian souls only one, John Freeman Walls, had crossed the border with his white wife, the legacy of his master.

The warm sun touched the faces of John and Jane as they lay on the green grass in each other's arms. John's jet-black complexion contrasted with Jane's soft, white skin. Jane looked into her husband's eyes with love. Her lips quivered as John touched them with his fingers. Out of the reach of slave patrollers, they were free to be themselves and start a new mile on their long road. Angeline Walls was conceived.

---

*Some of these communities were: Amherstburg, Fort Malden, Anderdon, Marble Village Union, Gambia, Haiti Village, Brion, Dawn, Dresden, Shrewsbury, Maidstone, Puce, Elmstead, Little River, Gosfield, Gesto, Gilgal, New Cannan, the Matthew settlement, Edgar, Mt. Pleasant, Rochester, Harow, the refugee home society and Windsor.

PART III

1845–1909

*Life in Canada of fugitive slaves
through the eyes and hearts
of John and Jane Walls*

MILE XVI

The road to the promised land was not finished for the black man with white family.

Even though it didn't matter to them personally, John and Jane were both very aware of their difference in skin colour. Others would often remind them with their stares. Nevertheless, most of the new populace who did stare did so out of shock rather than prejudice.

John and Jane had been through too much to fully realize this fact. They were definite about wanting to find the most harmonious and promising settlement in this new land. They wanted to raise their children and grow old gracefully.

They were two good, Christian people.

The town of Amherstburg had, in the early 1840s, a total population of more than two thousand people; the black population was almost five hundred. The fugitive populace was placed into mechanical and shopkeeping roles.[1] Some fugitives, however, had higher aspirations.

John and Jane Walls lived, for a few weeks, in one of the most progressive hotels in the town. It was run by a very enterprising former slave, kept in unparalleled condition for the area.

The Walls family had to make many decisions quickly; none of them were unimportant. Heading the list was finding a permanent home, a school and a place to take religious training. To this end, Jane visited the town's separate school, and did not like what she found. The books were tattered and worn-out; the interior was comfortless. The lack of blackboards and chairs made Jane's European education seem even more unique than it had been. This small, low building had long benches on either side of the room and desks of corresponding length in front of them; such an unequipped building would just not do for her children. The black teacher watched as Jane discovered the scantiness—and bad quality—of the ink stands. She knew what Jane was thinking. Jane was diplomatic: she smiled and uttered words of encouragement to the teacher. However, they both realized that the school was one more dreary chapter in the history of difficulties encountered by black people in their pursuit of knowledge. The teacher proudly told Jane of the rumour that the Colonial Church and School Society had proposed to establish a school for the benefit of the black townsfolk, but open to all.[2]

Jane related to John the need to look elsewhere for a permanent location. She had based her opinion on the poor quality of the existing school, the uncertainty of forthcoming schools and the possibility that ambitious slave patrollers were more likely to find them in this easily accessible water port. John knew what he had to do.

The next day he was ready, apples, dried venison and other staples neatly packed away in his packsack. What pleased him most was the fact that he did not need the travelling papers that had been a legal necessity under the cloud of slavery.

John had even said to Jane without thinking, "Where are my travelling papers?"

Jane laughingly replied, "We are in Canada now, John, we're free."

At 5:00 A.M., the usual time John had wakened and, with other "Les Miserables," done chores prior to entering the tobacco fields, he was ready to enter the interior of the heaven he and others had sung about in their songs. As he kissed Jane on the cheek in farewell, he laughingly uttered, "God save the Queen," and they both smiled.

They knew that any settlement he found would be a

paradise compared to the raging fire they had fled. However, they still considered their black man-white woman relationship to be a psychological hurdle for strangers; they felt they had to approach the situation with prudence, even in this new land. They loved each other and were willing to rise to the challenge.

They were too conditioned to ill treatment by the lower-class mentality of some whites to refuse to search for a superlative area of racial harmony in this free land. On this foggy morning John waved goodbye to his lovely wife, a wife who had given up so much to be with him. He was determined to explore this new land, to attain the very best for her.

By the time the fog had lifted, he had walked to a settlement called Sandwich. The beautiful, serene village of fifteen hundred people, John was to learn, was home for perhaps one hundred black refugees. John's pure African descent was complimented by a few of similar heredity; most of the refugees were of various shades of black, attesting to the fact that miscegenation had already occurred—but he knew his mixed children would be conceived in gentler circumstances.

Jane had instructed John to look to the school conditions as a priority on his checklist of requirements.

By talking with a few of his brethern, he learned that, legally, the black population had the right to send their children, when qualified, into the town's grammar school. But no one had taken advantage of this right. John asked why and, as he listened to their answers, his face lengthened in sadness.

The African race, his race, was still carrying the burden of prejudice. School taxes had not customarily been levied on the black people. However, a prejudiced trustee levied a school tax as a concrete expression of his feelings towards the people he did not understand. In retaliation the black children were sent from their separate school to the public school. As the African children sat down in the public school, the white children deserted it. Within a few days, they were boycotting the schoolhouse, leaving it to the teacher and the black pupils. The whites reacted politically and made a sign that read SELECT SCHOOL. It was displayed prominently on the schoolhouse. The whites selected themselves in, and the blacks were selected out.[3]

Despite this, the black populace was quick to defend their white neighbours; they cited examples to prove that the whites' prejudice was only skin-deep.

The strong, old-fashioned English hatred of oppression had, not more than a fortnight before, sent an ambitious slave holder packing. He had come to their community to kidnap one Jerry Hasley and carry him back across the Detroit River into slavery. The story made John smile and say, "All whites aren't bad." As he spoke he thought of his beloved friend Daniel, and shook his head to fight back the sadness Daniel's death had caused.

After collecting himself John asked, "Are there separate schools only for blacks, or are Catholic or Protestant minorities allowed in them also?" He was made to feel somewhat better by the answer: "Yes, they all are allowed to attend."

At this point a Mrs. Jones enthusiastically interrupted the group of people crowded around John to interject some gossip she had heard from one of her white neighbours. "The people here would feel ashamed to have the Detroit people, who live so close by, know that whites are sent to school with blacks.[4] Isn't that crazy, Mr. Walls? But that's what she said." John could only nod his head; he realized that some of the prejudice caused by slavery had even washed up on the Canadian shore, like the smelly, dead fish he had seen earlier as he walked along the shores of the Detroit River.

One church, the group announced, an English Church, "has thrown open its doors to us."[5]

"But we prefer our own Methodist Church," one sixty-year-old man said. He, and indeed all the townspeople, were touched by this new, yet slightly polluted, air of freedom. As the old man spoke, he opened his mouth wide, showing missing teeth. John sensed the pride with which his words were uttered.

That night John slept in the comfort of Mr. Ed Taylor's home, thinking of the pleasant dinner he had shared with the family. He had been fed well. Mrs. Laura Taylor had been a house slave in Frederic County, Virginia and was renowned for her good cooking. John smiled at the thought that her master must be missing her fine southern-fried chicken. At the supper table he had remarked, as he wiped the tasty remanants from his lips, "Slavery's loss is my gain tonight, Mrs. Taylor." All laughed in happiness.

The next morning John continued along freedom's road to the terminus of the Great Western Railway, the settlement of Windsor, located in the township of Sandwich. This small town was the Canadian counterpart of Windsor, England. Of the one thousand residents, approximately two hundred fifty were fugitive slaves like himself.[6]

As he walked down McDougall Street and Mercer Street, John was awed to find that blacks occupied very neat and handsome homes. Although they were not pretentious, by comparison to the slave quarters he had run from the homes were mansions.

John learned that his fellow refugees had acquired such dwellings because they were skilled, and hard workers. John also learned something that would make Jane very happy: Mrs. Mary Bibb, widow of the very ambitious Henry Bibb, had dedicated her life to teaching. The result was a very successful private school.

As John peeked in the school window, his nose pressed against the glass, he saw about forty pupils. Seven of the pupils were white.[7] He thought of Amherstburg, and the school problems there; then he thought of his own white stepchildren, and turned again to this scene of racial harmony.

He waved at Mrs. Bibb, who would have been frightened had it not been for his kind, black face, which forestalled any apprehension or fear. She waved back, not knowing why but feeling it necessary to return his kindness.

John walked along the streets of Windsor and could almost feel one long part of his journey along the Road to Somewhere coming to an end.

But as he stood on the wooded river bank, the sight of Detroit, a city still striving for harmonious race relations, made him think again. The memory of a reward poster (Black man, White woman—Nigger Dead or Alive) alerted him to the need to seek a more inland shelter for his family. "But where," he thought. "But where?"

That night John found hospitality in the home of William Holland. When he heard that John was a skilled carpenter, he said that in a place called Buxton, a Minister King had hired one of the most dextrous blacksmiths in town. He was sure John's skills would also be appreciated and rewarded. After John had explained his circumstances and the peace of mind afforded by inland settlement, William told his eager listener about another place besides Buxton. Eleven miles from Windsor, in the township of Maidstone and Sandwich, an organization known as the Refugees' Home Society had made a purchase of nearly two thousand acres of land.

Mr. Holland, flattered by John's attention and sincerity, told his guest all he knew. "The lots are sold in twenty-five acre parcels, and a school is maintained eight months of the year."

To John, eight months of schooling a year sounded lenient. He almost stopped listening to William's story, but then allowed his host to continue out of courtesy. Perhaps the lenient school system could be changed, and, he thought, his wife, Jane, was educated enough to start another school herself, if necessary.

"This same Mr. Henry Bibbs, whose widow you mentioned having met, originated the idea to establish a society that would eventually purchase thirty or forty thousand acres of land from the Canadian Government, in the most suitable sections, for the homeless refugees of slavery. John, the obtaining of permanent homes in the township of Maidstone, and the encouragement of our social, moral, physical and intellectual elevation was Mr. Bibbs's concern."

"How do we—or how can they—afford to purchase these thousand of acres?" John asked.

"Well, now," William replied. He pulled on his greying beard with a feeling of importance, knowing he knew the answer but wanting to seem nonchalant, to impress this inquisitive stranger whom he liked already.

"Contributions, let's see now. Half or a third of the monies from the sale of the land are to go towards the purchase of new land, other monies for the support of the schools, which his wife is so enthusiastically trying to keep running. I know these things myself, John, because I almost did it myself. They would have given me five acres if I cleared it within three years. For the other twenty acres, they wanted nine or ten equal-part payments—I am not quite sure. But then I would get my deed.

"But I couldn't sell the land, 'cepting to who they said, John, or to my heirs. But what if I don't have none?" William paused momentarily, then continued. "If I jump up and leave back to Kentucky, for instance, if the slavery thing ever ends, the Refugee Home Society owns my land again. I don't think this is fair do you, John?"

John agreed. "No, William, you're right. Let me share something with you—I have a wish that I haven't even told my wife, Jane, about."

"What is it?" William wanted to know.

"Well, my family, my father, Hannabal—and Lord only knows about his father in Africa—we have never owned land to call our own. I want to leave some land to my heirs, and

115

then have a family cemetery on it that is never to be sold. And—and—" John stuttered, excited by the possibility of a former slave actually owning and giving land. "I want as many of Jane's and my descendants as desire resting there, in a family cemetery, when Judgement comes."

John smiled a shy smile, as if worried that his thought might seem silly. William only nodded with respect.

"Another thing, John, listen to this. Like in Buxton, there is a bylaw. It says, 'No one owning a lot can own a still, or sell liquor.' Ain't that something? We's good people, ain't we?"

John, who was usually a quiet man, was true to form and only nodded his head in approval.*

William continued to bombard John with pertinent information regarding his fellow refugees. With pride, William announced that refugees would often refuse money and request that no money need be raised on their behalf. "We can do pretty good here in Canada, John. Mrs. Rock just told me the other day that she was paid a half dollar for

---

*The second report of the Anti Slavery Society, presented in 1853, was to reinforce John's and William's remarks.

There is doubtless a better state of things amongst the fugitives, than existed at the time when the refugee home plan was proposed. The panic produced by the fugitive slave-law having subsided, the poor refugees have more time allowed them to prepare for the change, and, in consequence, their wants have diminished. The true principle is now to assume that every man, unless disabled by sickness, can support himself and his family after he has obtained steady employment. All that able-bodied men and women require is a fair chance, friendly advice, and a little encouragement, perhaps a little assistance at first. Those who are really willing to work, can procure employment in a short time after their arrival, so that what is specially needed, is such association of friends at different places where fugitives land, as will interest themselves in the coloured man, put him in the way of finding employment, and extend to him such encouragement in the way of grants of land or otherwise, as his altered circumstances may require. In some places, fully to accomplish this, aid from abroad may be necessary, though in most places local charity will prove sufficient.[8]

John and Jane were, within a few years, about to provide this local charity to weary travellers at the end of their underground railroad journey. The idea of that underground terminal was paramount in John's mind as he stood, with William, under a slightly overcast sky in the village of Windsor.

washing and others like her, who are willing to work, are in such demand that it is difficult to hire them." At this point William noticed fatigue on John's face.

"John, you must be tired, and it looks like rain. Please come and spend the night with my family, and tomorrow we will send you on your way."

On their way home, they saw an elderly gentleman tip his hat and William recognized Derek Patey, clerk of the courts for the County of Essex. "Mr. Patey, Mr. Patey, come here a minute." The words came from William's mouth while a smile of pride covered his face.

John was impressed at the confidence with which his new-found friend addressed this obviously important white man. More than a few times, John had noticed how timid and stand-offish many of the recent refugees had been when in the presence of their white neighbours. But he could understand their timidity—he knew what many had experienced, and he knew they did not have a Daniel to remember.

John had not yet found anyone to confide in who could, or would, believe the almost brotherly relationship he and Daniel had had. "Yes," he thought, "Daniel Walls, even though burdened by slavery, was ahead of his time. I wish he were alive and here to see this. This is where Daniel should have been born, not under the burden of slavery."

John's thoughts were interrupted by a hand extended towards him. He thought of what Daniel might have said, because it was the first white hand he had shaken since leaving the hotel in Amherstburg.

"Mr. Walls, you are in good company. Welcome to Canada! I can tell you will be like the other black people I have met in the community, good and honest, as moral as any people. I have found no fault in them at all. They and you will be good loyal subjects of the Queen."

Mr. Patey's words left John almost overwhelmed by a feeling of worth and belonging. He almost said, "You mean there are others who really actually want me, and think I am a Human Being?" He was glad, later, he had held his tongue, for he realized his words might have made him appear childish.

That night John shared William's hospitality, and some of Florence Holland's fine cherry pie.

As John walked to a place called Colchester the next day, the warm sun and the reality of the freedom he was feeling made him imagine many pleasant experiences.

He was a child again, running on the open African veldts with his father close behind. Both were free. At another fork in the road, he was an imaginary African warrior protecting his family from a wild animal, with a deer running, frightened, in front of him.

As he walked, the whole beautiful Canadian spring countryside was transformed into what he thought the Africa of his father, free and wild like this country, must have been. "I can see now why Hannabal died trying to reach this haven of potential peace and racial harmony. How did he know?" This was his last thought before the arrow pointing towards Colchester came into view.

It was early afternoon. He knew he must find out as much as he could about this settlement before nightfall, for he would have to sleep in the woods if he did not receive an invitation of shelter. As he entered the beautiful town, he could see that it relied heavily on agriculture for its livelihood. The town was on the northern shore of Lake Erie, and the great railroad had not yet been built. Of the fifteen hundred residents, a third were black.[9]

Much of the open land had been cleared by fugitive slaves. They were often taken advantage of by unscrupulous settlers, because of their lack of learning and their conditioned timidity. The portion of leased wildland was no sooner cleared than they were required to move on and go somewhere else. This psychological branding went as deep as the branding of slavery on their bodies; both wounds showed to mankind what bigotry and hatred could do.

Some people were afraid to talk to John, for fear he was the informant of some white man. These early black inhabitants of Colchester were not yet cured of slavery's hideous disease; thus even potential allies seemed suspicious and forboding. John almost felt like crying, but he had a job to do. The reeve of the town, Mr. Robinson, spoke to John in positive terms on the general improvement of the black race in his community. However, he went on to say that they had few friends among the white settlers.

"They ought to be by themselves. If we try to encourage them, we shall have to mix with them. You understand, John Walls, you are welcome as long as you know your place."[10]

John Walls understood only too well. He could see the skin-deep prejudice very clearly, having lived in a country where racial bigotry went much deeper, into the very heart and soul of the victim of slavery's infection.

John told the reeve that the warning against mixing was advice given too late for him, as he had already married a beautiful, Christian white lady, and neither he nor she needed the reeve's half-hearted benevolent acceptance. "We will find a place all right, even in this beautiful land of freedom, that is safe from such as you and some of your bigoted white settlers. I bid you good day!"

The reeve nearly fell off his rocker as he looked, in shock and disbelief—and also respect, at the back of this proud African descendant.

As John walked on he thought, "I would rather be respected for courage in stating my true opinion than liked, and I certainly proved that today." John Freeman Walls felt good and free inside. He was proud to be black, and also to be able to say, as he walked away from the reeve, "I am a loyal subject of the Queen. I'm a free man."

John walked from the lakefront and saw that all the farms belonged to white settlers, pioneer Canadians. Behind the cleared farms were more farms, owned mostly by whites. These went as far back as the Fourth Concession. Here and there were farms owned by blacks. He noticed these farms

119

were not generally as thoroughly or neatly cultivated as those of the whites, though the lack of proper equipment would have contributed to this. He was, however, almost pleased to notice that there were some white men's farms in the same condition. John was a proud man, proud of himself and of his race.

Beyond the Fourth Concession, farms belonging to whites and blacks were mixed. This newly-settled area came closer to meeting John's standards for a new home for his beloved family.

Here the black familes, he noticed, had penetrated further into the woods than any of the whites. In one settlement, New Canaan, this was especially true. The refugees had settled both north and south of the old Malden road, where none but the most stalwart and persistent would have ventured. They were determined to own a piece of heaven before they died. Fugitive slaves who had nothing but their lives looked upon this land as the Canaan they had sung about in their songs. "O Canaan, sweet Canaan, I am bound for the land of Canaan."

Follow the drinking gourd, follow the north star, remember the side of the tree the moss grows on. To the fugitives, this free land was the promised land. However troublesome, no matter how many rocks had to be cleared, no matter how many trees had to be felled, this land meant freedom from oppression. This was all they cared about. They were not envious of the black loomis earth of other neighbours. These newcomers to Canada had been some of their masters' most valuable possessions. Courage, defiance and skill were common characteristics; unfortunately, lack of education was another.

John felt bitter when he heard stories of low-class whites taking advantage of his brothers' ignorance, and depriving them of the land that had become a symbol of the freedom they had all but given their lives for. One black settler told John he had taken a farm of one hundred acres, appraised at two hundred dollars. He was given ten years to pay. He paid twelve dollars a year for ten years, presuming that he was paying the principal debt and that the land would be his, free and clear. At the end of the ten years, he was told that he had paid only the interest on his debt: he must pay two hundred dollars immediately. The man lost his land and all the "interest" he had paid.[11]

John shook his head in sadness when he heard the fifth variation of this swindle. All he could say in response was, "We need schools, we need schools."

John slept in the woods under a lean-to/wigwam that his father had showed him how to make. Without thinking about it, he knew his father would not have meant for him to settle in this portion of Essex County, an area not yet completely free from subtle racial prejudice.

As he fell asleep the name Buxton, which he had heard the day before, came to his mind; then he saw a vision of Jane, whom he loved and missed. "Yes, before I continue, I will go back to Amherstburg and fetch her. Corliss can mind the children." Sleep was peaceful, as it blocked out some of the stark realities he had encountered.

MILE XVII

The journey to Buxton and inner Canada, as it was thought of by those who had more modest means of travel in those early years, was a journey that John and Jane enjoyed. They had rented a horse and were quite confident that he was strong enough to carry both of them on his back.

As they rode they talked husband and wife talk. John's conversation dealt with the excitement he felt about their eventual permanent settlement; Jane's dealt with the well-being of the children. She would oftentimes say all their names in a row in order of their ages. This morning, with the warm sun beating down on them and the mild spray from the waves of Lake Erie touching their faces, was no exception. The names of the children were proudly spoken as John and Jane rode under the hanging boughs of the willow trees. The eeriness of the heavily-wooded path and witches hair, as John called the long branches of the willows, was magnified on this crisp May morning by the sound of hounds baying.

"My God, Jane, my God, they're after us." An instinctive rap on the horse's rear made it leap into full stride; Jane would have fallen off had it not been for John's left arm reaching back to hold her.

"John, John," she cried, "this is Canada, this is freedom." The word "freedom" registered in John's mind and made him slow the horse down, slightly embarrassed, but with plenty of laughter.

The smile on John's face indicated he had forgotten that, on the north shore of Lake Erie, hounds hunted animals, not people. They had crossed paths with some Indian hounds, who were running a group of ten to twelve deer into the lake. The interested riders, having shed their fear, reached a clearing and saw the scurrying of mocassin-clad Indians into beached canoes, and watched in amazement.

The deer were swimming for their lives, close to the shoreline. The canoes were filled with the original inhabitants of this North American continent; they had learned to survive in this wilderness, which had not changed much since the beginning of time. The look on John's and Jane's faces made the Indians think the two on horseback had never before witnessed this simple necessity of survival.

Tomahawks were strategically and expertly aimed; the women would then take the deer by the horns and paddle ashore. The men would bleed and prepare the meat. That evening, a portion of the meat was shared by John and Jane, who were pleased to learn that Indian hospitality was not lacking.

A couple of the braves who had served as guides after the American Revolution and the battle of Stoney Creek could speak intelligible English. The names of the various tribes were relayed with pride: Oneida, Huron, Seneca, Onondego and Iroquois.

The Indians were proud of their ingenuity in deer catching, and boasted truthfully, "Even the white men, the lower class ones, envy us. They sometimes say that their hounds scared the deer into the water, therefore the deer belong to them, and they must have the meat. But we would not give the meat up."

John and the Indians could feel a sort of camaraderie, which came from the suffering resulting from being part of a minority. But John, who had married a white lady, had known a Daniel Walls, had seen what that benevolent man had done on his death bed, would not judge all white men by the actions of a few—especially in this new country.

A young princess named Kazar was a favourite of John's and Jane's. As they bounced the princess on their knees, John said, "I would like, someday, a son of mine to marry a girl like you." His words were prophetic.

They slept under the moonlit sky, by the fire of their new-found Indian friends. John looked up at the sky. "Jane," he said, "my father used to say, 'If you remember nothing else I tell you, remember the side of the tree the moss grows on and the north star are the way to Canada and freedom.' Jane, until now, I couldn't even imagine how important those words were." Jane fell asleep in John's arms, but not before kissing him on the cheek.

The next day proper farewells were made, and the two freedom seekers entreated Kazar's parents and their friends to keep in contact. Jane realized the Indians had given of their hospitality unselfishly, just as they were now giving fresh venison, but she felt she must repay the hospitality of these people who had been so kind. Her new friends, who were by chance born Indians, were not savages but human beings with hopes, dreams and aspirations—just like John, of African descent, and Jane, of Irish and Scottish.

John and Jane continued along their road. The physical road, which they at times had to literally pioneer, became very winding, but it was straightened somewhat by the congenial instructions of settlers, mostly white, whom they came upon. Nevertheless, a wrong wilderness road was taken, and, although the two travellers heard many reports of the Buxton Settlement, they would have had to retrace their steps to see it. The wrong road led them to Chatham, and they learned from a Mr. Oates about the potential benefits that Buxton could have afforded them.

The Buxton settlement was more commonly called the King Settlement, in appreciation of its founder, Reverend King. It was in the township of Raleigh, in the county of Kent. The eight hundred black townspeople were a mixture of former slaves and residents of the free states. The settlement comprised some nine thousand acres of land, six miles in length, and three in breadth.[12]

Mr. Oates commented that, had they taken the right road, which led to Buxton, they would have found that the settlement would have likely lent itself nicely to their general and specific requirements. The founder himself, they learned, was a former slave holder in Louisiana but, like Daniel Walls, was not comfortable in the role to which he had been born. He had acted immediately to correct the wrong he saw: he manumitted his slaves, fourteen in number, for whom he had been offered some nine thousand dollars, and brought them to Canada, to settle on land bought from the Crown.

The Elgin Association was started for the settlement and moral improvement of the black population of Canada; its purpose was to purchase land in this township of Raleigh and to settle the land with black families who had good moral character.

John and Jane Walls would certainly have fulfilled this requirement. The added qualities of a good carpenter and learned lady would have dismissed any possible reservations about their skin-deep uniqueness.

Mr. Oates went on to say, "Fugitives in and around these parts are as thick as blackbirds in a cornfield." This comment made John laugh, as his jet-black complexion would have rivalled any other of God's creations.[13]

Mr. Oates also told John that there was prejudice in Dresden, a community nearby, where whites and blacks attended separate schools. He thought that white settlers might not favourably accept the union of a black man and a white woman, at least not in this lifetime.[14]

But John and Jane were impressed by the overall conditions of the fugitives in Chatham more than in any other area they had visited together.

Of a population of six thousand, the former slaves numbered two thousand. John, with his wife at his side, walked the streets of Chatham, meeting members of the African race who could only stop long enough to exchange light courtesies or to wave. They were too busy working in mills, painting houses and blacksmithing—they were employed in every trade. One street was occupied by black shopkeepers and clerks. All through the town, blacks were busy with their gardens and farms.

At one point, Jane, with a specific purpose, left John's side long enough to strike up conversation with one white lady entering a shop. She asked curiously, "Why don't you shop at the white stores?" She wanted to test the true inner feeling of the white stranger.

She was curtly told, "These people are as good a body of souls as you can find anywhere. You, dear lady, should not be given to prejudice!"

Jane smiled thankfully, for more reason than the information contained in the woman's answer. She readily related her conversation to John, who was almost beside himself with fun. He said, "If the lady only knew, Jane."

However, within an hour John and Jane were to discover that this lady was not, as a whole, representative of whites in the Chatham community. Certain whites, of lower-class mentality, were afraid of "uppitiness" spreading, like some contagion, among the black race.

Jane talked to one of the Chatham farmers, again without John. She learned as much as she could about the true state of racial harmony in the town, and she found that the farmer's prejudice was founded on one incident. Apparently the disease of prejudice infected him when he witnessed a white man who had tried to pass six or seven blacks on the sidewalk, but couldn't get through. He had been obliged to cross the street.

The farmer did not stop to consider that the blacks were probably deep in conversation with each other and, not noticing the passerby were, therefore, not concerned with diplomacy or courtesy and did not let the white man pass through their midst. The farmer's words echoed in her mind: "The uppity niggers will soon rebel."

The farmer's words were too strong to allow her to continue her spying into the prejudice of men's hearts. She quickly replied, "Sir, where I have come from, I have seen hundreds of black men whipped and kicked. The smallest of insults was having to leave the sidewalk to let impudent white fellows pass. You cannot blame the entire white race for this, just as you cannot judge all blacks by the actions of a few. This is what so greatly upsets me—and, being white myself, I can clearly see how unfair people can be. If a black man does anything out of human error or weakness, all others of his race are blamed for his fault."

John, seeing his white wife in some type of altercation, walked to her side out of instinct. The enraged white man, a victim of the disease of prejudice, struck out. "What do you want, nigger?"

Jane, knowing the physical and psychological hardships John had been through, sensed he might not be able to stand much more insult to his worth as a human being. She also remembered the scene she had witnessed in the woods, the wolf's jaws being torn apart by the incredible strength of her

126

husband. She realized that even an armed assailant would probably require more than one bullet to quiet the rage of a man whose temper was so seldom ignited.

Jane looked into her husband's eyes and saw that the farmer's insult had aroused John's temper. She placed her small body between the two men and said with pride, "This is my husband. He is John Freeman Walls, and I am Jane King Walls; we are just as good as anyone."

The words so shocked the prejudiced farmer that he turned and walked away. He did not know what to say; he only realized that his mind was not ready to accept the Christian principles of racial harmony in his lifetime.

John turned to his wife. "Who was he?"

"John, the laws are strong here, we do not have to worry about the likes of him. I know it is hard, but we must try, as it says in the Bible, to love him."

John's rage was quieted. Like so many former slaves in Canada, he was too wounded to love all white men, but he was learning to love more than a few.

The thoughts of the farmer's problems turned to more constructive and positive areas; they had to erase prejudice, animosity or revenge from their minds. They delved deeper into the history of this potential home. In 1832, all that Chatham could boast of was a few houses and as many shops. The oldest street in the town had been built in 1801. In 1837, the steamboats commenced travelling to Detroit and Buffalo. With the advent of the Great Western Railway came an increasing number of blacks; the ratio of blacks to their white neighbours was increasing. They attended separate churches and a separate public school, but were generally welcomed by the white populace. "They are as good a body of people as you can find anywhere," the lady had said to Jane; her statement had typified the sentiments of many white Canadians.[15]

John and Jane travelled home towards Amherstburg,

127

guided now by a compass to prevent another wrong turn in the wilderness. They agreed to check out Buxton at a later date, because they didn't want to leave the children for too long a period.

John said to Jane, "In Chatham, there seems to be a happy medium between the timid ex-slaves, too unsure to mingle with the whites of this country, and the young black bucks. Young blacks feel so free when they first arrive in this country that they go beyond good limits and cast courtesy aside, until they realize the laws are strong and they need not overreact to a few low-class whites. They get over these feelings after a while." John was silent for a moment. Then he sighed contentedly.

"Yes, Jane, I like this country, Canada."

MILE XVIII

Canada in the 1840s could be likened to an innocent child. She was more untrained, inexperienced and pure of heart than her neighbour to the south, which, during its young, impressionable years, had been ravished by slavery's disease. But in Canada the vaccine of Christian laws and judicial avoidance of race hatred had kept the disease of slavery below the forty-ninth parallel. As John and Jane rode, they realized that their new country had to work hard to remain morally strong, to resist the destruction and decay caused by prejudice.

The horse, who was beginning to feel the burden of two riders, began to tire. John and Jane looked up at the sound of a horse and buggy approaching from behind. It was guided by Doctor Fisher, a dedicated travelling country physician.

His knowledgeable eye took one look at the horse and the

good doctor realized that rest was a good idea. He extended an invitation to John and Jane to join him in the buggy, since they were obviously travelling in the same general direction. John felt at once that he was in the company of another Peter Redmon, a quality person. He was to find he was not mistaken.

Dr. Fisher's family, they learned, had emigrated from England at about the same time the first Governor of Canada, Graves Simcoe, had—in the late 1700s. As a matter of fact, they had come over on the same ship, and Dr. Fisher took great pride in that fact. The Fishers were of the same mould as the illustrious Simcoe, and agreed with his unprejudiced accomplishments in the field of human freedom and dignity.

As the buggy rolled along, with the three travellers aboard and the horse behind, a rainstorm threatened, forcing them into a barn that offered immediate protection.

The barn's rafters were laden with a mossy green material, which created an eerie atmosphere. The rain dripped through the cracks in the roof, increasing the gloom. As the three entered the barn they felt uneasy; their unease turned to alarm when they saw blood dripping from the straw-laden loft. Although Dr. Fisher was used to the distinct smell of death and quite capable, if it be God's will, of turning back the grim reaper, he was as startled as his companions. "What in God's name is that?" he asked. As they ascended the ladder leading to the hay loft, first John, then Dr. Fisher, the sight they were greeted with made John yell, "Stay back, Jane, stay back!"

A man opened his eyes. He lay face down with his head turned sideways. The sight of John's black face made him sense all was well. The sight of Dr. Fisher's white face made him utter, in a voice too weak to show its real fright, "Don't kill me, massa, don't kill ol' Sam Lucas. I'se a good nigger, I'se don't want to die, I'se just want to be free." The man's mouth was dripping blood, which made Dr. Fisher wonder if his black bag carried the necessary instruments to save his life.

Jane, who was waiting in the barn, wished she knew what was happening; then she heard John's voice. "Please come up now, Jane, we need your petticoat." Jane reacted immediately, ignoring her modesty in an attempt to help a fellow human being.

Dr. Fisher tore the petticoat into strips for bandages. The three worked fervently to close the man's wounds and stop the bleeding.

As the last wound was being bandaged, John's bent back felt a sudden jar; he heard a scream that sounded as if it came from a crazed animal. "Leave my husband alone, leave him alone." John rose with a small but courageous woman swinging on his neck. She had just returned from foraging for food for her husband and, thinking he was being attacked, jumped instinctively to counter attack.

Jane's soothing words quieted the hysterics of Bertha Lucas, as was her slave name. As she realized that the intruders were trying to save Sam's life, Bertha's fears were replaced by thankfulness.

For three days the doctor and his new friends nursed the physical and psychological wounds of a couple who had been so given to fear and running that they had actually reached the refuge of Canada without knowing it. Only after three days did Sam Lucas learn that he had almost died. It would have been the ultimate irony: to die a free man, convinced that he was still in chains.

MILE XIX

As Sam's life returned to his body, he felt compelled to speak, and speak he did.

"Four masters have bought and sold me, each more cruel

130

than the last. The greenness of Virginia could not compensate for the reality of the whipping posts. The auction post saw my naked body four times. My whole body had been measured and felt, even my genitals, as if I was a dumb hog or mule.

"I did work like a mule, so maybe they weren't all wrong." The sarcasm of Sam's more articulate phrases proved he had two languages: one he had learned for the ears of the slave master, and one he had learned from books he had hungrily acquired.

"My mother, yes, my mother.

"I was a dog—no, more like a flea, slapped and spat on just because I was black, not because I was a bad person. Damn, damn, damn, I didn't even know if I was human.

"Word came to me that my mother was dying and, not wanting to be disrespectful to my master, I approached him for travelling papers, almost knowing he would allow me to travel the twenty miles as quickly as possible.

" 'If I let you go, everybody wants to go; she is just an old nigger woman.' Had he just said no I might have understood, on the grounds that the plantation needed me or something, but because he let me know that he felt my mother, too, was less than human, I turned and walked away.

"As soon as nightfall came I ran all but five of the twenty miles. When I reached my mother's bedside, she only had time enough to tell me to go north to Canada before she died. I cried, but not all of it was sadness. I was half glad she had been removed from this world, which had afforded her little happiness. What scant happiness she had felt made the sadness of its loss more profound.

"Like a proud man, not like an ignorant slave, I walked back to the plantation of the hardest of all masters in the vicinity. I had used ignorance to my advantage, but just then I didn't care to be ignorant and dumb. My mama didn't birth no dogs.

"The first fifty lashes hurt me terribly. The last fifty were unbearable, because my master had soaked the whip in salt and water. I almost died. I have seen men die, I have seen men turned to lumps of meat—raw meat—for no worse crime than being late to the fields because of bodily excretion. Damn slavery, my blood boils, then runs cold.

"Iron chains. He whipped me with iron chains, wearing my skin to the bone. I almost wanted to die, but my mother's words—'Go north to Canada'—meant possible freedom—and gave me the desire to live. My Bertha also helped me want to live."

Dr. Fisher looked at John, with whom he felt a sort of closeness already, and asked, "Could this be really true?" John only nodded.

"I should have died—slaves have died for much less. I was uppity and insolent. I said, 'No one whips Sam Lucas again,' and I meant it—even if it meant I had to pay with my life.

"Two months after I married Bertha, my master thought it would be great fun to sell me south. 'Ha, ha,' he said, 'let's see how uppity you will be now.' For the first of a very few times I thought it necessary to be humble and I said, 'I will do better, masa, don't separate me and Bertha, I be learned my lesson.' The hysterical laugh that followed served to make up my mind.

"Suspecting that I was not going to cooperate—by the way, I just now realize why they may have decided not to kill me. I was such a challenge that, like a great wild horse, any and all wanted to try to break me. I was a challenge to the nigger breakers. Ha, ha. . . . Yeh, that's it.

"Anyhow, they threw me in jail and, before daybreak, I had knocked a brick out, which afforded me leverage to pry more loose.

"I ran across the road and a devilish dog started barking and chasing me, alerting everyone. I heard a gunshot—my shoulder and back felt it. The whole town was awakened and came out armed; you would think it was an army of redcoats they were after.

"I jumped into the creek that ran in back of the town and buried myself in the mud after first burying that damn dog.

He wasn't a big or vicious dog, so I buried his body beside me and held his jaws closed with my right hand. I layed in a spread eagle fashion, with just our noses sticking through the mud.

"If they had found both of us in daylight, with patrollers all around, I am sure they would have laughed from pure ridiculousness before shooting me. We must've looked pretty funny. I don't know why I didn't kill the little mutt, it would have been easier. Oh, well, maybe that's why the Good Lord let me be here, and not permanently buried under all that mud.

"I stole a rasp from a blacksmith shop and cut myself away from the irons. I know their big manhunt was casually organized, they thought I was still in shackles and that I would be easy prey. But I doubled back the next night and borrowed the rasp. I left the chains and the rasp in the woods, where they would be easily found.

"I also printed in the mud—Sam Lucas says goodbye. That *was* uppity, wasn't it?" Sam laughed. "I went back to my old master's plantation, stole Bertha right out of the field from under the overseers' noses, and took off with my wife and came north.

"I never was much good at directions, as I am certain you three can attest to. Can you believe it, Bertha, in Canada and we didn't know it. Remember when we crossed the river to Cario, and footed through to Chicago, laying by day and travelling by night? I ended up so lost and bewildered I had to go up to a house and ask directions. And we were so lucky— he was an abolitionist, and showed me the route.

"That was the only white man I asked anything of. I had suffered so much from them my confidence was gone. I knew I must push on without their help. Even my own race had betrayed me at times, one shuffle-butt black betrayed me for ten dollars. Can you believe it? I had to cut somebody with his own knife is all I know, in order to get away. Bertha, you remember?"

Bertha, a quiet woman, only nodded. She was a strong

woman, but not talkative. She acted rather than talked. Sam acted also, and did enough talking for both of them.

"Dr. Fisher, you are the first really kind-hearted white man I have met. Most of the others were in that slavery thing, maybe that's why; they don't represent everybody in the states. I almost feel—yes, I do feel there are a lot like you in the United States. Except I haven't met them, and I don't intend to go back to try to find out."

John agreed with Sam. He told the Lucases the story of Daniel Walls and his own wife. "So you see, Sam, there are some good whites, even in slavery."

"Yeh, but few," Sam retaliated quickly. He continued his story. "When I crossed the Ohio bottoms we rode across on a raft I found. At times I had to swim, pushing the raft before me, trying to make sure Bertha didn't fall off and sink. Worse than death was behind us, I thought, and then it happened. Slave patrollers—ten-dollar patrollers. They would, I am certain, do anything for ten dollars.

"I was like the old hunting dog I had seen with my first master—the kindest of the four—when he had treed a coon. I couldn't believe I was really safe, like the dog couldn't really believe the coon was in the tree; he would look back, then scent all around to make sure the coon had not left the tree, even though he was in clear sight.

"This day I was wrong about safety. The four patrollers came upon me as I walked—I was only two hundred yards from my wife, making certain sleep was safe. I knifed one and beat the others off with a stick. I yelled the worse profanities at them—I'm sure that helped to frighten them, as they had never before heard a nigger talk so insolent.

"I travelled the last four days to this barn not really knowing I had reached Canada with—what did you say, Dr. Fisher? Buckshot and five knife wounds in my back?"

Sam would not give Dr. Fisher time to answer. "Yes," he said proudly, "I will take these shots of freedom to my grave. But it won't be as soon as I thought it would be, thanks to you three."

Bertha added that they had been hunted like wild animals in the woods, and they began to think like one, being more afraid of humans than was normal.

"Even when a dog barked, we expected a man to run out on the porch with a gun, like they do down south. We were scared—and even though we didn't see anyone, we wanted to avoid meanness, or worse, getting caught. We see here in Canada the men work in the day and sleep soundly at night, as opposed to laying half awake at night waiting for the bark of the dog, signalling the rebellion.

"We truly thank you good people for coming along; we would have surely died not knowing we were free. The river we crossed to get here we thought took us into another slave state. Thank goodness it didn't."

Bertha's eyes turned to Jane. She could not resist speaking what was on her mind. "You know, I thought at first, Mrs. Jane, you and the good doctor were married. I did not think I would live to see racial harmony in my lifetime, maybe not even six hundred years in the future."

Shaking her head in happy disbelief she exclaimed, "How can it be? How can it be? I hope you raise fine children and have descendants who will do you proud for what you have done for them."

These words filled John's and Jane's hearts; never more than now were they appreciative of being able to travel on the road to somewhere. Dr. Fisher smiled, realizing he had seen the reality of what many men like himself thought only fabrication.

MILE XX

The Lucas family was made comfortable enough to continue their lives in freedom.

The Walls family continued their temporarily interrupted buggy ride with Dr. Fisher.

Dr. Fisher could not hold back his questions about the length slaves would go to to be free. Jane related her experiences as an abolitionist and underground railroad activist, to further his knowledge of the way things were in the early and mid 1800s.

"Dr. Fisher, when we are settled, I must write to Mary and Ephraim Stout in Indiana, the abolitionists who helped us to freedom. Once I have written them of our permanent residence, they will use our home as one of the terminal stations of the underground railroad. We will aid those like John and I, those who are in need but ready to start their new lives. When our first travellers arrive, we will invite you over for some more sharing of reality. Possibly you will tell your children of the need for racial harmony and they will tell theirs, right into the twentieth century and beyond. You are a good man, Dr. Fisher."

As Jane finished speaking, the Puce Road Maidstone Township came into view. The blacks called it the Maidstone Refugee Home Society Settlement—and a good place to live.

Dr. Fisher was stopping his horse, getting ready to turn. "Well, folks," he said, "Amherstburg is but a day's ride away, but I live here. By the way, there are a lot of new settlers moving into this area and taking full advantage of the land made available through the Refugee Home Society. You wouldn't have to pay for the land for a few years, John. You might want to consider this."

John was quick to ask, "Will they accept me and my white wife?"

"What the devil difference does that make? No one really cares what colour you are if you are Christian, law-abiding people." These were the first harsh words Dr. Fisher had spoken to John, and they were soothing to his spirit.

John and Jane looked at each other, not needing to smile to communicate their happiness. "You must understand, Dr. Fisher, we have been through so much that we just want to raise our family, grow old and die in peace."

Dr. Fisher's unbigoted mind did understand, and he

replied, "This is definitely the place for you. I can't speak for all, but what you will have to deal with in terms of prejudice will be no more than I have to contend with, being an Englishman in the company of many French-speaking people. Maidstone is the end of your road. You have found a place where you can grow old gracefully together."

John and Jane looked at one another, not needing to speak. Finally, their long, hard road had led to somewhere.

MILE XXI

"Jane, you would think the children were going to Timbuktu. Bless their little souls."

"They're just happy, John," Jane replied peacefully.

The feelings the adults were suppressing equalled the children's. Were it not for dignity and deportment they, too, would have turned cartwheels with the young ones. The respect they had gained in the hearts and minds of the residents of Amherstburg had grown quickly. The residents of the town were saddened by hearing the Walls family was moving. John and Jane felt that too much display of happiness on their part would have possibly insulted the freinds they had made in Amherstburg. The people of the Nazery AME church John and Jane would definitely miss.

The buggy wheels turned; the compass John was looking at showed that the path through Windsor headed south. "My goodness," Jane remarked, "is it broken?"

John proudly related a fact he had learned from Derek Patey, the friendly clerk of the county of Essex. "Windsor is one of the only Canadian towns south of the United States but, my dear wife, I assure you this Maidstone Puce Road settlement is not like the south we came from."

In 1848, the census taker found the Walls family in possession of a log cabin, two oxen, eight cows, three sheep, six horses, two dogs and twenty-five acres of land.[16]

However, on that warm day, at the end of their ride, John and Jane saw woodland and trees on all sides. The children jumped out of the buggy, each trying to be first to reach Puce Creek. As John walked hand in hand with Jane, they could not help thinking back to Troublesome Creek, North Carolina.

"What does Puce mean, Jane?"

"It means 'flea' in French," was her reply.

"Yes, that is about as big as our troubles are going to be," John answered happily, laughing as they finished their walk and stood looking at the free-flowing waters of this free land, soon to be owned by John, a free man.

The Walls family unloaded their supplies from the wagon—clothes, blankets, bed quilts hand-stitched by Jane, flour and pork. As John was carrying the last pots and pans to the bank of Puce Creek, he thought out loud, "Never has a saw been used on these trees." The first to fall that afternoon was used for fire wood, and slats were placed to form a wigwam; cedar boughs from the creek flats provided a mattress for the Walls family that night.

They kept a staggered watch on the fire to ward off the bears, deer and wolves that had been seen on more than one occasion as they forged their way towards this spot. Pheasants, quail and rabbits were welcome sights as they meant immediate food.

Amidst the noise of wild animals, the crackling of the fire and the rushing of the stream, the Walls family slept in peace and harmony under the north star.

For the next few weeks, as the morning sun rose in the eastern sky, John was already busily chopping wood with Jane at his side. Four rocks had been rolled into a stragetic location to serve as cornerstones for the log cabin.

Cedar boards were split for the roof in the next weeks. They covered a small, two-storey edifice with one bedroom up and one down; one main room, with stove in the centre, served as kitchen and living room. The clay floors were level, and covered with the same boards as the roof.

The night their home was finished the whole family knelt in the warmth of the main room to give thanks for this humble and glorious new beginning. "My son, forget not my law; but let thine heart keep my commandments: For length of days, and long life, and peace, shall they add to thee." John continued by saying, "I certainly hope the good Lord does help us live long to enjoy this heaven on earth." She nodded, as if to say, "I am sure God will reward us with long life in the shelter of Queen Victoria's dominion."

As Jane finished, John walked towards the door that he had recently made, and tapped it as if to determine the quality of his workmanship. "This house will last over a hundred years, Jane," he said with pride. All members of the family looked proudly around the cabin.

Then they all looked at John as he walked through the door; their feelings of pride were directed more towards him, the builder, than to the cabin he had built.

John walked fifty yards towards Puce Creek, turned and looked back at his creation, smoke rising from the chimney. His black hands closed together in prayer; his eyes looked towards heaven, along with his thoughts. "Hannabal, Hannabal, I wish you could see what your son has built! Hannabal, Hannabal, I wish you could see where your son has built his log cabin."

John was surrounded by trees. He reached down and picked up some rich earth. He rolled the moist clay into a ball and threw it as far as he could into the air, in the direction of the drinking gourd in the sky, whose handle pointed directly at the north star. He then felt the first tree within reach and scraped the green moss, his symbol of freedom, which grew on its bark. He lifted the moss to his nose, smelled its pungent odour and manipulated it in his hand. It was as soft as velvet. As his black hands, with palms almost as dark, squeezed the moss between them, he realized how important, significant, beautiful, rewarding and precious these two landmarks of sky and earth had been to him, and to others who had settled in the back woods of this country.

John heard a branch breaking behind him. His survival instincts were alerted, and he tensed. But he quickly relaxed as he turned and faced his wife. Her skin glistened in the light and shadows of this clear, bright evening.

Jane's eyes went to her husband's hands, and she saw the moss falling between his fingers. Realizing the significance of what she was witnessing, she spoke. "We must help others, John, as soon as we have sufficient means. We must help freedom runners. We must be like the Quaker Stouts of Indiana. I hope they received our letter."

"One thing for certain, Jane," John replied, "bounty hunters won't find us here."

The two travellers who had reached the end of the freedom road walked hand in hand into the house, preparing to continue down the road that led to independent support and respect.

MILE XXII

John and Jane Walls knew that the vehicles that would carry them toward their goal were hard work and prayer. Over the next years neither was neglected. In a few years' time the former slave, who started with only hoe and rake in hand, boasted of raising five hundred bushels of wheat, one hundred fifty bushels of potatoes, seventy-five bushels of peas, one hundred bushels of oats, five tons of hay and to other produce of less consequence. The barn housed horses, oxen, cows, hogs, sheep and poultry in abundance. And John was one of the first men to grow tobacco in the area.

The man who, to many back in North Carolina, was a "bad nigger" was, here in Canada, an independent farmer, respected by the best men in the community. John's apple

140

orchard, which gave him the most satisfaction, often made him think back to the south. He remembered how he promised himself he would, in the new land, someday own one of the best orchards around. It made him smile to think of how his dream had come true; he cried to think how the dreams of his friends in slavery never would.

The land he had purchased from the Anti-Slavery Society would soon be paid off, but he knew the Refugee Home Society would not expect the final payments until the early 1860s. Therefore, he was making preparations for a downpayment on more land. He could lend or borrow money any time. Those who borrowed from him might hear him say, if they were negligent in repaying their debt, "I know you only owe me a penny, but it's my penny and I want it!" John Freeman Walls was taking care of himself and his family.

He would laugh at the remarks he had heard to discourage ignorant slaves from coming to Canada. When he looked into the sky and saw migrating geese, he would tease in a loud voice, "You mean these are the same geese that were supposed to attack and pluck my eyes out, just because I am black? It would be pretty hard for them to reach me from two miles in the sky. The worst they could do from there is splatter my black old head with droppings, but I suppose I can live through that. Never have froze to death, or starved because the ground could not produce crop. My poor brethren in the south, the lies they have been told."

Poor brothers and sisters in the south turned to poor brothers and sisters in free northern states when the Fugitive Slave Law was signed in September 1850. John was concerned when he heard of its signing; he was worried when he thought of its effect. "How can a man who is in the northern states, the so-called free states, be carried back into slavery just because someone else says he ran? I have even overheard of how a bribe of ten dollars would be enough to encourage some low-life individuals to swear by oath that this was their slave. How can it be, Jane? How can it be?"

141

"John, I know it's wrong. . . . There is nothing we can do to prevent it—but we have to be ready to help fugitives who might arrive."

John, who was in a frenzy, paced back and forth in the main room of the house, muttering. "But Jane, how can such injustice take place? This is the middle of the 1800s! Remember Sam Lucas? Remember the friend who stayed with them a while before moving to Buxton, Jane? Remember when the law of 1804, known as the Ohio Black Law, was revised in that state, and carried out? Listen, Jane." Jane very caringly turned her attention to her husband, whom she realized was labouring in psychological pain. John continued, "Here he was a free black, clearing $800 a year, forced by this law, this unjust law, to put up a $500 bond, not only for himself but for each member of his family—nine in total. And then, as if that was not enough, they passed a law forbidding anyone—under penalty of $100 fine—to employ any black man or woman. They were forced to flee to Canada."

John's jet-black complexion almost turned red from frustration and the sense of futility he felt because he could not reverse injustice.

Jane, realizing her husband needed some cheering up, brought out a surprise that would ease the situation. Jane had been saving the surprise—a letter from the Stouts—for Sunday, after a specially prepared dinner, but she felt it would serve a better purpose now. "Read this, John." The smile on Jane's face made John shift his attention from concerned, frustrating thoughts to a better, more constructive purpose.

When John saw the envelope postmarked Indiana, he got up from the table and read. He walked from one side of the room to the other, too excited to sit down.

As John's happy eyes focused on the letter and he began to read aloud, four fugitives who had been aided by Jane on her abolitionist missions to North Carolina were making their way northward. They, along with many others—including the several who died of the cholera mentioned in the letter—

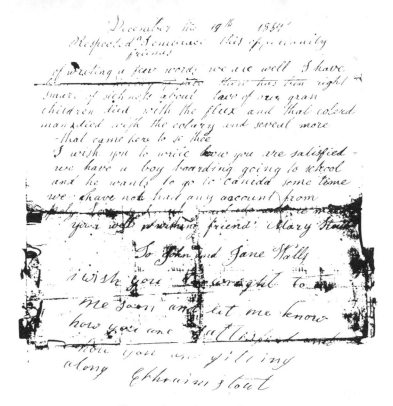

December the 19th 1854

Respected friends I embrace this opportunity of writing a few words we are well I have not been healthy of late there has been right smart of sickness about two of our gran children died with the flux and that colerd man died with the colary and several more that came here to see thee. I wish you to write how you are satisfied we have a boy boarding going to school and he wants to go to Canida some time we have not had any account from you of late

Your well wishing friend:
Mary Stout

To John and Jane Walls
I Wish you to wright to me soon and let me know how you are satisfied and how you are gitting along

Ephraim Stout

had, once they had oriented themselves in the free state, sought Jane out to thank her and bid her best wishes. Jane had been complimented with the name "the white Mrs. Moses; but, thinking it too glorified for her humble nature, she asked them to call her Jane.

The four underground travellers had a map the Stouts had given them and it marked in code the end of their journey: Mr. and Mrs. Moses, Maidstone, Canada.

As John continued reading he had no idea that, within a fortnight, he would have opportunity to relieve some of his feelings of frustration and futility. He would be able to combat the fugitive slave law and the other unjust laws which he had just spoken so vehemently against. His home was to become a final terminal for the underground railroad.

"The hounds barked and ran through miles of bottom land and swamp—five of the best nigger hounds, but they didn't catch us, John."

These were the first words John heard from the three fugitives as they were escorted into his barn. He would have taken them into the house were it not for their smell. Neither John nor Jane could keep their hands from their noses. They both realized that the three fugitives were not more than twenty-four hours into Canada and probably had had no chance to wash.

While Derek and Murray were busily devouring the first food they had eaten in three three days, Joseph made their apologies. "I know we smell bad but to us it is one of the sweetest of smells, as it saved our lives."

"What do you mean, it saved your lives?" John asked curiously.

"We ran, John and Mrs. Moses, I mean Jane, till our legs felt like they would fall off. The dogs were good. Nothing, not even the swamp water, would keep them from finding our tracks again and again. We even used a paste of red onion, spruce and pine on our bodies and feet but they kept coming."

"They must have been some kind of hounds," John was quick to remark. Before he could ask "What did you do?" Joseph continued his story. "John and Jane, we don't want you to think any less of us, but the Lord was with us and we did what we had to do. John, we came across an old graveyard and the three of us decided to try something we had heard of back on the plantation." He paused, watching his audience.

By this time, Jane was overpowered by curiosity and urged Joe to continue. "Sorry, Mrs. Jane, not trying to be rude. Just old Joe is excited, but I tell you what we did, we dug up an old grave and took the dust from the skeleton and made a paste with water and mud and rubbed it all over our bodies. The face still had some skin on it and I think he was a black man, but I'm not quite sure. But if he was, we felt sure he would have died in prejudice and would not mind helping others to escape to a free land while still here on earth.

"Our other partner, Jack, was too supersititious and would have nothing to do with the cemetery. He left us and we hope and pray he is free. He said he was still going to try to reach Canada, God willing. Anyhow the hounds didn't follow us and the bounty hunters went back with empty pockets."

As the three freedom runners bathed in the warm waters of Puce Creek, they were laughing and talking like children who had outwitted cruel adults—who had underestimated their intelligence, and underestimated the lengths they would go to in order to be free.

Jane lovingly nursed the practically starved individuals. "Putting meat on their ribs," she called it—her expression for the ample dinner of pheasant, duck, rabbit and vegetables galore that graced the table.

MILE XXIII

That night Jane lay within the protection and love of John's strong, black shoulder, his rippling muscles serving as her pillow. Her husband's eyes stared into the darkness of the bedroom he had built. He did not wish to move too abruptly, for fear he would wake his wife, whose sleep he wished to guard. John's thoughts were too overpowering to allow him to sleep. The story of his three guests, men who wanted so badly to be free that they would paste themselves with the smell of death, weighed on his mind. "My God!" John thought, "when will mankind give in to reason? When will a man treat his fellow human beings with at least the same dignity he gives to his animals?"

This emotion-packed thought caused his huge biceps to flex in such suddenness that Jane's slight frame felt the movement; she immediately sat up. "What is it, John? What's wrong? What—" Before she could finish her sentence, John seized her arms with a firm gentleness and half wrestled her now awakened body under his rippling muscles, being careful not to bruise her.

Jane could only see a shiny, black face with eyes shining with love, and as her eyes closed her ears heard quieting words that chased away any thoughts in her mind that all was not well.

They were oblivious to the freedom runners they were helping. They were proud to be able to be themselves. They were sheltered by the darkness of the room; outside the log cabin on the Puce Road, the north star glittered brightly in the clear, midnight sky.

Henry, their first-born son, had been conceived.

The next morning the sun broke through the cracks in the walls of the log cabin. John and Jane were sheltering each other with their arms, welcoming the opportunity to yawn a most sincere thanks to this Canadian sunrise.

"Jane, we've got company." John's words were all that was needed to motivate the Walls family into full swing.

The three travellers, who had hardly slept because of conditioned fear, felt no sensations of tiredness in their excited, free bones, but plenty of hunger pains in their stomachs. The aroma of Jane's eggs and Canadian bacon filtered up the stairs and into their comfortable bedroom. Derek was the first to speak. "Do you think we have died and gone to heaven?" His question brought hysterical laughter and a look of thankfulness from his companions.

Jane recognized this look as they came down the stairs; it was the same look she had seen on Caesar's face, and the faces of others she had helped from the slavery fields of North Carolina. The mere thought of Caesar, who had died to let his little Sammy and others be free, brought a tear to her eye. Her tear sparked uncontrolled tears of joy in the eyes of the three underground railroad travellers, who were instinctively wiping the water from their cheeks.

John, who had just come in the cabin with some kindling, felt almost like an intruder who had unexpectedly come upon a party. It did not take him long to add to the fun and frivolity with a song that had just come to his head.

The Road That Led To Somewhere
Has brought us all the way to where we are
Follow the side of the tree that the moss grows on
And the light of the north star.[17]

The third time around the others had caught on to the words and were all joining hands and dancing around the room, as if a holiday had been created in honour of all fugitives escaping from the baying of the hounds.

Only the smell of burning bacon caused their merriment to

cease, and they all sat down at the table John had made, and ate the food Jane had prepared.

As Murray began to feast on Jane's sumptuous breakfast, he looked at his friends gathered at the table. "Freedom is happiness; happiness is former slaves who are free." All were at the Walls's breakfast table.

After breakfast the travellers eagerly discussed the business of finding work and independence.

John had planned to hunt for deer to add to the family's meat supply; he invited the three recently-arrived fugitives to join him.

John slung his gun over his shoulder, the same gun that had been brought up from slavery; with excitement in their hearts, the men left the cabin as the women waved and the children jumped up and down. They implored the grown ups to bring back a tame baby deer, a request that brought laughter from the Canadian hunters of African descent.

John's decision to stop and check on his good friend and neighbour, old Bud Piercell, who had broken his leg a week back, made the trip even more enjoyable.

They entered Bud's yard amidst barking dogs and running chickens and Susan, Bud's wife, came running onto the porch, smiling and waving them into the house.

"John, come on into the house and have some breakfast, and next time bring Jane."

Susan's words made him shake his head and say to his companions, "She's just like my Jane, she's just like my Jane."

The four former slaves entered the comfortable kitchen. They knew they weren't hungry after Jane's sumptuous breakfast, but they soon learned they would be eating anyhow, in order to avoid insulting Susan's good, Canadian hospitality.

As John was asking Susan how Bud's broken leg was healing up, Bud came hobbling into the kitchen in more than a sour mood, pretending he was as fit as a fiddle. Susan looked at John, shaking her head and commenting on how

Bud had practically thrown Dr. Fisher out of the house when he was told to rest for a few weeks, to allow his broken leg to heal properly.

They sat down to a meal of steaming biscuits, washed down by a pot of coffee. John was deep in thought: he was trying to figure out how he could convince his good friend to curb his hard working spirit, and give his leg a chance to heal properly.

John's face beamed as an idea came into his mind; his white teeth contrasted with his black face as he spoke.

"Bud, you know I came over and plowed the field for you last week. I didn't do that for my health, you know. I need you to be my partner again at the horse-shoe pitching contest in the fall."

Bud's white face had been touched with light redness, partly pain from his leg, but also embarrassment because his huge pioneer spirit and pride had been injured by the devilish wild horse he was trying to break. At John's words, his face lit up happily.

John, seeing this change in Bud's face, knew he had hit on a winning argument, and continued.

"Bud, you know we're the best horse-shoe players in Maidstone County. What good you think I'd be if I have to take on all comers by myself? I need your one or two points a game to win." John's joking raised Bud's eyebrows—and his Canadian competitive spirit.

"John, what you mean, one or two points? You know if it wasn't for me throwing a guaranteed two ringers a game, we wouldn't have a chance." John smiled with pride: he had won.

Before long everyone at the table was laughing spontaneously, and the three newly arrived fugitives laughed loudest. Even though they didn't know what the game of pitching horse-shoes was, they sensed the feeling of fun that this game must give.

As the visitors bid farewell all were happy. As he left the

149

kitchen, John smiled as he watched his good friend hobbling back to bed. He knew his words had been all the motivation needed to get his Canadian friend to rest.

"Slavery was never like this," John's friends commented as they travelled in the direction of Lake Erie, hoping to meet up with the Indians who had befriended John and Jane. Their paths did cross after half a day's walk and plenty of singing, joking and back-slapping, through woods that were possibly being pioneered for the first time.

The campfire was blazing and crackling, but its warmth was temporarily disregarded at the sight of John, their friend.

A few of the white settlers, who had been invited to join the deer hunt, could hardly believe the enthusiasm with which John and his companions were welcomed.

The white settlers, even though at ease with their Indian friends, were uncertain how to react to these people of African descent.

One of the settlers was forced to react when the blackest of the three, and the most kinky-haired, walked towards him and extended his hand in a conventional handshake.

As John's strong, black hand was extended, the white settler could almost see himself, at age four or five, being warned never to touch a black man for fear the colour would rub off; he could almost see his grandmother pointing at him and frightening him with prejudiced old wives' tales. "Can this be the heathen, the whatever, that Grandma told me about? I can't believe. . ." His thoughts had taken enough time to turn the smile on John's face to a look of concern and embarassment; as John was withdrawing his hand the white settler reached out, and as their hands touched, a gap was bridged. The white settler and the former slave, who met in the Indian village, were at the beginning of a lifelong friendship.

Then the Indian chief, White Cloud, motioned that the hunt was about to begin. As quickly as it began, it ended. The hunters had not travelled more than a quarter of a mile into the woods when a frantic voice cried out. "Daddy, Daddy, papoose, papoose, please come back!" The Indian chief's oldest daughter, Kazar, was panting breathlessly and pulling on his clothes, too young to realize that childbirth was more a natural occurrance than a sickness.

White Cloud's stoic expression turned into a grin of joy; his smile eased the minds of the white settler and the black hunter.

As the three friends waited outside White Cloud's teepee, John thought of Jubil, his mother, and Hannabal, his father; he realized how important he had been to them, and he remembered their words: *If you remember nothing else I say, remember the side of the tree the moss grows on, and the north star, are the way to freedom.* Those words had allowed him to be sitting with legs crossed, as he was now. He looked at the native Canadian on his right and the white settler on his left, and the peace pipe seemed unnecessary.

His head turned towards the skin-covered teepee in front of him, and he tried to visualize what must be going on inside, and he smiled.

He could almost see the hips of the Indian Queen—and he could imagine the hips of other women—heaving, her widened legs straining under the pressure of childbirth. But just as she would refuse to cry, so would they. This was too momentous an occasion to cry.

He imagined he could hear the midwives slap the buttocks of his descendants; he could almost hear his descendants' cries, just as he was now hearing the cries of the little Indian princess, Parthena, his future daughter-in-law.

Tears were in his eyes, tears of joy and thankfulness to the Almighty; he was thankful that, because he and Jane had followed the road to freedom, his descendants would follow their road to somewhere.

151

PART IV

1845–1909

*Life in Canada of
John and Jane Walls*

MILE XXIV

The popcorn flew halfway to the ceiling, but no one cared. Relaxation was a necessity after the daily struggle to survive. In fact, the popcorn was a special bonus; the friendly euchre game was what the men had been waiting for. The card game was an almost weekly tradition between John's new and old friends.

Jane was smiling as she bent over the hot stove. The sweat poured from her brow and she was mumbling under her breath about how perturbed she was to have to watch four grown men laughing hysterically and even, on occasion, jumping up from their seats.

"You fellas ready for some more popcorn?" Her question brought no response until she added, "John Freeman, did you hear me, John Freeman?"

Half annoyed, John turned in his chair, more upset at losing a hand of euchre than at Jane's interruption. He knew, however, that his euchre game would be interrupted—he had to help his wife carry in the pan of corn. He was worried about her, and did his best to help her whenever he could. Hearing the words "John Freeman" at least twice from the other room made him move—he did not wish to test her Irish temper.

As he lifted the pan off the stove and pecked Jane on the cheek, he knew she was not overly concerned about the happenings in the next room, and her indulgence served to make these weekly sessions even more exciting and fun.

The smile on her husband's face made Jane glad she had offered to find the aging pan and pop some corn.

As John walked back to the living room he chattered

happily to the men, corn falling over the sides of the pan he carried. He looked back at Jane and said, "Honey, please go to bed before you have my boy right here in the kitchen. Me and old Bud won't be long sending Charley and Wayman back to Elmstead with their tails tucked between their legs, ha, ha!"

John looked at Wayman with a friendly grin, and Wayman said, "Deal."

Charley mumbled, "Good thing this isn't poker. I don't like playing this old euchre anyway. Damn! Excuse me, Missie Jane."

Jane just shook her head and smiled, as if to say, "Grown men acting like children." She walked into the bedroom, but before closing the door behind her, she bid good night to the men. Jane then put on her increasingly tight nightgown and, as was becoming a Tuesday night custom, lay on the straw mattress and placed a feather-stuffed pillow over her head to drown out the laughter but a few steps away.

White Cloud had come over to sit in one of the loser's seats, and his presence added extra fun to the affair. He nervously pushed a whole handful of popcorn into his mouth before the other four had a chance to put down their cards. The Indian chief made John laugh, as some of the popcorn streamed from the sides of his face and fell to the clay floor.

"Here, White Cloud, have some of my water."

"Thanks, John," the chief stuttered as his red hand patted John's black shoulder.

The game continued as the atmosphere in the cabin was charged with excitement. "Euchre!" The exultant cry bounced off the logs again and again and rang in the losers' ears. At one highly emotional point, White Cloud could hardly believe his eyes. The turn of the final card decided which team would win and claim championship for the night. White Cloud watched John stick what the black man thought to be the winning card on his sweaty forehead to dramatize his victory. John gently placed the thought-to-be-winning card on the table and was about to go into his Walls victory dance. The chief saw Charley frantically pointing at Wayman, who was sitting back in his chair with arms folded and a smile on his face. He had the real winner stuck to the sweat on his nose. John could see only the corners of Wayman's mouth, grinning triumphantly; in a matter of seconds, the card was flying across the table as Wayman burst out in uncontrolled laughter.

John laughed so hard he nearly fell off his chair. Charley was standing up, pointing at Bud and crying, "We won! We won! We're finally the champs!"

Bud hated to lose, and his face turned red as Wayman, between laughs, tried to impress on him how "No Walls or Piercell was going to beat the team of Scott and Stewart again."

Jane awakened, half afraid and wondering how they could be so loud. And how would she ever get used to the recreational pastime of John and his friends? "Have they ever considered reading a book?" she thought, but then remembered that most of them couldn't read. The thought of John—"My John, he certainly must be enjoying freedom!"—took her back into a most peaceful sleep again.

The next morning as she was half waking, her arm fell over to John's side of the bed, but her husband was not there. He had, despite his late-night frivolity, gotten up at six and was working. "John really knows how to make the living for us," she said to herself sleepily.

John was busy chopping wood, clearing land and making his dreams come true.

One of his most important dreams was to come true before the setting of the beautiful red sun. That evening the sunset was a tapestry of colours, but its beauty went unnoticed as the cries of his first-born son reached his ears.

Henry was slapped on the buttocks and he cried.

John was standing outside the cabin he had built; inside lay the newborn son he had fathered. As the music of Henry's cries continued to float from the cabin, John reached down and touched the ground. He walked proudly back to the creek lost in his dreams. He was a happy man. Doc Fisher walked up behind him. John had already sensed all was well, and he knew a son had been born to carry on the Walls proud name, a son who was healthy, a son who was wealthy with love, a son who would be blessed with the positive qualities that only he and Jane could produce.

They both walked back from the creek, into the house and straight into the bedroom. John looked in and saw Wayman Scott's Guinea wife, and the brown infant she held in her arms.

"Jane, Jane," he cried, "we did it! You're the best woman in the world!" Jane had saved enough energy just for this moment to give John a big smile.

"Are you proud of your son? John, are you proud?" John answered with a kiss. The other children were running into the small bedroom, making it almost burst from the vibrations of good.

"Hello, little brother, hello, hello," they all said excitedly.

"Look, Ma, he's already got a tan," little Mary said, taking them by surprise. Unexpected ideas were not uncommon to the child. Jane would usually criticize her for being outspoken, and John would usually defend her. He did not need to defend her today, because they were all too busy laughing.

Daniel Junior was daydreaming and hoping his new brother would hurry up and grow, so he could take him fishing. Angeline was mumbling the excited, incoherent words of a toddler as she reached to play with the baby. The family was hugging each other in celebration, and the cabin was pulsating with their feelings.

The good doctor wiped seldom-felt tears from his cheeks as he turned and left the room. He departed quietly, not because he was embarrassed but because the room was becoming too full of emotion. The good doctor felt like an intruder in the family's happiness. Even the cabin itself seemed to express joy: it was personal; it was alive; it was real. The doctor had never assisted in the birth of such a special baby, a baby whose ancestry stretched from the mountains of Scotland and Ireland to the vast coast of Africa, journeyed across the potentially great nation of the United States and ended in a tiny cabin beside a peaceful stream in Canada. "This room," he said to the Guinea woman, who was crying with happiness, "is going to last for a long time." She nodded in complete agreement, as she also realized the room's significance.

Thus, into this world, Henry Walls (brown) was born.

MILE XXV

After three days Jane's small frame, which had been through many more physical hardships than childbirth, was returning to normal. John realized this when he heard her call his name twice; when she called, John Freeman came a-running. He felt at first like kidding her about being well enough to fuss, but was too concerned for her health. "What is it, Jane? You all right, girl?"

"Get me the blanket over there in the corner, John."

"You mean you called me running in here for that? Don't you know I'm trying to put some vittles in you and the children's stomachs?" John answered.

John looked at Jane, trying to appear hard and annoyed, but knowing he really wasn't. She beckoned him over to the bed with a smile on her face. Before he could even think, she had bent his head towards her lips and said, "Give me a big kiss. I love you."

John knew, as he left the house, that she really meant what she had said, but he wondered why only briefly.

In the past three days of forced rest, Jane had had plenty of time to think about why she had borne John's child. She remembered how, on the first day of her rest, John had come in carrying Daniel Junior on his shoulders, both of them laughing to beat the band. John had been teaching Daniel how to farm, and the lesson for the day was ploughing.

Jane heard John's words again. "Now, Daniel, put the plough in the soil, pick an object in the distance and walk towards it, but first say 'Gitty up!' to the horse. I'll be back in an hour or so, to check on how you are doing."

She remembered how John, when he related the story to her, could hardly get the words out of his mouth, he was laughing so hard. She remembered starting to laugh herself, without knowing why. When she learned why, minutes later, she practically split her sides laughing, which made John try to calm her down, worried about her physical condition.

John stopped laughing long enough to continue his story. Daniel had picked, as his object in the distance, a cow. When John and old Bud came back from hunting, they could scarcely believe their eyes. Instead of neat, straight furrows, Daniel had ploughed a path as crooked as the winding Puce creek.

Old Bud had started to roll on the ground with laughter; years later, he would jokingly talk about what good farmers those Walls boys were.

Jane remembered how, on the second day, little Mary, John's favourite, had almost drowned in the creek; John had risked his own life to save hers.

She remembered how, on the third day, she had, in a state of boredom, felt devilish and decided to test John's patience and love for her. She had called him away from his important carpentry for mere play.

She didn't need a fourth day to justify lying in this tiny log cabin with John, instead of in some mansion down south.

MILE XXVI

Seven days went by, and it was Tuesday night euchre again. John was reluctant to have his friends over, but Jane insisted she felt well enough for the fun, as long as she did not have to pop corn.

That evening the men did not feel much like playing cards, because all the women insisted upon accompanying them to congratulate Jane.

The women were rustling around the tiny cabin, the children were pulling at the men's pants, and all but the men were having a good time.

Then White Cloud suggested spearfishing the next day, as the spring run of pike was at its peak, and the men began to enjoy themselves.

John told them how high the current was, and how he had almost lost little Mary less than a week ago.

When Charley, who prided himself on being a fighter, heard John's story, he felt no shame in admitting he was not an outdoorsman, and had to be coaxed into agreeing to come fishing.

While they joked and kidded about each of the men's abilities—or lack of them—John could not resist beginning the story about how he and Charley had gone rabbit hunting last winter. Upon hearing John's opening remarks, Charley sat back in his chair, rubbed his bald head and smiled nervously.

"Well, fellas, it was like this." Before continuing, John asked one of the children to get him some water, knowing that his throat would be dry before he finished.

"We had crossed over the creek and about an hour out, Charley started complaining of frostbite on his bald head."

The other men started laughing, allowing Charley to jump in and say, "I did not, John. You're just making that up. You know I had my hat on."

John realized he was exaggerating slightly, and laughed. When the others realized this, the whole room was in laughter.

John continued, "It was some kind of cold, I will admit that, so cold I walked by a tree stump on the other side of which sat a rabbit that had frozen stiff, due to the cold weather." John stopped for a minute and took a sip of water.

"Get back to the story, John," Wayman's Guinea wife said impatiently.

John, realizing he had a bigger audience than he had thought, decided to really dramatize the story. He pulled back his chair, tilted his head slightly and continued.

Near the end of the story Jane yawned, then smiled quickly, hoping no one had noticed. She did not want to take away from the punchline of the story John was telling.

"He actually told me I had walked too fast—and missed the rabbit's tracks."

At this point John tried to mimic Charley's look; with white teeth showing and black face glowing, he also tried to mimic Charley's voice. "Yeh, I shot him between the ears, John. That devilish rabbit was really speeding through the woods. You should have seen him!'

"I said to Charley, 'I did see him—the durn thing was frozen solid!'"

Jane laughed, even though she had heard the story at least four times. She enjoyed the atmosphere of laughter John's story-telling brought. The women sewed, the children sang and the men, who had worked hard all day, forgot their responsibilities and cares, and played.

The next day's fishing expedition was a combination of work and play. The work was getting the fish on the table; throwing spears in the water was play. Charley, who had often bragged that his father's native tribe in Africa had some of the best spear throwers in the world, realized he had to temper some of his claims to world rights when the native Canadian arrived.

White Cloud was smiling at the others and beckoning them to hurry back to the fork in the creek, where he had found a waterfall. They saw not only a beautiful natural sight—but also enough fish to feed their families for a week. Spears were whistling through the air, men were shouting and fish were jumping.

John yelled, "The only jumping you fish will be doing tonight is in Jane's frying pan."

Charley had overcome his reluctance, and could hardly believe how exciting this was; he wished it would never end.

"There goes one," someone yelled, and all five men ran along the bank of the Puce Creek, trying to keep their balance to avoid falling into the cool spring water.

They had travelled at least three miles from the cabin when they decided they were tired and had caught enough fresh fish to turn back. As they discussed what to do, White Cloud spoke. "My friends," he said, "always conserve the natural resources of this beautiful land—waste is not a good thing."

John understood and they decided to turn back. As they walked, he overheard Charley asking Bud what Puce meant.

He heard the reply, "It's French for flea."

The conversation his friends were having went unnoticed as he thought about the name of the creek. In his mind "flea" led to thoughts of "troublesome". As he walked, he remembered his boyhood and the boyhood of his friend. He could almost visualize himself and Daniel running barefoot along a creek, laughing and playing in the North Carolina sun.

Then he saw the cabin he had built, and his new son held tightly in the arms of his wife. He knew he was a thankful man, a man who had really come a long way.

MILE XXVII

John's new son was growing older and maturing, and so was one of his proudest achievements, the apple orchard.

Jane had the reputation of being the best apple pie maker in the country. One day she was out getting apples for her pie; looking for the best fruit, she climbed higher up the ladder.

"Hold it still, Henry. I've got to get this best one."

Henry knew only too well that his mother would have him sit on the lower rung of the ladder at least fifteen times before she was satisfied.

His mother's secret, or so she claimed, was that she didn't pick all the apples for her pie from the first tree she came to; instead, she took the best from many trees. She would explain this to her children, speaking maturely to make them feel grown up. She would add, "The way I prepare pie is the way to do business. Always remember, children, to take the best people from different trees. This makes a strong team."

Henry always thought his mother must have made a mistake and meant to say "apples," because he had never seen a person growing on any of his dad's apple trees. He would make the correction in his own mind and not correct his mother; he didn't want to make her feed bad.

By the time the pies were made he was almost too full to eat, because he had eaten more than a few apples while sitting on the ladder. But his brothers and sisters were more than willing to keep him from getting a stomach ache by eating his leftover pie.

He gave his pie to Daniel Junior, using it as a bribe to make Daniel promise to play tag, Henry's favourite game. "Oh, all right, let's go," Daniel said when reminded of his promise, and the two headed for the barn.

Daniel was determined to rid Henry of his obsession for playing tag by making it a really tough game.

The boys decided to play a game of free-for-all tag with Red Squirrel, one of White Cloud's sons. There were no holds barred, and no places outlawed or off-limits, anywhere in the barn.

Henry knew his smaller size would keep him from climbing to the top rafter of the barn but he agreed to the rules anyway. He was really anxious for a game of tag. "Besides," he thought, "I don't know when I can coax Daniel with more pie again."

Daniel tried everything to escape Henry, who was "it"; finally, when all else failed, he took to the top rafters of the barn.

Henry saw a rope and figured, since he couldn't climb high enough, he would swing and catch his brother in the middle of the beam.

Daniel watched in shock and disbelief, as his little brother grabbed the rope and began to swing in desperation to reach the narrow beam. "No, no, Henry, don't try it! You'll fall, you'll fall!"

All Henry replied was, "H-e-l-p!" His voice got fainter as he fell. Fortunately, he fell into a few bales of hay. If Daniel had already fed the horses, as he had intended to, those bales of hay would not have been there to save Henry's life. Daniel could see his brother roll off the hay and onto the hard, clay floor; Henry seemed unconscious—or lifeless.

He and Red Squirrel rushed down from the rafters and over to the quiet figure on the floor. "Are you all right, Henry? Are you all right?"

"Let me get my dad's medicine man," Red Squirrel stammered.

"Are you all right?" Daniel asked again, beginning to panic. At that precise instant, Henry jumped up, tagged him on the shoulder, screamed, "You're it!" and ran frantically to his secret hiding place.

"You forgot what Dad said about how an opossum plays

dead. Ha, Ha!" he yelled as he ran. Daniel was too shocked to laugh. From that day on, he refused to eat Henry's leftover pie.

The journeys to the apple orchard were enjoyed by family and friends. One newcomer to Canada, whose long journey had started in Kentucky, ended on a bright, warm and sunny day, in the Walls orchard at the foot of Jane's ladder.

The man had started his journey with Derek, Murray and Joe; his superstitions in a cemetery had delayed his escape to Canada by a few years.

As he walked into the orchard and looked up at the woman picking apples, the only words he said were, "Thank goodness. It's better late than never."

Henry, who was startled, stood up from his seat on the ladder; then he quickly grabbed the ladder to keep his mother from falling to the ground. Jack aided his attempt and grabbed the other side of the ladder.

"What in tarnation?" Jane said, when she reached the ground. "I can't believe my eyes! Jack...is it really you, Jack?"

His mother's words, and the grin on Jack's face, told Henry there was no need for fear. But the stories he heard later that night made him too frightened to sleep.

John and Jane wanted the children to hear Jack's story so they would know what prejudice was all about, and how good people in the United States and Canada formed the underground railroad.

"I would travel but twenty to thirty miles between each brakeman, but sure enough, Missie Jane, slave patrollers would interrupt my journey. I even once tried to mail myself in a box, when I heard another slave had tried this. You would have been quite surprised to have gone to the post office and found me, wouldn't ya, Missie Jane, huh?

"Mary Stout, the Quaker lady you first helped us escape to,

sends you greetings and this letter. Here it is. I don't know what it means, but maybe you do."*

Jane looked at the letter and saw that it was a personal one. She was prudently silent, and appreciatively, as Jack was doing most of the talking. To him, human company was a luxury; he had lived for years in the wilderness. His enthusiastic conversation was often interrupted by his coughing; the sound was so harsh it made John and Jane look at each other, each knowing the sound was not normal or healthy.

Jack talked on, despite his coughing spells; the good feeling that began when he had entered the Walls's apple orchard that afternoon had put him in a trance: a trance of happiness, which only he, an escaped slave, could feel.

"Indians in the United States helped me hide when I broke away from the others, and I even married a squaw lady, but she died giving birth to our child. There were thousands of us, Missie Jane, living in the woods together. Some were by themselves, but we all knew we couldn't be truly free until we reached Canada. I knew I would reach it some day, but I didn't know when. After my wife died, I heard of a cause for freedom in Florida through my Indian friends. It made me sad—I wanted to give up my life, if necessary, for freedom. I really miss my wife—she was a good lady."

John and Jane immediately thought of White Cloud's wife but they said nothing, allowing Jack to continue.

"My Indian chief friend married the daughter of a free slave woman—you may have even helped her to freedom, Jane. I forget her name for the moment, but it will come to me shortly. Anyway, an agent of the government kidnapped his wife and took her right straight back to slavery. The chief had his revenge and he waged war, with the help of other fugitives like myself. Hundreds of my friends were captured. And at

---

*The letter Jack refers to has been carefully preserved and is reproduced at the back of this book.

times, believe me, I didn't know where I was. Were it not for the north star and the moss on the side of the tree, I would not be here right now."

These words made John smile, and Jane clutched her husband's right arm even tighter. The children were almost frozen with excitement and desired to hear more from this interesting newcomer.

Jack continued his story. "You know this war cost the United States millions of dollars. Can you believe that? What is the sense in fighting and killing? Can you tell me, John? The government needs to spend its money on more freedom and opportunity programs, I think."

"Yes," John replied. "Would you like to stay here and work for awhile until you get on your feet?" The words made Jack grab his handkerchief so the children could not see his tears of joy.

The family invited Jack to join them at the County picnic, and he gratefully accepted. As their buggy pulled up to the picnic area, Jack could hear an even stranger sound. "Clink. Clink. Clink," he heard; it was the sound of horse-shoes landing on target.

John and Jane could hardly believe how quickly the children had taken to Jack. "This," Jane said to John "is because Jack has suffered so, and his heart, like the hearts of other fugitive slaves newly arrived in Canada, is so thankful it has softened rather than hardened. He doesn't want to kill; freedom and opportunity are all he seeks."

John understood why his wife had become a "brakelady" in the underground railroad chain, and why his heart was attracted to her.

But his serious thoughts ended quickly when he saw old Bud waving at him to hurry; their turn had come to pitch horse-shoes.

"Jack," he said, "come on over and watch me and Bud send

two fellows from the Elmstead settlement scooting back home."

Jack enjoyed the sight of four men playing horse-shoes; two of the men he would see each week at John's Tuesday night euchre games. The freedom runner quickly got the impression that winning the horse-shoe championship was almost as important as freedom.

These and other first impressions of Canada were so overpowering that tears could often be seen coming to his eyes at routine family hospitality.

The only thing that marred his enjoyment of his new life was his much too frequent coughing, which was getting worse.

Within six months, Jack died. Within two days, John and Jane had to make a decision.

"No, John. You know I liked Jack as well as anyone, you know that. I helped him from North Carolina to the Stouts in Indiana, I risked my life for him, but to bury him right on this land, when our church cemetery is down the road, and to start a cemetery right over yonder— No, John. What if you die first, John? I couldn't stand to be constantly reminded of your loss. No!"

John knew it would be hard to relate his feelings to her, feelings he had never before communicated. He had often wished to, but could not find the right words.

"Jane, I want our descendants with us when Judgment Day comes." It was the most eloquent argument he could think of.

Jane's answer, which she had so adamantly proclaimed, was not changed by John's argument; she changed her mind when she saw the look in John's eyes. His eyes reflected the feelings in his heart, the heart of a fugitive slave in Canada.

She remembered the months of happiness that had filled Jack's heart and the desperate attempts he would make to stop coughing. She could remember how he would seal his lips, his cheeks filled with air and saliva. She remembered how he would run out of the cabin and to the outhouse. Dr.

Fisher could not cure what Jack's wilderness living had caused. Of all the fugitives they had aided, no one had been more appreciative than Jack.

Had it not been for this fugitive slave, the family cemetery by the Puce Creek, near the cabin John had built, may never have existed.

Jane realized her husband would not have wanted her to look out of the cabin window and see his tombstone. The stone would remind her of their escape from North Carolina, the fight with the wolves, outwitting the slave patrollers, their flight on *The Pearl*. Then she thought of the years of fruitful toil in a land where Indians could join hands with white, and neither would shun the black hands of her husband.

The word "yes" made John realize Jane would be at peace with the decision to allow the family cemetery on their property.

Slaves from all over came to pay their last respects to one of their brethren. The procession to the spot John had chosen was made difficult by mud and intermittent rain. The Scott clan from Elmstead was there in force, as they often were when called upon by the Walls family.

Reverend Floyd stepped up on the stump of one of the first trees cut for the cabin. This was the area John had chosen for the cemetery, an area the Reverend called a place "of new spiritual beginning."

Reverend Floyd startled all ears with these words:

This good man, Jack, has been freed twice, once by escape from slavery, and twice by death. You who came to Canada, be thankful that you have already been freed once, and prepare your lives cleanly and decently so that when twice comes, you will be ready.

Rain began to pour from the heavens at the precise moment Reverend Floyd was about to step off the stump. He hesitated a second, then turned again to his flock. The smile on his face did not go unnoticed. He bent his head back and opened his mouth to let the pure water enter his throat. He raised his arms towards heaven, and with all the power his voice could muster, let forth these words from his lips:

> Thank you, Lord, for blessing our dearly departed and we who are still alive. Bless the United States, from where we have come. Bless this property in Canada, on which we now stand. May both countries never forget that we hold no malice, and wish no ills, for our rewards are those that man cannot give us. May both countries never forget why, I say never forget why we were among the first newcomers to Canada. Praise His holy name. Amen!

As Reverend Floyd finished speaking, John Freeman began to sing.

"Swing low sweet chariot,
Coming for to carry me home. . . .

A whole parade of singing voices followed John, Jane and White Cloud through the rain and into the log cabin, to begin their drying and finish their crying, mindful of all their blessings.

MILE XXVIII

As the sweat poured from John's brow year after year, each day brought him closer to his most sought-after material blessing. He worked as though everything depended on him, and prayed as though everything depended on God. His philosophy was putting him ahead of schedule.

Jane was busying herself about the kitchen, mumbling about how her house should be called "The Walls Hotel" because of all the people John would invite over, for whom she had to prepare food.

John was only occasionally reminded of this fact, and Jane always phrased her complaint politely. "Please give me more notice, John. I am only human, my goodness."

171

John would sheepishly change the topic of conversation, knowing his wife was right. But once in a while he would feel compelled to retaliate.

"Now Jane, be quiet. You know how I am. I just get with people that I like and can't resist telling them how good your apple pie always is. Your pie is famous, Jane."

Jane knew well enough when she was being sweet talked, but she always kissed him on the cheek for his valiant attempts.

This day, however, as the steam rushed out of the stove and touched the grey and red hair hanging over her eyes, she muttered angrily, "John Walls is not going to sweet talk me today, believe me."

The sight of John and the children coming up the lane in one buggy, and White Cloud and his family in another was beginning to smooth some of her ruffled feathers—for all her grumbling, she was happy to see her friends. The Scott family and old Bud and Susan bringing up the rear put all her feathers in place.

John could not believe how quickly his wife had added vegetables and trimmings to the largest turkey he had ever shot. Thanksgiving dinner would be hard to beat this year.

Jane's visitors hesitated to step on her clean floors, and more often than not would remove their shoes. Today was no exception. But, as she always did, Jane insisted her guests make themselves at home. She wanted her guests to be themselves, and come in as they were.

She had only broken her rule once, years back, when Jack's three friends had arrived with the smell of a dead man rubbed over their bodies to keep the hounds from tracking them; even then, she had felt guilty when the refugees had been escorted to the barn. John saw tears in her eyes the day the three fugitives left. They were destined to be some of the first black pioneers in a place up east called Toronto. Realizing the cause of his wife's tears John assured her he would assume the guilt; as he said, "No one enters my home smelling like that—

172

especially when the Puce Creek is running right behind the cabin."

Today Jane was entertaining clean, smiling old friends, not newly arrived fugitive slaves; and all was well.

Things were even better before the apple pie had been completely consumed. John had hurriedly finished his piece and excused himself from the table. When he returned, he held a piece of paper in his hand, and asked Jane to do him the honour of reading a little surprise he had saved just for Thanksgiving dinner, to share with their friends.

"Jane, this is why I didn't give you more notice of company, as I know how smart you are—you might have figured it out if you had more time, but read, read."

Jane carefully opened the paper, her hands trembling. "My God, John, you don't mean it's our deed!"

John stepped back with a smile on his face and folded his arms. The emotional impact upon Jane made her eyes water and her hand go to a fluttering heart. Susan fanned air towards her nose and John helped her sit back down on the chair.

"My part-time jobs is what did it, Jane. Kinda proud of myself."

Everyone seated at the table, family and friends, was proud of John Walls, but none was more proud than Jane.

The owning of land was a momentous occasion, and caused all adults to kneel and give thanks. The kids were out playing and the adults were praying.

Parthena, White Cloud's youngest daughter, ran into the cabin just as they were rising from their knees. Tears were streaming down her cheeks and a bump was welling on her forehead: she was crying so hard she could hardly talk. What the puzzled adults finally understood was that Henry had caused the bump on her head by "showing off."

John immediately peeked out the cabin door and saw Henry trying to pretend nothing had happened.

Seeing John instead of his mother made Henry realize it

had been a bit more serious than he thought, and that he'd best act more sorry. This he did; it saved him from a spanking, but not from serious words, which would become more significant as he and Parthena grew older.

"Henry, play gentle with Parthena; she may be your wife some day, boy." The reprimand was light. Great, Henry thought. "I'm never going to marry the crybaby anyhow."

"Yes, father" he said.

The company went home, the children went to bed, and John sat in the kitchen eating cold turkey and apple pie, while Jane read the deed out loud four times in a row.

Sleep that night was long in coming.

MILE XXIX

Canadian life, for John and Jane, was not without hardships, and these hardships were shared by their neighbours. Neighbours worked together in time of trouble; this sharing exemplified the fullest definition of neighbourly love. Canada was a heaven.

The snowstorm of sixty-two, the flooding of seventy-three, and the ravishing of the flux added wrinkles to their aging faces. Their children offered them many rewards; they hoped their descendants would carry on this tradition.

Day-to-day life brought much that was unexpected; there was much to be dealt with in this strange, yet beautiful, new country.

The Tuesday night euchre games relieved pressure; the lighthearted fun would carry the men through the more serious work of building a country. Even Jane would smile when she remembered the exceptionally dark night Charley had gone out to the outhouse. John went running after him to warn him that the seat was being repaired and it had not yet been replaced—but he was too late. It took all four men to pull Charley up from his unusual resting place; he went for a swim, clothes and all, in the peaceful creek.

Their laughter that night could be heard for miles. All were laughing except Charley and Jane. She was sobered by the memory of another strange happening in the outhouse, one that had been frightening.

The children had found a surprising house within the outhouse; it was called a bee hive. Their curiosity got the better of them; the stick whacked at the hive and before a few seconds could elapse, children and bees were pouring out of the outhouse. The children headed straight for the protection of their mother.

When Jane saw the hurried procession of her sorry offspring, she realized that dealing with the unexpected was becoming a rule rather than an exception.

She ran out of the log cabin, shouting and imploring the children to rush into the house as she swung her arms and flapped her apron madly at the bees, trying to distract their anger. Some of the bees got into the house, but the majority followed her running figure to the bank of the creek. She dove in and held her head under water, intermittently coming up for air, until the bees were weary of their attempts at revenge.

Just as Jane was climbing out of the creek, John arrived home from a hunt, gun over his shoulder and a smile on his face. The smile became even wider when he saw his wife, hair dripping water down her face and clothes clinging to her body.

"Jane, girl, you're supposed to be preparing supper and here you are taking a swim. Must be nice to have life so easy, ha, ha!"

His last "ha" ignited her Irish temper, and her face started to turn red. She ran to the top of the bank but, before she could vent her anger or tell John about the bees, she felt her body being lifted into the air by strong black hands. John swung her around twice and before her toes touched the ground, he kissed her until she forgot all about being angry, and almost forgot about the bees.

John carried her into the house. When the children saw their mother they thought she had been destroyed by the bees.

They all gathered around her as John gently placed her on the bed. The children stopped worrying as soon as they saw the smile on her face.

Then John spoke, and Jane's face took on an added glow. "Jane, lay right here after you get out of those wet clothes, and I'll fix the children's food." As he walked out of the room, she felt a tear come to her eye.

"I can't stay here too long," she thought. "I have to welcome those new people down the road." Before John had finished fixing the dinner, he felt his body being moved and a hand reaching over his shoulder.

"Excuse me, John."

"What! Jane, get some rest; you're not the strongest woman in the world, you know."

Jane ignored his words as she pulled an apple pie from behind a pan.

"I didn't know that was there."

"I hid it from the kids because I want to take it to those new neighbours who moved in next door to old Bud."

With a shawl around her shoulders and a scarf over her head, she was hoping to make a good impression on her new neighbours.

Henry and little Mary felt as if they must go with their mother to protect her although they could not say from what. Jane laughed and took their hands, and continued on her expedition of welcome.

What she heard as she walked onto the porch made her stop. The door was partially open and she could hear the conversation coming from inside the house.

"Mama, what are they saying?" little Henry asked.

"I don't like it here," Mary said at the same time.

Jane did not answer. As if frozen in time, she heard words she thought she had long before left behind.

"There are a lot of those blacks around here and I certainly can't understand how a black and a white can live together."

She had to deal with yet another of those unexpected

situations. The bees she had escaped by running into the creek. But the sting of bigotry could not be outrun. The children were pulling on both her arms in an attempt to encourage her to leave. This helped her regain her composure, and she knocked on the door.

The faces of the new couple went pale, as they saw the lady, the wife of the man who had been the topic of what they thought was private conversation.

They could not speak as they were welcomed into the community and handed a fresh apple pie, compliments of Mrs. John Freeman Walls.

Jane walked off the steps, took both of her children by the hand and went home. John was smiling as she entered the kitchen, but Jane's face was serious, resolved and completely at peace with the reality of the world around her. Later on that evening she related the incident to John, and ended with the words, "I simply do not care. Prejudice is their problem, not mine. We have been graced with too many blessings."

MILE XXX

The community expressed thanks for the blessings of God during Sunday church services. Until just recently, these church goings had been conducted in the Walls home itself. But John and other members of the Maidstone Black Community had constructed a log church with money loaned by John. The Walls family was more than proud, on that warm, Sunday morning, to invite two of the many other fugitive newcomers, who were walking, to ride and attend the service with them.

The buggies were decked with ornamentation and full of seated men and women of different shades of black, all anxious to give thanks for being able to ride, like the white folks, to their own church.

The two newly-arrived men were looking in all directions, John asked them what they were so concerned about. Their answer reminded him of something he had almost forgotten: here in Canada, when such a gathering of blacks came together, they were not surrounded and harassed by overseers.

"This is Canada, brethern, no need to worry about whips." John's words quieted the apprehension of the two, and made them begin to realize how sweet a society free of racial bigotry could be.

On this dry, hot, summer day the dirt road was making all church-goers, riders and walkers, slap their Sunday-go-to-meeting clothes sharply, to remove dust prior to entering the place of God. .

John had built fifteen rows of pews on the left and ten on the right. Those on the right were separated by a large, pot-belly stove; it allowed the parishioners the luxury of holding church services at night and during cold winter seasons in comfort.

As the congregation began to sing the old, black spirituals, Reverend Floyd walked to the hand-carved pulpit, which had been created by John's gifted hands. John was proud of his handiwork, and he was even prouder to be the first deacon of the Puce First Baptist Church. As the deacon looked at the gleaming pulpit and the articulate man behind it, he looked forward to the first convention of Baptist black churches which would be held here in the Maidstone County community. John crossed his arms, satisfied that the convention would be impressed.

As he heard his fellow freedom runners sing "Hallelujah," he seized Jane's white hand with his own black one; he was praying silently: "Thank God, for how far we have come."

The service lasted two and one half hours. The minister preached about hell fire, damnation and brimstone with such sincerity that the parishioners were moved to shouting.

Maggie Lucas, an emotional lady at the most quiet of times, shouted, praised the Lord and spoke in tongues as she danced up and down the aisle, filled with the Holy Spirit. As Reverend Floyd's spirit-filled voice summoned the choir to sing "Joshua Fought the Battle of Jericho," she tumbled out of her seat, and started a chain reaction of inspired, free blacks who thankfully praised God as loudly and unceremoniously as they wished. They were not going to let the rocks cry out, as it said in the Bible.

Many had waited all week to share the sincerity and music. Deborah, the best female vocalist in the black community, was accompanied by Lillian; they sang the Gospel song "Go Down Moses into Canaan Land and Let My People Go" with such emotion that few could hold back their tears.

John remarked to Jane, "Good thing Maggie is too tired out to shout." Jane smiled back, realizing that no insult was intended; the religion of people who had been so deprived and oppressed took the form of great emotional release and uninhibited praise of God, and was often unmistakeably entertaining. The entire congregation felt goose bumps as Deborah's high notes bounced off the rafters of their precious new log church.

The two recently-arrived fugitives looked back over the congregation; they were used to Jane's white face, but they looked frightened upon seeing the other white faces that dotted the pews.

Jane noticed their concern and nudged her husband. He spoke to them during the offering portion of the service, pointing out that Dr. Fisher, the Perkins family, the Piercell family and other white families meant no harm. Their attendance reinforced the reality of freedom: the fugitives were beginning to shed the psychological shackles of slavery.

As they walked out of the church, John pointed to the log school house across the dirt road and said, "This school was given to us by the Queen and, even though it was for former slaves, black and white alike attend the classes sitting side by side. Jane was the school teacher when it first started, but now we have a black teacher."

Everyone shook hands after the services, and they gathered

around to tell stories of how well they were doing. They took pride in reaching their never-before-imagined material goals, and discussed their success with so much exuberance, that Reverend Floyd, even though he understood their excitement, felt it necessary to remind his flock to be thankful to God rather than themselves for their blessings.

John noticed that his two new friends were listening, fascinated, to the conversation; he repeated to them Reverend Floyd's inspiring words of three Sundays ago. "I do not want any of you two to build any golden calves like Moses' people did when they left the land of Egypt. You all are free blacks now, but remember from whence you came. Don't try to intimidate good whites, or those less fortunate than you, black or white; be thankful to God. Just as Jane and I are rewarded with the good feeling of helping you, you in turn help others. Our people have to learn to help one another more, and not act like crabs in a barrel—just as soon as one tries to get out, the others pull him down. You know what I mean, don't you?"

Both understood, having seen how slavery had alienated their brothers, even in suffering. House slaves looked down on field slaves, and field slaves looked down on each other.

John repeated his words: "Help others, and don't be like crabs in a barrel!"

This idea of charity among fugitive slaves led to a political discussion on the merits of membership in an organization known as True Band!

The recently-arrived fugitives listened on in earnest as Wayman Scott stood on the back of his wagon and explained the importance of this organization.

"I joined an organization when I was out in Malden last week, and I think we should all join."

Sam Lucas asked, "What is it, Wayman?"

"Well, Sam, you know how we have heard of thousands of dollars being raised for us by good whites in the United States, but we never received any of it. Also clothing, which we never received. I heard first hand last week from some representative in the States that one guy who was begging for us had taken advantage of others of his white race, and built himself a home. We black Canadians do not want people begging behind our backs and then using the monies un-Christian like. If we do need any money, it's only in the first few days after we arrive, and often as not, good people like John and Jane Walls standing over yonder will help, as they are helping these two underground travellers standing beside them."

All eyes turned to John and Jane. None of the onlookers noticed whether the people present were black or white. Nor did they notice—or care—that John was black and Jane was white. The church members saw only the halo of good, God-fearing human beings having enough love in their hearts to love others.

Wayman continued to speak. "Men and women can join this organization, and the purpose is for our improvement here in this new country. We're going to help each other, by building schools like this one across the road. We want to tear down prejudice everywhere so people and places can be more like here in Maidstone.

"Look at us," Wayman said proudly. "Dr. Fisher is here, and white neighbours, and anyone else regardless of race or colour. We even have Methodists and Baptists attending the same church. We know the Methodists intend building their own church on the next road. Our's is getting too small but, anyway, they know they are welcome. This True Band organization will decide minor differences and disputes among ourselves by a committee. And we want to stop the begging system going on in the United States, which is taking advantage of the growing number of those who sympathize with racial harmony. We can, through this organization, raise such funds as may be necessary for our own poor, sick and destitute fugitives newly arrived."

All eyes again turned to the Walls family.

"And lastly, but not least important, we must prepare ourselves for the vote and get some political power. There are over six hundred members already paying small monthly dues. The money is overseen by good men like Reverend Floyd, and will be used for the purposes I have mentioned."

As Wayman Scott jumped from the wagon to sign up members, all could see that he was a leader, like John Walls and countless other black Canadians.

MILE XXXI

As John and Jane Walls travelled the road from the church back to the log cabin they were thankful yet melancholy. They were sad because next Sunday was seven days away, and even sadder that for many, many years they and others had been deprived—by the disease of slavery—of knowing the feelings they had just experienced.

To be free, spiritually as well as physically, to build a tabernacle open to all denominations, races, creeds and colours, was an unparalleled experience in their lifetime.

The unparalleled hardships associated with pioneering in a new land had become insignificant, compared to the joys brought by this taste of freedom.

All fugitive slaves in Canada realized that the road they were travelling home was painfully short when they counted the miles of hardships they had endured on the road that led to somewhere.

None was more aware of these miles than John, black man, and Jane, white woman. They had been born at a time not of their own choosing; and again not of their own choosing, had been forced to flee like animals before a raging fire, to a place where only the waters dividing one country from another kept the flames from engulfing them and their innocent family.

John lived to be ninety-six, Jane died at eighty-eight. They were buried in the Walls' cemetery beside the log cabin he built and is still standing on the Puce Road, Maidstone Township, County of Essex, Ontario, Canada.

PART V

1945–1979

Freedom's Mile

OSSTF/FEESO

A news digest designed to keep OSSTF members abreast of trends, issues and the daily success stories in public secondary education.

*An estimated 40,000 escaped to Canada through the Underground Railway, out of whom 20,000 remained. Bryan Walls has written a documented novel, The Road to Somewhere, based on the Underground Railway and his slave ancestor.

May 10, 1989   Volume 16, No. 7

Hi, champ!

Earl Walls, right, former Canadian boxing champion, congratulates nephew Bryan Walls, OSSTF's 1989 Lamp of Learning winner *(Inset: Earl Walls in 1953, Canapress photo)*

MILE XXXII

Earl Walls woke from a profound sleep. Amnesia was his only salvation. What his mind's eye had seen was meant to be used for the betterment of mankind. The view of his ancestors his sleep had given him would have made him question his sanity. *You are a black, be proud, and the slave's descendant, just as good as anyone.* His mother's words graced his thoughts as he awoke. As he rose from the feather mattress, he realized that a loud knock had awakened him from his sleep. "Are you all right? Ain't you all right, Earl?" he heard Cliff, Lylia, Freida and June shouting loudly.

Earl's absence on Christmas morning had aroused the suspicion of his family, and also a genuine concern. They knew Earl had walked over to visit the homestead; they did not know his reason, but were respectful enough not to ask. However, he had been absent for five hours and the worry they felt was too much to bear.

Cliff, the oldest brother, and the women drove over the concession to the log cabin. The snow was too deep to drive back the laneway, which made them even more concerned. "My God, he had a heart attack," Freida said.

"More like food poisoning from your cooking," Lylia laughingly retorted, trying to lighten the mood. She could not hide the real concern for a brother she deeply loved, but she tried to quell the tears in June's eyes.

Cliff had many times protected his younger sisters and brothers at school; at fifty-two he again rose to the challenge. "Earl's too ornery to die, you know that." However, Cliff himself had had open heart surgery not more than a year before; he too was concerned.

The walk back to the cemetery was a long one; at any moment they expected to see Early lying in need on the ground. The women's walk turned into a half run while June, still in tears, held onto Cliff's arm. Cliff could not run.

Tracks led from the cemetery to the log cabin that John Freeman had built. As Cliff, Lylia, Freida and June went through the cemetery, they saw that Earl's fingerprints had moved the snow from John Freeman's name. This made them pause, but only briefly, for their attention was focussed on the cabin itself. They ran to the cabin door and, seeing it was locked, they knocked loudly. "How did Earl get in?" they thought. Cliff knew: it was the kitchen window, void of nails for probably a hundred years; they used to sneak through it as boys and borrow—in their minds—some of Aunt Stella's lemon meringue pie. As Cliff was perched half in and half out of the window, Earl came into the kitchen, "What the heck are you doing, Cliff?" he asked, laughing. "You haven't changed since you were a boy."

"Darn you, Earl," Cliff replied and boyishly finished his ungraceful entrance.

They both opened the cabin door and asked the girls what they wanted. The laughter from the five on that bright, clear, snow-covered Christmas morning could be heard for miles.

Once Earl had been reprimanded for scaring the wits out of everyone, a lighter mood prevailed; the five became nostalgic as they sat around the kitchen table. The table was over one hundred twenty years old and capable of withstanding many more years: it had been hand-made by John Freeman himself.

They talked about their childhood in Puce. Cliff and Earl remembered fights they had with neighbouring farm kids as they tenaciously fought for an education at SS Number Nine Maidstone Public School. The school had been given to the slave settlement by the Queen, but had undergone a change in complexion over the years.

The cold from the wind whistling through the cracks in the cabin made them wish their coats were heavier. "How could you have fallen asleep in this cold, Earl? You certainly are tough," Lylia remarked. The five decided to continue their pleasant reflections and reminiscences of their childhood in the warmth of Olive's house.

As they shut the cabin door behind them, Lylia's inquisitive personality felt the child come to the surface; she wanted to visit the creek to see if the ice was hard enough for skating. So, dressed in her full-length brown mink coat, she persuaded the others to follow. They did, lovingly shaking their heads at her childish whim.

The five grown children headed along the same path their great grandfather had travelled many times, to a creek physically not much different from Troublesome Creek, but certainly not as troublesome in significance.

As they approached the creek a wondrous thing happened, lightening everyone's mood. A flock of pheasants, possibly the same one Earl had disturbed a few hours earlier, ran and flew. On impulse Lylia ran with them. Her relatives remained on the path, June huddling in fright in Earl's arms. She was a city woman, not used to country life. But even the three who had grown up in Puce could scarcely believe what they were seeing: a beautiful, intelligent woman, regional director of Opportunities Industrialization Centres of America, was running down a pheasant. And because of Lylia's indomitable character and the wire fence, that pheasant did not have much of a chance for escape.

With burrs in her mink coat and the hapless pheasant under her arm, Lylia smiled a radiantly happy smile. She caught the look in her family's eyes and laughed; soon Frieda, June, Earl and Cliff were laughing, too.

Lylia insisted on showing the pheasant to her father before letting it go free. The others knew better than to try to dissuade her, as Lylia had many of the characteristics of Jane King.

Snow started to fall lightly, making this Christmas day even more pleasant. The soft flakes momentarily distracted everyone's attention, except June's. She was still voicing her concern about riding in the same car with this "wild animal."

187

The others laughed caringly, realizing the country wilderness was too much for her city upbringing. Earl knew she would insist upon sitting on his lap, with his arms tightly around her body, and he felt a slight sensation of pleasure.

As Earl walked through the snow behind his sister, he thought about their schooldays and how they'd grown up together. He remembered many things that had happened to his sister, and how she had always managed to learn and grow, even in the face of adversity.

Lylia had been born about 1934 (like most women, she was reluctant to give a definite year; if she did it could have been one of the few times she stretched the truth.) Earl could almost see his little brown sister sitting in the one-room schoolhouse that held eight grades and one teacher. Lylia was being reprimanded for her occasional daydreaming. He could see the yardstick landing, unceremoniously and unexpectedly, on her knuckles. A tear had almost come to his own eye as he watched his little sister crying; he knew she had received more than physical pain. "Why can't I travel to Europe and be educated like my Daddy and Aunt Stella Butler told me my great grandmother Jane was?" Lylia thought painfully. "The nerve of the teacher striking me, Lylia Walls. Don't she know who I am?"

The different-cultured white teacher did not know the potential or the power of the little black girl who was crying in front of her. However, the teacher did know that Lylia was more than just another little black child, who added a little colour to the integrated country school.

The teacher was not like certain members of her race who fail to research and review the records of black history. Instead she did realize that the very school she was making her livelihood from had been donated to the former black slave settlement by the Queen. And the first log school built on this location was built by Lylia's great grandfather, John Freeman Walls.

All these facts were uncovered in the teacher's historical perusal into the background of the school and certain of the young students whom she had been hired to teach. She did not assume incorrectly that the complexion of all achievement blossoms from a lily white seed. The teacher stood beside little Lylia. She was not insensitive to the human tears falling onto Lylia's small, black cheeks. Instinctively, like a mother with a bad child who had suffered enough, she wrapped her arms around Lylia's tiny shoulders and kissed the girl on the cheek. As she did this, she whispered in Lylia's ears: "Little lady, I am sorry I hurt you, but please pay attention; I don't like to be mean, but, in order to be smart, you must learn your lessons and pass into grade four."

Earl, though in a higher grade, was only two rows over from Lylia. As he watched the teacher hug his sister, he knew he liked the new teacher already. He could see his sister's tears quickly drying up and her eyes, even though still red, beginning to glitter.

Lylia, excited by the teacher's compassion, anxiously told the teacher how she was going to be a nurse someday, and move to the United States, and help heal all people, and that this was what she was daydreaming about, not something bad.

Earl overheard the words of his little sister and waited for the teacher to laugh—but the laugh did not come. Earl and the other black children had been scarred by the previous teacher; she had lost her job because of her racism. On more than one occasion she had been bold enough to call the little black children "stupid pickaninnies," and had once cuffed a young, innocent black's ear.

Frank Walls, who was on the school board, could not and would not tolerate any expression of this form of ignorance; he had taken steps to have the teacher removed.

Lylia's young, impressionable mind had already felt the psychological scarring in white-black relations that had so stifled the growth of harmony between races. Only good deeds such as the hugs and love given by this new teacher could begin to heal her, and others', psychological wounds before they permanently scarred her mind with misunderstanding and fear, the same misunderstanding and fear that had caused her ancestors to flee north to cold Canada, in search of warmer hearts.

By the time recess came Lylia had lost all feelings of animosity towards the teacher and happily sought the companionship of her white and black peers for the fun and frivolity of jumping rope, hopscotch, and other little-girl games.

The children, black and white and brown, hugged and played, their young, innocent minds ignorant of any but the purest thoughts.

There were a few older, less fortunate students whose tainted minds need only call Lylia "nigger" once or twice before feeling Earl's or Cliff's fist as reminders that the Walls family was just as good as anyone, and would not stand for any white ignorance, nonsense or other reminders of slavery.

"Not the descendants of John Freeman and Jane King Walls, no, Lord." Seven voices spoke as one. Cliff, Earl, Irvine, Alger, Larry, Winston and Allen spoke defiantly.

The white comrades eventually came to understand that it was all right for blacks to use the word "nigger." To blacks this word meant, "Never forget where you came from, no matter how high you get in success or society, remember to reach back and help somebody else."

When the word was used by whites, however, it had a different meaning and provoked a different response, as many white faces with black eyes proved.

Lylia paid her dues through many recesses and school days until, finally, grade eight graduation came. She passed with honours, and the compassionate school teacher of five years beamed with pride. "Yes, Lylia, you will be a nurse," the teacher told her as she handed Lylia the diploma.

Lylia was only thirteen years old when she walked up to the front of the one-room schoolhouse to receive her diploma. Her clean but not completely patch-free dress rustled as she walked to the front blackboard. Earl had been at her graduation and he could remember, as vividly as if it was yesterday, the tears in her eyes. He remembered bowing his own head to hide his own tears. "Yes," he had said to himself; only one word, but what he meant was, "I may not be able to be a lawyer, but I will damn sure do something to make sure Lylia can afford her education to become a nurse. As a matter of fact, she will be the best and one of the first black nurses I will know."

Lylia walked home that night with Cliff on one side and Earl, her second oldest brother, on the other. Their father's car had broken down; it had been through three or four owners by the time it had reached the Walls barn, so anything other than guaranteed transportation could be expected.

The road home led them past the cemetery. Lylia said, "It's light enough, let's go back and visit John's and Jane's tombstone!" Her suggestion brought no eager responses. Earl was first to break the silence and in his most masculine and assertive voice he blurted, "Lylia, we're in a hurry. Besides, don't you want to hurry and show off your diploma to Ma and Dad? They couldn't come 'cause Allen was sick, but you know they're excited and anxious."

"No," Lylia answered, and she continued, "Earl, you and Cliff both know what Ma has always said, *We are black, strong and proud, John, the slave's, and Jane's descendant, just as good as anyone.*"

"Oh, brother," both Earl and Cliff muttered. She had outwitted them, and placed before them an unanswerable argument.

The brothers and sister stood in front of the cemetery marker of John Freeman Walls in the bright moonlight. Earl, as he had many, many times before, felt compelled to touch the stone. As he ran quivering fingers over the almost smooth stone, Lylia broke the silence with a yell, a yell that sprung from her soul, a yell that, as she waved her diploma in the air, carried far into the night: "You are proud of me, ain't you, John and Jane?" The words travelled as if drawn in the direction of the north star, which glittered brightly and almost proudly, as if realizing the part it had played so many years before in Lylia's present achievements.

The three knelt down in the dew-covered grass and, with their hands on the stone, prayed as if compelled to do so. Their voices quivered as they volunteered a prayer that they would unembarrassingly remember as one of the most meaningful ones of their lives.

The atmosphere, as the three descendants arose, took on almost spiritual connotations. *Black man, white woman, mid-eighteen forties, slavery, slavemaster willing, how could it be, how could it be?*

As they walked home each was oblivious to the peaceful night. Each waged his own mental battle between his inner thoughts and the distractions caused by the world of reality around him.

Lylia began her career in the environment of her forebears, in the agrarian community where John Freeman and Jane King Walls had grown, dreamed, aspired and died. Nevertheless, she found it necessary to lovingly depart Puce, Ontario to better fulfill her destiny. That destiny was helping people to help themselves. Lylia was continuing along a road that had been travelled long before, in the pages of her family legend: the journey had been started by Jane King, her abolitionist great grandmother.

And Lylia had inherited her grandmother's determination and strength of character. She found an outlet for these inherited characteristics through her association with an organization known as Opportunities Industrialization Centres [OIC]. The relationship was a rather incongruent one because Lylia was, by first choice, a registered nurse; she had only recently come to be one of the leaders of the powerful self-help program, one of the greatest ever in the history of the United States. She was still searching to understand her second choice of occupation.

Lylia had a natural ability to make other people feel important and by so doing she became even more important to them. Lylia was a capable individual who, just as she refused to feel any inferior feelings because of her blackness, refused to feel superior to other people.

Nevertheless, she made it clear to her colleagues at OIC, by her gentle but firm manner, that it was better to love and respect her than to seek confrontation. Jealousy towards Lylia, or envy of her position, only served to increase Lylia's determination to continue to make the best of her talents. She had walked down a long, long road since her days in the one-room schoolhouse in Puce.

"Yep," Earl muttered out loud, "Jane King's great granddaughter sure has been walking."

Like a pendulum, his mind's eye quickly swung from thoughts of her early public school country learning to the ultimate manifestation of her achievements: last year's Washington, D.C. 15th Annual OIC Convocation. He had gone to the capital to see his sister, and they had arranged a meeting at a hotel. He could remember her sitting in Room M500 of the Sheraton Park Hotel, surrounded by people who were friends first and employees second, all hanging on every word she said.

"Earl, are you going to attend the luncheon and dinner? I want to introduce you to the founder of the OIC, Dr. Leon Sullivan."

"Oh, brother," Earl said under his breath. But when his sister said, "Jump!" Earl would often laugh and say, "How high?"

Lylia had always been definite, but not overpowering or demanding. Those she loved and was close to knew that she was tireless in her energy and devotion to help folk; her invitations always resulted in rewarding experiences. "Be there" meant "share with me something I am sure you will enjoy, and be better because of the experience." He knew that when Lylia said, "Be there," he could only nod his head and fake a smile.

So Earl nodded his head and accepted his sister's invitation. He remembered sitting beside her at the OIC Convocation Luncheon; he remembered looking into her face. Although his pride was almost too overwhelming, he did not wish to appear too emotional. He could not—and did not—resist patting her on her shoulder, but spoke no words. Lylia understood his meaning and smiled.

As Earl read the brochure in front of him, he could understand why Lylia, whose growth had begun under the protecting and healing arm of her white and black Canadian forefathers' precedent of racial harmony, had gravitated towards this organization, which proposed to advance peace and harmony among mankind.

He thought of Lylia's boss and the founder of OIC, Reverend Leon Sullivan. Reverend Sullivan had six principles for achieving racial equality in South Africa, a country, like Canada, affiliated with the British Empire, but, unlike Canada lightyears behind in its apartheid philosophies and bigotry towards the black race.

As he stared at the brochure, Earl felt almost like fighting his way into their white senate rooms, and telling them about Lylia Walls's achievements and Leon Sullivan's six principles, which were explained in the brochure he was wrinkling between his strong, black fingers. He shook his shoulders, being careful not to disturb Lylia, who sat with her chair almost touching his; then he continued to read Sullivan's six principles in order to quell the rage in his heart.

When he had finished his reading, for the moment at least, his apprehension was gone. It was replaced by a feeling of pride in Canada, and in being a Canadian, pride in the United States' Emancipation Proclamation, which had allowed his sister to move back to the land of her forefathers, and pride in Reverend Sullivan's principles aimed at liberating African brothers and sisters in slavery. He felt proud of his ancestors for watering the seed of racial harmony and peace.

That evening, Earl was not sitting with Lylia. He looked around the room towards the distinguished head table, and at the two thousand delegates.

Lylia sat at the head table during the OIC banquet, with Reverend Jessie Jackson, reformer, and Elton Jolly, National Director of OIC, to her right, and Dick Gregory, the comedian-activist, and Reverend Joseph Lowery, the president of the Southern Christian Leadership Conference, to her left.

The nervous feelings that were starting to well up inside of her were reduced when the words *slave's descendent, just as good as anyone* echoed in her mind. These words gave her the strength to rise from her chair and begin an eloquent speech as regional director of the millions of black, white, red, brown and yellow people, under OIC's jurisdiction, guidance and wing. She could hardly fight back the tears coming to her eyes.

She paused to take a deep breath and to gain a certain measure of composure.

Her beautiful eyes looked out over the crowd and were drawn, as if by a magnet to Earl, her brother, who sat with arms folded. The grin on his face made her feel like shouting, "Look at me, Earl, look at me, look at what your sister has accomplished. Remember the public school diploma, remember the high school diploma, remember the nursing diploma, remember, remember, remember. . . ."

Lylia controlled her childlike burst of enthusiasm and began a dignified speech.

Reverend Sullivan, Mr. Jolly, distinguished head table guest, fellow labourers in the vineyard for racial harmony and peace, region nine of the Western United States, I bid you greetings. And, more specifically to our host, OIC here in Washington, D.C., my condolences.

Earl and the multitude in front of her were confused by the word 'condolences'. Earl thought to himself, "I don't know what she means by 'condolences', but at least she got their attention."

We of the Seattle, Washington OIC, home of the champion Seattle Supersonic basketball team, wish to say sorry to the home of the Washington Bullets, who made such a valiant effort in their attempt to bring the highest honour in professional basketball away from where it belongs, namely Seattle, Washington.

The crowd was in a frenzy—the stuffiness of a formal affair had been dispelled. Harmony and happiness were on the faces of the black, white, yellow and red delegates in front of Jane King's great granddaughter.

Lenny Wilkens, basketball coach of the Seattle Supersonics and long-time friend of Lylia's, was out of his seat—along with OIC members of the one hundred forty American cities and African and Caribbean countries.

Even the local Washington, D.C. Bullet fans could not help but applaud and smile in delight.

When the applause had died down, a new feeling of relaxation and camraderie was in the hearts of the delegates. They were united in the common cause of the good that OIC represented. They were further united in the reality that no branch of the OIC anywhere in the world need be at odds with the accomplishments of another. Lylia, indirectly and subtly, had, in her few brief opening words, united the Opportunity Centres of the world.

By referring to competitive sports, she had implied that all teams and all fans win as long as their hearts are relaxed and free of jealousy and prejudice. The audience knew that competition encouraged excellence and created one keeper of the cup each year. And they realized that excellence meant doing the very best one was capable of, not feeling the futility of continually seeking perfection.

That night, Lylia's words created a harmonious attitude. The cup of excellence, from which all peoples of the world, no matter what their nation, race, creed or colour, could drink, was placed before the audience by the great granddaughter of Jane Walls.

Lylia finished her speech and, as she did, she put in a good word for OIC, Canada, women's rights and, most of all, the need for harmony and peace among people, the same harmony and peace shared by John and Jane Walls.

After the banquet, Earl related to Lylia a few of his nostalgic thoughts. Lylia did not need much prompting to remember the night of her graduation, the night she and her two brothers fought back immature feelings of fright, aroused by cemeteries, ghosts and goblins. That night, they had matured in the knowledge that the deeds of their forebears had made their freedom possible. They were the African John's and the Irish and Scottish Jane's descendants, not needing to take a back seat to anyone. The appreciation of their lineage made them capable of facing life's hurdles in a positive manner.

"Earl, Earl, did you hear Lylia? She wants to take the bird back to show Pa. Quit daydreaming. You haven't been quite the same since we woke you up from the cabin. Are you all right?"

"Better than you can imagine," Earl answered his wife.

To quell June's fear the pheasant was placed in a green garbage bag they had found in the cabin, with a hole made for his head to stick through. He had a look in his eye as if to say, "It is a good thing I can't talk."

There was a devilish look in the eyes of Cliff, Earl and Lylia: only June would have nothing to do with the fun and frivolity, and she walked ahead of them into the house.

Laverda, Cliff's wife, shook her head; she perceived what June felt and could only mutter, "Olive's children." But she laughed as they entered the house behind June, triumphantly carrying the garbage bag.

Lylia went into the living room where Frank was playing euchre with three of his sons, Alger, Allen and Winston. She placed the bag on the living room floor; the pheasant's eyes were rolling in confusion and fright. As she reached down to pick up the bird, his instinct to survive came to the fore and gave him the strength to take flight, garbage bag streaming from his legs like a kite tail.

The sight of Frank's euchre chair tipping over as the bird flew over his greying head was surpassed in comedy only by family members ducking and hiding under anything that hinted of shelter.

The one certainty amongst the lighthearted confusion was that Frank was not going to be the one to catch the pheasant—and not just because of his bad knees either. As he was being unceremoniously helped from the floor by Allen and Winston, he thought, "Bad knees or not, if I hadn't so much love for my heirs, I would put someone over my lap for a good spanking."

The pheasant flew into Freida's bedroom. The excuses the family members made for not going in after it were various; finally, Earl was elected to retrieve the bird, which had managed to get stuck under the bed.

"Why me?" he exclaimed. "Lylia brought the bird." He found no allies, and Lylia retreated behind her brother Larry. Even Larry, the actor-cowboy and owner of Rolling Acres Ranch in Durham, Ontario would not come to his aid.

"Damn," the others heard Earl say from the bedroom; then all was silent, except for the croaking of the bird and the clapping of feathers.

When the door closed behind him, Earl felt much like he had many times before, entering the ring during his professional boxing career. But this time, when the final bell rang, he opened the door carrying a bird; it looked innocent of the disruption it had just caused. As Earl walked out of the house uttering mild profanities, the others could hardly hear him for laughing.

Earl carried the shivering bird across the yard and threw it high into the air. The bird flew straight as an arrow from the homestead property of John Freeman Walls and Jane King Walls, towards the cabin Earl had just left, a refuge in 1978 just as it had been in 1848. For a brief second Earl froze as he remembered the words of his mother. *You are a black, be proud, and the slave's descendant, just as good as anyone.* He thought of Olive's words as he walked back into the house and sat at the kitchen table.

Hero privilege lasted for approximately five minutes; then he was just old Earl again, which suited him just fine. June came to him and asked, "Are you all right, Earl?"

He looked at her with a loving smile and said, "Yes."

The family sat around the kitchen table and talked. Some of their stories were traditionally repeated; others were surprisingly new. Their storytelling was prolonged by another meal: sausages, cheese and the remnants of the Christmas Eve turkey.

Earl sat grinning with arms crossed, his flexed muscles still hinting of pugilistic potential. But fighting was the furthest thing from his mind as he listened to Cliff relate escapades with local farm boys on his daily walk home from school through the fields. "If it hadn't been for them I may never have become heavyweight champion," Earl thought. "I was always skinny and didn't really fill out until fifteen years of age." Earl had had to rely on speed and quickness to offset his lack of strength, and would welcome reinforcement from Cliff during boyhood rivalries.

Cliff would often laugh and say to Earl, "You may be the fighter, Earl, but I am the lover." They would both laugh and walk off, arms around each other.

Everyone was always interested in fighting stories: they would perk their ears and smile at Earl with pride and respect. Earl responded with a look of humility and embarrassment, especially on this day, when Frank walked out of the bedroom with two magazines, which he had saved for just such occasions.

The proud father said, "Gather around, you younger ones, and let me read to you something to tell your children about." Frank's proud face was beaming as he opened the *Boxing Fan Gazette*. The cover of the January 1953 issue stated: "Earl Walls, Greatest Threat to America's Claim on the World's Heavyweight Championship Crown."

The family members knew Frank could recite the whole article by heart; he turned immediately to the proper page, which had been read hundreds of times. The magazine's yellowing pages and wrinkled corners attested to this fact. Frieda commented softly to Nathan, her architect boss, "Dad is in his glory now."

The sweat flowing from Frank's brow increased along with his enthusiasm. His glasses slid further down his nose and his eyes peeked over the top of them. Frank's seventy-eight-year-old voice quivered with excitement, and excitement was soon generated in his family and friends by his words.

Earl Walls—Boxing's Next World Champ. Chances are you never heard of Earl Walls, the Canadian Champ, but he is climbing over his knockout victims, the greatest KO artist since Joe Louis. He can knock a man out with both fists.

"Set still, Geoffrey," Frank said lovingly to his first-born great grandson, who was fussing on the floor with his other relatives while adults sat and stood in doorways. The family knew from Frank's words that any further fidgeting must be suppressed if at all possible. The head of the Walls family had spoken.

Who is Earl Walls? Ask any American, and chances are the man on the street won't know. He is just the hardest puncher in the ring today. He may not be known because he, up to now, has done most of the knocking out in Canada and the British Isles.

Earl not only punches harder than the Rock, meaning Marciano himself; but, his hook is said to be more annihilating than Joe Louis', when the Brown Bomber was at his best.

Earl, who uses Louis as his idol, would not admit this; but, these facts can be verified by most of the twenty-three fighters still trying to regain their senses.

Of these—one has fought Marciano, the other Louis. In thirty-two professional fights, Earl has fourteen, can you believe, fourteen one-round knockouts. Four more than Louis had in his entire career of sixty fights.

At twenty-five years old, Earl Walls has finished and won fights with a broken right knuckle. This is but one of the reasons that managers are eagerly trying to buy his contract from Jones, his manager. But Jones knows only too well he would be foolish to sell, as too many unwary opponents were foolish to step in the ring with this "hooded terror."[1]

Frank looked up; his glasses, with one arm missing, were perched delicately on his nose. The room was filled with a mosaic of beautiful colours, white, black, tan and brown, all his descendants and friends. The response to the reading further cemented the harmony that existed in Frank Walls's family.

Earl fell asleep that night with a smile on his face and a peace of mind that came from years of family tradition. The next morning he got ready to leave for Toronto. He would be stopping at the home of Mr. and Mrs. Palmer, his in-laws, in Brantford, Ontario on his way home. June was not quite ready to leave when he entered the kitchen, and asked him to help wash dishes. Earl jokingly replied, "That is woman's work," and ran out of the house followed by a wet towel and laughter.

The chilling wind on the twenty-sixth day of December was whipping at Earl's pant legs and nostalgic thoughts were stimulated in his mind, as he walked along the dirt road leading to old Highway Two. He wore rubbers, which guarded his feet from the effects of previous winter days. As he looked down at his feet treading through the white blanket of snow, he felt pride welling up inside him; he was thinking of his father's reading of the night before. He thought nostalgically of past boxing accomplishments; his thoughts made the walk he was taking even more significant. He remembered when he was seventeen, and was running down this road referred to as "the slave's road" by his grandparents. Memories of his early boxing career continued to occupy his mind. These thoughts carried him some half mile from his home. The dust-like snow made him look down at his feet, and within his mind's eye, instead of rubbers and snow, he saw running shoes and puddles of spring water. The portion of Earl's mind that controlled his subconscious thoughts turned back through the pages of Canadian and American boxing history that he helped to write. The year was 1946. He could visualize his running feet splashing through the puddles and leading him in the direction of Windsor and the Drouillard Boxing Club.

MILE XXXIII

As the seventeen-year-old Earl Walls ran, he could feel the pebbles and small rocks of crushed stone, periodically placed by an efficient town Council of Maidstone to reinforce the dirt road, through the soles of his running shoes. "I am certainly glad it isn't new gravel," Earl thought as he ran on, knowing he would soon reach the smooth surface of Highway Two.

His skinny legs were pumping fiercely; Earl was trying to gain some measure of credibility as a fighter. He gritted his teeth with determination as he remembered the night two weeks ago, when he had suffered the embarrassment of defeat.

202

The Brewster recreation centre, on Detroit's east side, was teaming with potential Joe Louises and spectators hoping to see the making of one. The three Canadian boxers, Eno, Don and Lou, were in their dressing room apprehensively awaiting their turn to pit their prowess against their neighbours from across the Detroit River. Their turn finally came. Eno lost by a decision; Lou was not as fortunate, and when the stretcher came in carrying his unconscious body, fear followed. The young and inexperienced Don, the third contender, felt the pressure to save the Canadian pride weighing on his shoulders.

The coach, Mr. Swinhoe, could see that Don's head was moving not up and down but back and forth; to his chagrin, the young boxer confirmed his worst fear. Said Don, "No, coach, I can't go in there. Did you see the guy I am supposed to fight? He is an animal."

Mr. Swinhoe realized he was dealing with inexperienced amateurs; from them, anything was possible. "Darn," he said, shaking his head. He knew that words like coward, scaredy-cat or other derogatory remarks would only leave unnecessary psychological scars on the young boxer.

His eyes focussed on a chocolate-coloured spectator standing in the corner, a friend of Don's; the coach briefly thought, "I wish."

The chocolate-coloured spectator was Earl Walls. During the day he worked with his three amateur boxing friends at Ford Motor Company in Windsor. Earl was a proud member of Local 200 of the UAW in Windsor; little did he realize that he was destined to make his union members even prouder of him. He was at the recreation centre only for something to do; as far as he was concerned, life was great. It hadn't cost him anything to get in, and he had even been invited into the dressing room, which made him feel important. Earl left the room a few minutes after the coach to allow his friend time to take off his gloves and change in dignity. As he walked down the hall, the strangest thing happened.

Coming toward him was a relative of his brother's future

203

wife, Laverda; Joyce lived in Detroit, and was spending some leisure time with her relatives. They had come to watch an evening of boxing. "You boxing next, Earl?" Earl spoke too quickly, hoping an affirmative answer would bring a smile to Joyce's face and a feather in his cap if he decided, in future, to ask her for a date. "Yes," Earl boyishly replied, his desire to impress outweighing his prudence.

"Oh, great, I will be watching and cheering for you." As Joyce faded into the crowd again, Earl stood half paralyzed with fright. "What the hell have I said?" His strong family pride compelled him to tap Mr. Swinhoe on the shoulder. In as masculine and strong a voice as he could muster, Earl said, "Let me fight in Don's place. I used to fight at SS Nine Maidstone practically every day. I can fight."

To Earl's surprise, the exaggeration of calmness worked. The coach smiled and said, "You've got the makings of a champ, son. Get your gloves on!"

When Earl entered the dressing room he was more aware of how his friends must have felt. He could understand the inner pressure that mounted before a fight, pressure that could force even the most apt physical specimen to fear the ring. Physical prowess and pride kept Earl from changing his mind about fighting as he was helped into the Brewster ring for the first time. The sight of the crowd and the stench of sweat, blood and vomit almost made his own stomach turn. "What am I doing here?" he thought and, as he looked into the eyes of his experienced opponent, he knew he had made a mistake. He would have to pay the dues.

Until he was in the middle of the ring, standing toe to toe with his opponent, Earl forgot what had attracted so many spectators to the centre that night. His idol, Joe Louis, had agreed to referee since he was in town. "I have really made an ass of myself this time," Earl thought. "Going to get it kicked, too, in front of Joe." Earl did not have much chance to think about his bad timing—in a matter of what appeared to be an eternity but was really only fifteen seconds, the bell rang. "I don't even know what to do. What do I do, coach?" he asked desperately as he got up from his chair and moved to the centre of the ring. Bip, bip, bip—Earl's head vibrated with his opponent's punches. Anger welled up inside, anger that could not be satisfied, because he did not have the necessary training. His frustration only served to increase his opponent's confidence. Earl's arms were like windmills as he hoped, by some miracle, one of his punches would connect. The country boys at SS Nine Maidstone Public School would not have had a chance—but he was not in the schoolyard now. This was the Brewster recreation centre with Joe Louis refereeing.

The end of round one brought a frustrated Earl Walls— with one black eye—back to his seat. Earl sat in his corner swearing, as if he hoped pure vulgarity and meanness could replace boxing skills. Mr. Swinhoe could only say, "Doing good, Earl, you made it through round one."

Sheepishly, Earl answered, "Thanks."

The bell rang, round two came and Earl charged out caring nothing for style or looks. He would throw his arms around his opponent and hold him, wrestle him to the canvas— anything to win this round. He wasn't worried about being popular with the crowd or Joe Louis—he was fighting for his life. "Thank God Ma isn't here," he thought, and found himself in the centre of the ring with his guard too low. He walked right into a left hook, a left hook that Earl could remember started from somewhere near the floor and moved up at the speed of light, stopped painfully by the side of his face.

As Earl lay on the canvas, with Joe counting over him, he could almost hear his mother's words: *You are a Walls, be proud, and the slave's descendant, just as good as anyone.* An inner strength made him leap up from the canvas, which had felt so comfortable to him. Joe Louis could see that it was not a second wind—Earl's young body was in excellent physical condition. Joe could not realize that the rippling muscles and sinew underneath were not the product of training and body building, but rather the result of years of baling hay, planting crops and running miles to school each day to be in time after morning chores.

Earl came back at his opponent like a wild man. He cared little now for his own safety; he wanted revenge. As he lunged forward he felt his opponent's right hand land; it had been laying in wait for Earl's jaw. Earl had heard the phrase "saved by the bell" many times, but he hadn't truly appreciated the words until now. He crawled from the centre of the ring and draped his elbows over the middle ropes wondering if he could last even ten more seconds. Suddenly he heard a beautiful symphony of sound—the bell signalling the end of the round. He walked to his corner, his knees working more from instinct and habit than from any conscious direction. He scanned the crowd, hoping he didn't see anyone he knew. He was embarrassed by his poor show—he just wanted to go home and stick his head under the pillow. He saw Joyce's face; suprisingly, she was jumping up from her chair, cheering him on. "Maybe I don't look so bad after all," he mumbled to himself. The thought held him together until he reached his stool again. "Is it round ten, coach?" Earl asked. The question drew a smile from the coach.

In the back of his mind, Mr. Swinhoe was impressed— certainly not by Earl's pugilistic skills, but by his indomitable heart and determination. "Earl, do you want me to throw in the towel?"

"No, no," Earl replied, not really understanding what throwing in the towel meant. He only knew it was some form of quitting, giving up, and the idea was alien to his personality.

The bell rang, signalling the start of round three. Earl's style had not changed, but the young man was not even breathing hard. His stamina was a surprise to his opponent, who was panting with the confidence of a victor but glad he didn't have to face ten rounds with Earl Walls. The trained boxer was tired, and could not move quickly enough to ward off a haymaker; the punch glanced off his forehead with enough force to cause him to stagger back. He was kept from falling only by the ropes.

Earl could scarcely believe he had actually landed a punch. He began to get excited about the fight; he was awed by his own natural strength. But his natural talent was not enough: to win a refereed boxing match he needed much more skill and experience. His closed right eye kept him from seeing his opponent's left arm, which was down. Had he seen this, he could have delivered his lightning right punch to the chin—a punch that had, during his young public school years, devastated any unwary individual who dared mess with him—or his brothers or sisters. But Earl missed his knock-out opportunity and the bell rang, ending the third round. Earl walked back to his corner dejected but not broken. He would never be broken. He saw, with his good eye, his opponent's arm being raised in victory, and every bit of sinew and muscle in his body tensed as his pride was wracked with pain, a pain greater than the physical pain in his body. A tear came to his open eye: defeat and humiliation were too bitter an experience for Earl Walls.

His friends from the Ford plant patted him on the back but their words of encouragement were little consolation. As he rode back through the Detroit and Windsor tunnel he was silent. The coach drove him to his home so he wouldn't have to hitchhike—the way the boxer looked he couldn't expect even the most sensitive good samaritan to give him a ride. Earl shut the car door and Mr. Swinhoe called, "Earl, come to the gym, you have potential." The coach's invitation went unanswered, as Earl was trying to prepare himself for his family's reaction.

The defeated gladiator sported a lip swollen to twice its normal size, a black eye and wounded pride. As he had feared, his entrance was greeted with shock. His nine brothers and sisters could not speak for at least thirty seconds, and Earl stood in front of them, unable to speak himself. The tension was almost palpable; finally it got the better of one of the girls, and she giggled, seeing the comical side of Earl's plight. But Earl felt humiliated—and he got angry and even more determined.

Cliff had been staring at his younger brother. His first fleeting fear was that Earl had been run over by an automobile; then he thought the boy had been bushwacked by Windsorites. "Who did this to you?" Cliff asked. "I will kick their butt, Earl. No one is going to mess with my brother." Cliff's words made Earl feel somewhat better. Olive ran and hugged him, as Frank listened to his story.

Frank's reaction was predictable. "Earl, I should spank your butt for being so stupid. What do you know about boxing?"

As the words left his lips, Frank saw images of himself, some twenty years earlier, standing in front of his father, Henry, telling the same story. He was moved to sympathy. Olive was bustling about, preparing bandages. She dressed her son's wounds and tucked his now aching muscles into bed. "Ma," Earl said, as she walked out of the room, "I'm going to fight one more time and beat somebody. You can believe that." The words were spoken with hope and courage, but Earl knew he needed more than natural ability to make them come true. He needed training. He was determined to win one fight.

Two weeks later, the five-mile run over pebbles of crushed stone had become a routine part of his training. After the run he would hitchhike to Windsor, and the Drouillard Boxing Club. Earl Walls was beginning on his road to somewhere.

MILE XXXIV

Mr. Swinhoe was a good trainer and left a favourable impression on Earl's young personality. "Punch the bag, Earl, skip, Earl, jab, Earl, move, Earl." The coach's commands were engraved in Earl's memory. After a month of training,

Coach Swinhoe felt confident enough to schedule a rematch at Brewster Centre. Earl was one hundred percent improved as a boxer.

As Earl stood in the ring for the second time in his life, he could hardly believe how frightened he was. Ignorance had saved him from being overly afraid during the first contest; he had lost that advantage during his first fight. "I am some kind of nervous," Earl thought, as he looked into his twenty-three-year-old opponent's eyes through his inexperienced ones. He shook hands with the other boxer, then walked back to his corner to wait for round one. As he walked, he almost tripped over a shoe lace that had come untied, and he realized just how apprehensive he really was—he couldn't even tie his shoes properly. Mr. Swinhoe kneeled and did the honour, then, with a pat on the back and mouthpiece over the teeth, the coach sent a determined but scared Earl Walls into the arena.

Earl walked reluctantly to the centre of the ring, thinking of the words his mother had spoken as he left the house. *You are a Walls, be proud, and the slave's descendant, just as good as anyone.* The thought rejuvenated his wilting courage.

Earl saw the hair on his opponent's chest, the broken nose and the scarred face; then the bell rang, and the two boxers began to circle warily. Earl could feel the top of his forehead turning red from seven or eight quick, unanswered jabs. His eyes were focussed on his opponent's midsection. The older boxer was beginning to become overconfident, hitting Earl at will as if expecting no response. But Earl was still bobbing and weaving and stalking his prey. As his heartbeat quickened, sweat poured from his brow and his muscles tensed. His mind envisioned, instead of a human opponent, a wild animal—a wolf who wanted to tear at his throat. Suddenly Earl's opponent felt the wind leave his stomach as Earl's fist found its target. The older boxer was no longer the aggressor: he showed his respect for the younger man's power. The end of round one came and, as Earl walked back to his corner, instinctively felt his right eye, to make certain the cut he had received in his first fight hadn't been opened again.

Mr. Swinhoe was intense: he could almost sense the thrill of victory. But he remembered to heap instructions on the young boxer. As the bell rang and Earl entered the ring for the second round, the coach's instructions echoed in his ears: "Follow with the right after your left hook." Earl looked, saw his chance and did as his coach told him. The punch left his opponent crawling back to his feet at the count of eight. Earl could scarcely believe it had happened. But as the older boxer rose painfully, Earl wished two more numbers had been counted—namely, nine and ten—so he could go home.

The third round was fierce in intensity. The twenty-three-year-old boxer's ego had suffered, and all the skill he could muster—and a thirst for revenge—was directed toward Earl. Earl bobbed and weaved more from reflex than training, and caught his opponent on the side of the ribcage again, hard enough to knock some steam out of him and slow down his desperate attack. As the older boy staggered, the final bell rang.

Earl stood in the corner anxiously awaiting the judge's decision. "How did I do? How did I do?"

The question was asked with such sincerity and enthusiasm that Mr. Swinhoe hesitated to tell the truth. He knew it was going to be a close decision despite the knock-down which, in amateur fighting, counted only as another point. "Earl, you were great," the coach said truthfully. His praise brought a radiant smile to Earl's boyish face.

As Earl walked to the centre of the ring the decision was announced: "Winner by a split decision, the Canadian, Earl Walls." He felt his arm being raised above his head and the blood rushed to his face as the crowd cheered and booed at the same time. But Earl didn't mind the booing: nothing could detract from the feeling he had, winning his first fight. "And no black eye, coach," he said happily. The coach knew that Earl was gaining confidence, and that the boy's pride, devastated by his first fight, was healing.

A cocky Earl Walls entered his parents home with news of victory. His blow-by-blow description of the fight left his brothers and sisters and Ma and Pa certain that they were related to another Joe Louis, who had just fought for the heavyweight championship of the world, instead of an amateur Earl Walls who had fought at Brewster recreation centre. Earl saved the biggest news for the end: his opponent wanted a return match at the Windsor Arena in two weeks, and Earl and Coach Swinhoe had agreed. The family immediately began making preparations to be there, and Olive monopolized the telephone for the next day or so, telling friends and relatives that her son was going to box in Windsor.

For the next two weeks, Earl continued to get up at six o'clock in the morning and run four miles before breakfast. As he ran down the dirt road he would think of food, boyhood experiences, or anything at all to keep his mind off running. He would pass his grandfather Henry's farmhouse, set back a quarter of a mile from the road. He would remember his Indian grandmother, Parthena—the squaw, as she was sometimes called by others—and how she had always treated him with such kindness. He wished she were alive to see her grandson do well in the ring. He ran past other farms, many of which were still owned by descendants of former slaves. Earl ran on, thinking of the upcoming fight and of his responsibility to his family—he would have to put on a good show.

Earl reached the original homestead of John Freeman Walls. This would be the turning point of his run. He jogged to the cemetery, touching the tombstone of his ancestor, whom he had never seen but had heard so much about. Earl's thin, black hands would run up the side of the marker and he would repeat the words of the family legend his father had told him—"John Freeman Walls, born a slave in North Carolina, died a free man in Canada, was willed his slave master's wife." Earl thought of the family legend as he turned to start the second half of his run.

211

Earl returned home, where a hearty breakfast awaited him. Although he was now famous in the neighbourhood, Earl's status did not prevent Olive from demanding that he wash and change before he ate breakfast. "Do you want any more sausages, Earl? What about bacon? Did your coach say you needed any special food?"

"Ma, all he said was, 'Make sure your mother feeds you all you want to eat, and don't make you do too many chores, because you use the wrong muscles when you do chores'." Olive grinned with delight. Earl sheepishly bent his head towards his food-laden plate, having told a white lie.

But he didn't have to do the chores—Cliff did them, complaining good-naturedly the whole time. Every time he threw an extra bale of hay into the barn, Earl's bale, Cliff wished boxing had never been invented.

But as Cliff sat at the Windsor Arena with his parents and brothers and sisters, pride welled up inside of him as he watched his brother climb into the ring while the spectators cheered wildly. Earl danced around the ring, no longer the inexperienced fighter of a month ago; tonight he was the hero of Windsor and Maidstone Township, eagerly awaiting the bell for round one, sensing a victory. He was not to be disappointed nor was the crowd, for when Earl Walls won, he won with style. In a flurry of punches, seventy seconds into the second round, Earl's right hand moved his opponent's glove out of the way and continued with speed and power, into his opponent's hapless chin. The twenty-three-year-old found himself staring at the ceiling of the Windsor Arena from an undignified vantage point: the floor.

Earl dealt with eleven more opponents in a similar fashion, spurred on by the cheers of the Windsor, Chatham and Detroit boxing enthusiasts. Then the people from Toronto heard the name Earl Walls. Earl, who had started boxing almost by a quirk of fate and had stayed in because of pride and family approval, was gaining a reputation. Then he received a letter from some managers in Toronto, who indicated their interest in his abilities and enclosed a ticket to the city. He read the letter out to his mother, and both were in shock, not believing this new development.

Olive sat down slowly, her two-hundred-pound frame feeling the strain of psychological pressure. Her son sat down also, feeling dazed and confused. "Toronto? Why would I want to go to Toronto?" Earl thought out loud. And to himself, he thought, "I want to be a lawyer, not a fighter. But how can I become a lawyer? I had to quit school and go to work at the Ford plant to help the family." Then he spoke. "Oh, what have I got to lose? It's a free ticket." He paused, thinking about his decision. "But, Ma, I'm not good enough to fight in Toronto." The boys words turned Olive's ears red with anger.

"Earl," she said, "if you remember nothing else I ever say to you, remember this: even though we are poor, we are rich. You, Earl, are John Freeman Walls's descendant, and John Freeman came up here through the worst times and hardships. You, Earl, are just as good as anyone."

MILE XXXV

On the foggy morning of 12 July 1946, an emotional Walls family gathered in the Walkerville train station, Windsor, Ontario to send an important member of the family from the shelter of his home and out into the world—to make history. Lylia was crying; Freida was pushing fried chicken into the brown paper bag containing Earl's clothes; Cliff stood straight as an Indian chief, trying to look brave and the rest of the kids waved and yelled. Olive was hugging her son and patting him on the back at the same time. Frank waited till they had finished and shook Earl's hand. Frank spoke to Earl not as a son but as a respected equal. Earl boarded the train full of feelings of love and family harmony.

The train pulled out of the station and began to speed the boxer further along his personal road to somewhere. Four hours passed, and Earl slept; then he felt a tap on the shoulder and heard the porter announce: "Toronto!" Earl had never been this far from home before, and the sights that greeted his eyes were overpowering. Union Station itself, with its vast network of terminals and tracks, captivated Earl's imagination.

Then he walked out of the station and saw the Royal York Hotel, and was amazed all over again. He set off in search of Yonge Street, carrying his two brown paper bags. He had boxing trunks, boxing shoes and robe in one paper bag; the robe had been his mother's, one of her best second-hand acquisitions, and it was plain white and looked masculine enough. He had two changes of clothes and a Sunday-go-to-meeting suit carefully folded in the other paper bag. Earl Walls had arrived.

He found Yonge Street and walked along it in the only direction he could without ending up in Lake Ontario, looking at every sign for the cross street his directions indicated, called Bloor. He passed King, Queen, Dundas, Gerrard, College. By the time Earl reached College Street he was feeling a little dazed by the hustle and noise of the city. He turned right on College and walked a little ways, till he came to a restaurant, where he went in and had a glass of water.

Feeling better, Earl got up and walked out of the restaurant, looking around to get his bearings. Right in front of him was a huge building, bearing a sign: Maple Leaf Gardens. He thought, "Boy, would I ever like to see the inside of that place." He walked one block west, turned up Yonge again and continued to Bloor Street, and then along Bloor to Spadina, where he spent the night with friends of the family.

The next morning, the fellow who was going to train Earl came and picked him up to take him to the gym. The two men were formally introduced and Earl, remembering all Olive had taught him, was polite and respectful. The young boxer's manner impressed his future trainer, who felt instant respect and liking for the fellow from Maidstone. They walked to the car and Earl was introduced to another stranger, one Vern Escoe. Earl thought Escoe must be the Canadian amateur champion he would be working out with. The trainer took Earl and the other man to the gym. As they entered the ring, Earl noticed that the training gym was full of people who had come to watch. The sight of so many spectators confused Earl and for a fleeting second he thought back to the Drouillard gym in Windsor. He remembered how, after his eleventh victory, his fans in Windsor had started coming to watch him train. Finally Mr. Swinhoe had had to lock the door—the gym was full, and there was barely enough room for his own boxers. "Could these spectators have heard about me already?" Earl wondered nervously. But his question was quickly answered when introductions were made for the benefit of the spectators:

"Vern Escoe, current Canadian professional heavyweight boxing champion. Just returning from a fight with Archie Moore. Earl Walls, Windsor, Ontario sparring partner."

Earl's confusion must have shown on his face, because Vern smiled sympathetically, as if he understood Earl's feelings. Earl wanted to turn tail and run; then his mother's words ran through his mind. *You are a Walls, be proud, and the slave's descendant, just as good as anyone.* Earl stayed in the ring.

Vern was too much of a professional to hurt Earl. The young boxer, whose instincts for self-preservation were aroused, fought one of his best fights. In the fifth round, two rounds longer than he had ever gone, Earl bobbed when he should have weaved and Vern's right hand landed firmly on his head. It staggered Earl, but did not knock him down. The new trainer noticed it, and filed the information away for future reference. That punch had hurt, and as the bell rang ending the final round of training Earl thought, "I darn sure paid for my ticket, and I am ready to go home." But his trainers had other plans. They intended to keep Earl Walls around for a while.

215

For the next three months Earl trained rigorously. The training was gruelling, but provided the foundation he needed to be a great boxer. He was up early in the morning, running down the sidewalks and along the streets of Toronto, through Queen's Park, Hyde Park, Sunnybrook, anywhere he could run. He also trained at Deacon Jim Allen's gym on Queen Street, and the gym's punching bag was becoming like a person. Earl visualized a head, a ribcage, a stomach and—most important of all—a jaw. Skipping rope to the count of one thousand was routine. He worked hard for many months—harder than he had ever worked in his life. But he also found time to become seriously interested, for the first time, in a woman.

One night a phone number had been placed in his hand by the cousin of a girl in Brantford. Earl twisted the piece of paper with the number on it and threw it carelessly in a drawer. He went home after a day of training, thinking to himself, "I'm not too fussy about meeting her; what's her name again?" He picked up the paper and read, "June Palmer, Brantford, Ontario. I wonder what she looks like."

In the months that followed Earl was training constantly. The regular routine of skipping rope, running, and training had just begun to grow boring when Irvine arrived in Toronto for a visit. "Let's go to the Brass Rail in London," Earl suggested casually. Irvine, who was always ready for some fun, was a willing running buddy. And Irvine owned a car. Earl's curiosity about the girl in Brantford was growing; his brother's car was the key to satisfying it. "Irvine, we have to stop in Brantford first, to pick up June," Earl said, pretending he had known the girl for some time so Irvine wouldn't feel his car was being used for a taxi. But Irvine wasn't easily fooled.

"Earl, you know girls in Toronto. Get one of them!"

Earl looked at his younger brother with a confidence he was far from feeling.

"Irvine, you don't understand," he said haughtily, and went to search for the girl's phone number.

Earl rummaged through the drawer he thought he had tossed the paper in, panicking as his search failed to turn it up. "Damn, I lost it." Just then he lifted some clean jockey shorts and a tightly rolled paper fell to the floor. Earl smiled as he smoothed it out and he was dialing the number immediately.

"Hello, this is Earl Walls," he said, heart thumping madly.

"Earl who?"

"You know, the fighter!"

June's voice said dubiously, "What fighter?"

"Why did I do this?" Earl thought, but said nothing.

"Oh, yes, my cousin told me about you," June remarked, as she sensed a kind voice and struggling suitor on the other end of the telephone line. She searched her mind and finally remembered someone named Walls. Earl took a deep breath and asked her if she'd go out with him. She agreed, but said he'd have to meet her parents first. "Oh, brother," Earl thought.

Earl stopped at her place, met everybody and they continued on to London, to the Brass Rail. Earl was impressed with this girl, and the thing that impressed him the most was that she seemed to know how to act. She wasn't giggly, like other girls. He didn't find out until much later that this was her first time ever in a cocktail bar. They had a nice time and Earl took her home—and June wouldn't let him kiss her. He told himself he wasn't interested, and made up his mind not to call her. His resolution lasted one day. He drove the sixty-five miles to her house for dinner every Sunday for the next six months.

Then, one beautiful spring day, he was sitting with June on the porch.

Earl considered himself a big time operator, and he could scarcely believe what he was saying, but the emotion he was feeling was too overpowering to resist. "June," he said, out of the clear blue sky, as she was pouring lemonade and preparing to remove the ice cream and cake, "I don't want to get married and tied down, you understand."

217

June didn't answer for a moment, because this was the first time Earl had ever mentioned marriage. Finally she responded, feeling slightly confused. "I'm glad to hear that, Earl, because I feel the same way." She made her reply as she walked into the house, leaving Earl with the most threatening of thoughts. He had expected his words to initiate a lengthy discussion as to why June felt they should get married. In his imagination, she would convince him of the inevitability of marriage, an idea that had been haunting him for the past six months.

June came back on the porch. Without further thought, Earl asked the question he wanted to know the answer to more than anything. "June, will you marry me?" Her answer came thundering down on his mind like a left-right knock-out punch. "Oh, brother!" Earl muttered.

The next step was to tackle her parents. Earl approached them with the same confidence he had when he entered the ring, thinking, "They can't refuse me. I must be one of the best things that could ever happen to the family." When June's parents said they were going to sleep on it, his mind again felt the pressure of a left-right knock-out punch. "Oh, brother!" But Earl had what it took to be a great champion, and he picked himself up from the psychological floor and, the very next morning, went to June's home, making an impression by washing the dishes and lending a hand. After breakfast, Mr. Palmer took him aside and asked if he was still in the mood to marry his daughter. Earl wasn't in the mood for any lectures, but he was persistent, and said he was still interested. Mr. Palmer said, "Well, son, it would be fine with me." For Earl, it was the final straw, and Mr. Palmer found himself helping the young athlete to the living room sofa, to collect himself and shake off any possibility of fainting.

Earl had only three dollars in the bank, but he was determined to get married right away. June asked where they would live. The proud young boxer said, "I'll buy a house." Earl was determined to support her, even if he had to wash cars to do it. June didn't know anything about his finances, but she had a practical mind. Sensing his well-meaning and good intentions, but also his lack of funds, she suggested that they wait until they saved up at least three thousand dollars.

Earl continued his training, saving his money as fast as he could. Finally, after months of training, Earl was in the ring, again, for his first important fight in Toronto. His opponent was big news around Toronto, and an amateur boxing champion. A first-round knockout dethroned the surprised champion, and Earl's name began to be news in Toronto. Now he was an Ontario amateur champion, and his trainers, who were increasingly impressed by the young man from Windsor, had enough confidence in him to take him to New York.

"What do you mean New York? I think it's time for me to go home—I have paid for the ticket you sent me to get here." Earl's reaction startled his manager and trainer, and they looked at each other in disbelief.

"Don't you realize the opportunity this will give you?" Jimmy Jones, his manager, asked him. His trainer, Shirley Jackson, had begun to understand the young boxer, and knew what it took to motivate him.

He looked his fighter in the eye. "What's the matter, Earl? Don't you think you're good enough?" Jackson's question stopped Earl dead in his tracks. He thought fleetingly of Olive.

"I am just as good as anyone," he answered proudly.

The train pulled out of Union Station, its destination New York City. Earl sat beside Jones, looking out the window at the telephone poles flashing past. The knuckles of his left hand were bandaged, and Jimmy Jones looked at them as if he were inspecting a prize racehorse before the Kentucky Derby. "How do you feel, Earl?" The boy just nodded, indicating that all was well.

Jimmy knew how important it was to keep Earl's confidence up and his body in shape. His training in New York would be a challenge: meeting that challenge would take all Earl's ability. Stillman's Gym, New York City, was famous for training the fighters who boxed at Madison Square Gardens. Most of these boxers were "main eventers." In the 1940s, when boxing was really popular, the term signified fighters who had devastated a minimum of twenty-five professional opponents.

The boxing profession in those early post-war years attracted numerous candidates. Anyone capable of being rated in the ring magazine's top ten was a great boxer, considering the competition. This was the calibre of the fighters whom Stillman's Gym attracted.

Jimmy realized, when he planned the trip to New York, that Earl would gain experience as a sparring partner to many of the great boxers of the day: Ezzard Charles, Archie Moore, Gonzales and perhaps even the Champ himself. His boy would need good hands, and all other physical attributes boxing required. He smiled at Earl, not wishing to reveal too much of the future to his already homesick youth.

The train crept on from one town to another. At three A.M., they pulled into a village and Earl stared out into the darkness.

On that Saturday night the inhabitants were out in force, their black faces eager for a taste of Duke Ellington, Bessie Smith or perhaps Billie Holiday. Earl longed to join them as his train took on a few passengers. He was nineteen years old, ready for some fun, and his feet moved to the beat of music coming from an all-night club. "That club must be the where-it's-happening place in town," Earl thought. A pretty girl waved to him, sending goose bumps and shivers up his spine and making him think of June Palmer. "I'll have to save every penny I earn so I can call her as soon as I get back to Canada," Earl thought.

The train moved on to another small New York station. He heard the clanging of cans and other usual early morning sounds but he didn't pay much attention: his head was full of thoughts of June.

Finally his thoughts faded from June to his boxing career, and sleep was eventually his rescue.

The Big Apple was even more awesome to Earl than Toronto had been. The skyscrapers he had heard of were really there, and so was the Statue of Liberty, and the United Nations Buildings. His manager told him he wouldn't have to start training for two days; Earl should spend the time relaxing, and preparing himself mentally for the task ahead. Only two things prevented Earl from walking every street of New York: time and distance. He loved the city and the Americans he met.

On the third day he reported to Stillman's Gym, where he learned that American boxers were less friendly than strangers in the street. Never before had he seen such talent or physical stamina; this was serious business. Boxers had to line up, awaiting their turn in the ring.

Earl's turn came and he did well: he survived the five rounds. His hard right hand, his more unfortunate opponents were to learn, needed no training and was to be avoided at all costs. The little-known heavyweight from Windsor, Ontario turned pro in New York City.

Earl Walls won his first professional fight in a one-round knockout. Then, still green, he lost his next three fights; then he won ten in a row. Since he won seven of the ten victories by first round knockouts, his manager had reason to believe Earl did not yet have enough ring experience: he was too good for his own good. Some top-grade opposition would remedy that.

Sixty, seventy or even a hundred fighters might be training in Stillman's Gym on any particular day. Each time he arrived, Earl would count at least twenty-five heavyweights, fifteen of whom were main eventers who had taken at least two years to get where they were. Earl's personality, which even the most indifferent of fighters could not resist, helped him to make friends easily; he sparred with and learned the various styles of some of the best Madison Square Garden regulars. Earl Walls was continuing along his long, hard road, through the school of hard knocks.

While Earl was in New York, he lived with some friends of

221

his manager's, who were wealthy blacks and made his road easier. At that time the Dickens family owned several apartment buildings and, besides being wealthy, they were intelligent people.

When he arrived at the Dickens mansion Earl was introduced to Thomas Dickens, lawyer and future well known judge of the United States. As they shook hands, Earl was appreciative of the evidence that, given proper opportunities and freedom from financial pressures, minorities could take their place with the best. "Maybe someday there will be opportunity centres throughout the world for minorities," Earl thought. "If a person wanted to become a lawyer, doctor or make the most of other talents, it could be a reality, not just a dream." The Dickens family liked the youth who had shaken the lawyer's hand for so long. The family smiled in appreciation of the kind and thankful heart typified by such a warm handshake. "My mother would be pleased to know I am with such good people," Earl commented as he finally released his grip.

The Dickens family really liked their young Canadian neighbour, and they drove him to his fights and stayed to watch all of them, forming a cheering section. This support was as motivating to him as his own family had been in Canada.

Earl met similar families, white and black, all over the world who carried on the tradition of hospitality established by the Dickenses of New York.

MILE XXXVI

The Canadian boxing circuit could not produce an opponent worthy of the product of Stillman's Gym. Earl's professional bouts were deceiving. Many lumberjacks and Spadina brawlers challenged Earl, thinking he was inexperienced. They added to his impressive, first-round knockout record.

Earl could not find a courageous challenger in his own country so he began to look elsewhere: he planned a trip to Europe. Before leaving he wanted to visit the slave homestead and his family.

He received a spectacular homecoming. The women in the family—Olive and her three daughters, Lylia, Freida and Sandra—prepared what Earl liked best: fried chicken, black-eyed peas and chitterlings. He drove up to the house in his two-year-old, newly-bought car, a status symbol in itself and much better than the 1932 model he learned how to drive in. He could smell the chitterlings cooking as he climbed out of the car. His happiness and excitement knew no bounds. It was like Christmas all over again, and his friends and relatives were making certain they had given Earl proper praise and plenty of boxing tips. Uncle Wilfred bobbed and weaved as he gave his nephew instructions on how to handle the champ. Everyone smiled, everyone was excited, and a round robin of euchre playing served to enhance the event. Sleep was a luxury that night. The next morning, a tired but happy Earl Walls arrived at the Detroit Metropolitan Airport for the flight to London, England.

Earl, you are a black, be proud, and the slave's descendant, just as good as anyone. Earl heard the words as he boarded the plane and closed his tired eyes.

The plane ride was uneventful, but the first few days in England required all of Earl's conditioning, as he tried to recuperate from the family send-off party and jet lag.

In the ring, Earl was fierce, cat-like and all business. He landed punch after punch on his unsuspecting English opponents. Other European champions were flown in, to no avail. The Belgian champion fell in two rounds; the Italian champion was not quite as lucky.

Earl continued to show his punching power to the enthusiastic English crowds, but he didn't manage to win every fight. According to Jackson, two of his losses in Britain shouldn't have happened.

Jackson was adamant in claiming one loss came by a disqualification. Earl lost his temper and retaliated when his opponent butted him. He lost another to Barnett of Jamaica. He had Barnett on the floor five times—then he broke his hand. Earl finished the bout, broken hand and all.

Earl finished his European tour and came back to Canada. He had a few good fights, but he still wasn't setting the world on fire. He fought against both Slade and Aster, but lost both fights. Then, early in 1951 he began his long climb to the top. By May 1952, he reached his full stature, six feet two inches, and his best fighting weight, one hundred ninety-two pounds. That month he went to Edmonton to fight a supporting bout. Mostly he went just for the ride, to accompany his sparring partner, Vern Escoe, who was still heavyweight champion of Canada.

Earl sat in the car, watching the miles go by, thinking about his life; in his mind, he reviewed his whole boxing career. "Maybe I should go back to Windsor and work at the Ford plant. I enjoyed it there. But what would the family say if I gave up? But I should decide for myself, not for them—this is my life, and I must make my own decisions. I know I am just as good as anyone, white or black." The miles flashed past and still Earl thought. Then somewhere on the Trans-Canada highway between Winnipeg and Calgary, he said, "Jimmy, what is your feeling about a boxer giving up his career? When should he think about quitting?"

"I can't say exactly when for everyone, Earl, but I know there are two things to think about. Of course, a boxer should quit before he gets badly hurt. But that's the second thing. The first, and most important, is to stick with your decision. Look at the sad greats who didn't heed this rule."[2]

These words were one of the reasons Earl had great respect and appreciation for his manager, and in later years would resist offers to purchase his contract. Jimmy was a straight shooter who placed the interests of his boxers before his own. He had dreamed of Cadillacs and caviar, but had become used to bread and beans. The well-built Windsor, Ontario boy sitting beside him and interrupting his nap was destined to make Jimmy's dreams a reality: Earl would put the best cigars between Jimmy's lips. The manager would someday speak of his fighter with pride, and others would respect his opinions on boxing strategies.

As the car moved along the road, Earl heard again the words Olive had repeated so often.

"No, I am not ready to quit," Earl blurted.

"What's that, Earl? I didn't hear you," Jimmy muttered sleepily.

"It's all right, coach." Jimmy was satisfied with Earl's answer, and fell into a peaceful sleep again.

The nights before and after his boy's fights, Jimmy could get no sleep: his nerves were too charged with anticipation and excitement.

His co-manager, Shirley Jackson, always calmed him down. Jackson, like Earl, had great respect for Jimmy, a man who had helped Jackson leave his post as railroad porter and live out his dream of training boxers. The calibre of boxers did not matter to Shirley; he just loved boxing, and the action associated with it. Although he naturally wanted his boys to win, he was more interested in their conditioning and skills, and in keeping them from getting hurt. He would ride his bicycle right behind Earl as he ran through the Don Valley in Toronto each day; he would watch Earl eat a full breakfast and then, a few hours later, work it off at Deacon's gym.

It was here in Edmonton that Earl's training gelled. He scored one of his many first-round knock-outs, and his first victory since returning from England. In a voice that could be heard above the cheering crowd, Shirley yelled, "Three lefts is all Earl needed, three lefts flattened him! That's my boy!"

Like Earl, Escoe easily won against his opponent that night, and defended his crown. The shrewd Jack Berry, a hustling Edmonton promoter, signed Earl to fight Vern for the heavyweight title of Canada, realizing that their crowd-pleasing performance could be financially lucrative. After the contracts were signed, Berry revealed that the guarantees—

stipulated by Jimmy Jones—were the most substantial he had ever offered. Another facet of Jimmy's character emerged when he refused to train either fighter; George Dunn would be brought in to train Earl.

At 8:00 P.M. the evening of the signing the twenty-two-year-old aspiring champion lay in his hotel room after training hard under Dunn. Earl had a real problem, and decided to talk it over with his new trainer. "How can I try to knock out my buddy Vern, George?"

"Where's your killer instinct, boy?" his trainer exclaimed. "Do you want to keep on eating red beans and rice? Earl, you get your black butt in there and fight and forget all this friendly stuff. This is a job, boy, for cash money!" These words so shocked Earl that he buried his head in his pillow, too confused to talk. He tossed and turned all night. When he awoke he knew what he had to do.

MILE XXXVII

As Earl Walls made his way towards the ring, his head seemed to be completely covered by the dazzling white hood of the robe his mother had given him. The crowd tried to catch a glimpse of his face, but the hood screened it from their eyes, and they had to wait to see the serious look of business in the challenger's eyes. Someone in the crowd yelled, "Look at the Hooded Terror!"

A capacity crowd sat as if waiting for a kill. The spectators were hoping to see one of Edmonton's greatest fights ever. They were not disappointed.

One spectator was Cliff, Earl's older brother. He was turning the pages of the souvenir programme dated Friday, 13 June 1952, and praying that it would be an unlucky day for Vern Escoe. Cliff read to take his mind off the nervousness in his stomach.

Regardless of how the odds may look, Earl Walls is the sentimental favourite in tonight's Canadian heavyweight title contest against Vern Escoe.

This lean, well-proportioned specimen, who has been likened to Joe Louis in more than appearance, has caught the fancy of the fight gentry, even though he strutted his stuff for something less than a round when the chips were down.[3]

"What's this mean?" Cliff thought. But he was too nervous to wonder about it for long. "Oh, well," he said and read on.

They liked the way he handled himself in the gym and his easy one-round knockout in the last fight was enough to convince them that he had what it took.

Walls is as good a fellow out of the ring as he is a fighter inside. His fine personality and sincerity have won him a host of friends in the short time he's been in Edmonton.[4]

These words brought a smile to Cliff's face and he said, "That's my brother."

Lylia was sitting beside him. She nudged him on the shoulder and said, "Shut up, Cliff, people will think you're crazy, talking to yourself like that." Cliff was too absorbed in reading to deal with his younger sister's attempts to be a grown woman, as he would put it.

All this did not seem to bring any great flood of Walls money out in the open. As the gambling gentry puts it, the wise money is on Escoe.

It's almost impossible to count out this thirty-year-old veteran, who has the knack of pacing himself admirably. He makes a point of being only as good as he has to be.

The Edmonton fans have no way of knowing just how good he can be. He made two starts, winning both handily.

Escoe, the old pro, is the master of the situation, even when his opponent momentarily has the upper hand.

A Walls victory tonight might serve to brighten up the Canadian heavyweight picture and bring it back to the spotlight after years with the title resting securely on Escoe's capable shoulders.

No one has had serious designs on the crown because of Escoe's superiority as far as Canadian fighters are concerned.

With Walls in the throne, it might be a different story. Guys who shied away from Escoe might take on Walls. Actually the two are

pretty well matched, if you overlook Escoe's experience which, of course, you can't. That probably will be the difference tonight.
They both hit hard, but both can take a punch. Walls is a good boxer, but he's not quite in Escoe's class. So, it promises to be a thriller, as match-maker Jack Berry prophesies.[5]

Cliff's reading was interrupted by the sound of the bell marking the beginning of the fight. Olive grabbed Cliff's right hand and his left hand was nervously held by Lylia. By the end of the fight, both of Cliff's hands were red.

The first three rounds had Cliff on the edge of his seat. In the fourth round, Cliff watched as his brother threw a crashing right and left to the head. Earl felt as if his right knuckles were almost shattered. Cliff jumped from his seat, and before he realized he had climbed through the ropes, he was lifting his brother, the new heavyweight champion of Canada, as the crowd cheered and the tears streamed down his face. Cliff's mind, frenzied with happiness, could imagine the triumphant news clippings of the next day as he carried his champion brother around the ring.

Although he was nailed several times with Escoe's vicious, ripping left upper-cuts, he shook off the blows to score with his own beautiful lefts. Earl had a mouse raised under his left eye in the first round, which gave George Dunn, his trainer, some concern.

For the first two minutes of the second round, he landed some low blows, although unintentional. Late in the second, he caught Escoe with a thumping left that jolted his head back, and his body followed against the ropes. Earl attempted to follow up the advantage, but the bell sounded before he could again catch up with Escoe.

They slugged it out almost toe to toe in the third round, Earl skillfully covering up as Escoe appeared to have a momentary advantage. Earl was hit with a lightning right as he came off the ropes, but recovered quickly, owing to his great conditioning.

The fourth round had barely gotten under way when Walls caught his opponent with a left that spun him like a top through the ropes. Escoe took the eight count and was barely on his feet before Earl nailed him for the second time, again sending him sprawling across the inside stand.

Escoe took another eight count and with the mark of a

champion, came back with considerable fervor, but with not too much finesse. Earl waited for this break of uncertainty. He set a stunned Escoe up with a blazing right, one of the few he threw all night, and dropped him with a solid left. Earl didn't even look back as he walked to a neutral corner. Escoe raised to his knees at the count of nine, then toppled over onto the canvas.[6]

Olive and Lylia soon followed Cliff into the ring. And as Olive hugged the same fighter who had lost his first fight in the Brewster recreation centre in Detroit, she could scarce believe he was representing the whole Dominion of Canada—and with no black eye. "Didn't I tell you, Earl, you are the slave's descendant, just as good as anyone."

MILE XXXVIII

The Walls—Escoe rematch was scheduled for an outdoor card, 17 July but, because he received no cooperation from the weatherman, promoter Jack Berry announced that afternoon it would be postponed until the eighteenth. Tickets moved at an unprecedented rate for Edmonton and, because conditions were favourable, a new attendance mark for Western Canada was achieved. Those in attendance realized that something more than flesh and bone would be needed to stop Earl Walls that night. The newspaper reported:

A crow bar or a General Pershing tank were suggested as possible opponents, but one of the big names from across the border seemed the more practical answer. Earl's thundering fists proved again that he was top dog in the Canadian heavyweight picture. Only the bell saved the fight from ending in the fourth round like in the first fight. Escoe was down late in the fourth when the bell sounded. He was dragged to his corner where some quick repair work enabled him to go out again. Escoe, despite his courage, could last only forty-two seconds into the fifth round. Earl's second punch spun Escoe into the bottom rope.[7]

He wobbled to his feet at the count of nine, and was obviously hurt. His manager, Jimmy Jones, tried to throw the towel in. The referee ignored him. Knowing full well it was against the rules, Jones tried to climb in the ring himself when the towel was disregarded, to prevent a serious injury. Jimmy had never seen Escoe like he was in the fifth. Even Earl asked that the slaughter be halted. But the referee waved Escoe into the ring, and the fight continued.

As Earl stepped hesitantly to where Escoe was weaving on his feet, he thought, "What am I doing here? This is my friend! Is this what being a boxer means?" Training and reflexes brought Earl's right arm up and across to Escoe's jaw. The former champion crumpled.

Escoe's handlers rushed to the ring, and it was several minutes before Escoe came around.

Earl stood in his corner feeling no glory in his victory. He felt only sadness. He walked slowly to his dressing room, wondering if he had lost a friend. Finally Vern came out of his dressing room. He had shaved, showered and was much recuperated. Earl stood in front of him and gathered his courage. "Vern," he said, "let's go to the party together."

Earl extended his black hand towards Vern, who returned the gesture. The handshake was more than a mere greeting: it signified the continuation of a friendship. No words were necessary as the former and reigning boxing kings walked out of the stadium.

MILE XXXIX

For the next year the tall, handsome Earl Walls was the top main eventer on the Edmonton boxing card. Vancouver boasted of getting him for one fight, but otherwise he fought only in Edmonton. In a short time he had met—and bested— all challengers; he was running out of competition. Then Rex

Layne, ranked seventh in the world, agreed to fight the young champ. The Edmonton fight fans could hardly believe their luck. [8]

Earl Walls was twenty-five years old, a heavyweight champion and, according to veteran experts, Dempsey included, a good bet to become next champion of the world. When the telephone rang, the big fellow with the lightning fists was sprawled across his bed in a downtown Edmonton hotel room. His manager was excited as he told Earl the news, and his excitement was contagious. But Earl wasn't thinking about what the fight would do for his career, and he wasn't thinking about winning the fight.

He was thinking about money. He thought of how much he might get paid for fighting Layne; the thought made him jump from his bed and do twenty-five push-ups, smiling all the time. "With what I have saved from the Escoe fights," he was thinking, "and this Layne fight coming up, I will have the three thousand dollars I need to get married. June Palmer, you lucky girl, here I come!"

Early the next morning, Earl was in the gym training with an enthusiasm that made even Jimmy wonder. "Earl must really want to beat Layne, maybe so he can challenge Marciano," Jimmy thought. "Layne is the stepping stone to the champion." Jimmy didn't realize it, but Earl saw the fight, not as a stepping stone to Marciano, but as the stepping stone to June. And he was motivated.

Layne, who had made nine combat jumps as a US paratrooper in the South Pacific, had beaten Jersey Joe Walcott, the former heavyweight champion of the world, and was then stopped by Rocky Marciano. He was certainly not afraid of Earl Walls as he stepped off the plane into the waiting handshake of Jack Berry. [9]

He carried a folded newspaper, which had kept him occupied during his flight from Salt Lake City, Utah. One article on the sports page had caught his interest.

Walls wins Northwest title with second round TKO. Courageous Grant fights Canadian Champ, but is out-gunned. As his manager, Jimmy Jones, said in the dressing room after the fight last night, when Earl Walls and another heavyweight enter the same ring, somebody's got to go.[10]

"Ha, if somebody goes it sure won't be me," Layne said aloud, as the plane's engine whined to a stop.

One week later, on the fifth of July, 1953, Earl Walls was doing some newspaper reading of his own. He was in his favourite position, lying across his bed in his Edmonton hotel. He held the telephone receiver delicately with his shoulder as he talked. "June, we have enough money to get married now. Listen to what your man has done, babe! What John Freeman Walls, the slave's descendant, has done for Canada!" Then Earl read aloud from the *Edmonton Journal*.

Tan tornado needs only 63 seconds to stop world ranking contender. The audience was appreciatively silent while a great virtuoso hammered out a 53-second concerto of clout at the Edmonton Exhibition Grandstand last night.

When Earl Walls, "Maestro of Mail," pulled out all the stops on the key instrument, his ringing right hand, and chopped down Rex Layne, a great tearing mass of sound welled up and drowned out the feature artist. Ten seconds later, at 1:03 of the first round, a bright new star began to blaze in the world's fistic firmament.[11]

"That's me they're talking about, June. Listen to this, there's more."

Walls, Canada's heavyweight, and best bet Canada has for the world heavyweight championship since Tommy Burns in 1910, required a total of just sixty-three seconds to knock out Layne and take a long and determined step along boxing's rugged, rutted glory road. By the same token, Layne, the world's seventh-ranking heavyweight, was willfully shoved a pace closer to the dark pit of obscurity. A crowd of 4,885 paid $34,820 to see the tan tornado topple Layne with a shuddering short right following up a spearing left hook.

The great Salt Lake City pugilist, a second earlier, had clobbered Walls with a solid overhand right. Walls was shaken up by the punch and scrambled back up against the ropes on the north side of the ring. Layne hesitated for the barest moment instead of following up his advantage.

Like a great brown cat, Walls came off the ropes and straightened Layne with that driving left hook. In one fluid motion he came through with the other half of the combination, a flashing right hand that couldn't have travelled more than eight or ten inches.

The punch caught Layne in the side of the chin. As the crowd realized what was happening, bedlam began to break loose. Layne began to fall with all the awesome solemnity of a British Columbia fir tree put to the axe. As his knees crumpled he performed a grotesque pivot and went over on his back with a resounding thud. He lay stretched full length on the canvas and there wasn't even a tremor from him, as referee Johnny Beh of Chicago tolled the full count.

A howling mass of spectators rushed the ring, as Beh raised Walls's hand aloft in symbolic victory ritual. Excited fans stampeded through the press row on the side of the ring, and trampled the press table to splinters in their eagerness to get closer to their Canadian champion.

"Yeow!" a fan screamed in this writer's ear, "at last Canada has a real champion."

It is doubtful, even if Walls wins the world title, that he'll ever again be subjected to such an all-embracing spontaneous show of adulation.

Weighing 192 pounds, the big brown man was in superb condition. Layne at 206 pounds, appeared to be overweight. The Salt Lake fighter, who fought Jersey Joe Walcott and Ezzard Charles, both former world heavyweight champions, was out cold for more than seven minutes. And, when he did come to, asked what round it was. Upon hearing, remarked they stopped the fight too soon.

The victory was Walls's twelfth since coming here in May 1952. It was the tan tornado's eleventh KO in the long string of victories in his short career.

Walls rung up an amazing total of 13 one-round knock-outs, a better mark than that possessed by the redoubtable Joe Louis, his boxing idol.

A rematch is planned under the terms of the contract. Walls must fight Layne in Salt Lake within 60 days.[12]

"What do you think of that, June, what do you think of that?"

June had tears in her eyes and could only say, "Yes, I will marry you, yes, I will."

Her words left Earl wondering if she had really heard all that he had read.

MILE XL

Walls is headed East for peace
He's tired of work and training.
Layne is headed South to ease
His weary ol' head, it's paining.[13]

"It's just as well I got to him when I did. I did it for Canada," Earl said to his family. They were all sitting on the edge of their chairs around the traditional setting for all great Walls events, the kitchen table. Olive was smiling, and the rest of the family and friends smiled along with her.[14]

The three-week holiday her son was beginning meant twenty-one days of joyful life, or so she thought. Earl's announcement that he was getting married brought the Walls family to the brink of uncontrolled emotions—and Olive was on the brink of fainting. Frank was the first to make intelligible sounds; his words were coming somewhere from the Walls ancestral archives.

"Who are you jumping the broom with?"

As if understanding what his father meant, perhaps knowing instinctively that Frank was harking back to a description of marriage common in his great grandfather's day, Earl answered, "June Palmer, from Brantford, Ontario."

Olive loaded the table with soul food in honour of the happy occasion, and talk shifted back and forth between boxing comments and wedding conversation. Uncle Wilfred had been a real inspiration to Earl in the earlier, more undecided, years of his boxing career. He made another of his dry but jovial, remarks, comparing marriage to a sixty-three second, first-round knock-out. He explained he didn't know who was worse off, Earl or Layne. Everyone in the room broke into gales of laughter, and the discussion of marriage preparations continued.

The carloads of folks headed for Brantford had a good time on the road. They filled one whole side of the church, which had been set aside for the groom's family, and slightly infiltrated the Palmer ranks on the other side.

As Earl and June walked down the aisle, the congregation of black, white and in-between had eyes focussed on the heavyweight champion and his bride-to-be; the groom had rewarded Canada, and was now rewarding himself. *You are a Walls, be proud, and the slave's descendant, just as good as anyone.* The thought of these words sent a chill up Earl's spine as he looked at the tears of joy falling down his mother's chubby cheeks and into her handkerchief. Fun and frivolity was an apt description of the atmosphere that night and the day following. The whole wedding party travelled back to Windsor, Ontario, for an old-time good time.

Olive gave a special rendition of the charleston. Duke Ellington's records were at a premium and second choice was the latest rock-and-roll fads of the mid-fifties. The ring dancing brought laughter from all, aided slightly by the liquid spirits, which Olive usually frowned upon.

"Earl, you are really heading down the road to some-where," more than one proud relative uttered; and, as Earl looked into the face of his new bride, he was oblivious to the inhumanities of the past. He was oblivious to the hardships his great grandfather had had to endure in escaping to Canada with his master's widow. And he was oblivious to the hardships his grandfather and other early descendants of former slaves had had to face, once they arrived in Canada.

235

And, for this moment, he was oblivious to his own hardships, the hardships of coming from the obscurity of an agrarian community to world prominence, and oblivious to the future hardships he would endure as he moved closer and closer, on his road to the Boxing Hall of Fame.

His only thought was the love he felt for June Palmer Walls, and the love he received in return.

The new bride stayed with her in-laws for the remainder of Earl's holiday rest to encourage him in his training. He would keep in shape by running only, purposely avoiding sparring in the gym; his muscles were finely tuned, and so was his brain, and he didn't want to waste his enthusiasm in the gym.

June would run with him on occasion, on the pretext of needing exercise for her beautiful, lithe body; but everyone knew she dreaded the thought of not being near her new husband. Even more, she feared his upcoming motor trip to Salt Lake City, Utah; it would mean at least a month of second-best contact through phone calls or letters. When his wife accompanied him, Earl would reduce his running pace and mileage to allow her to keep up. The track from his Dad's farm to the original homestead of John Freeman Walls was sufficient distance for both and, as they would near the last quarter of a mile, Earl would sprint off, leaving June in the dust yelling after him to wait, but knowing that his boyish tendencies were surfacing. This only strengthened her love for him.

She would always catch up to him while he stood in the family cemetery, reading the tombstone of his great grandfather, which led into story-telling of the Walls family legends. His hand seemed compelled to touch the stone, as if hoping it would unleash some mystery of great import to himself and perhaps even mankind; a mystery that would reveal what could happen, were racial harmony allowed to exist. Earl could only shake his head; he realized neither he, nor society, was mature enough, as yet, to accept the significance of the worn cemetery stone beneath his fingers.

Unable to cope with the frustration his philosophical

musings would cause, his thoughts would turn to more immediate questions, such as how he could again defeat Rex Layne.

That night the entire family was looking at the new television Earl had purchased as a gift to his most loyal supporters. They waited eagerly for Wednesday night at the fights; they were indifferent to all else. The outcome of the fight was significant in terms of being a turning point in Earl's boxing career. Frank, Olive, Earl and June were practically glued to the set during the fight between Mentor and Zak; Earl gave a blow-by-blow commentary of the behind-the-scenes aspects, which many others would not have the advantage of knowing. This added to the interest. But a heavy silence fell over the family as Zak was knocked out, never again to raise his gloves or to be the head of the family that depended on him.

The blood ran from his nose and ears onto the canvas; even on the twelve-inch black and white screen, the death made Lylia and Freida run outside to keep from fainting. All Olive could say was, "I don't want that ever to happen to you, Earl; maybe you should think about quitting." The look in her eyes was one he saw for the first time that night. She had never shown fear before; she had suppressed it because she had felt compelled to indoctrinate him in the need to fulfill a destiny, and to continue along a road started by a slave over a hundred years ago.

To Earl, the look in her eyes indicated possible compromise and the need to stay alive—even if it meant changing the direction of his road. That look was not taken lightly.

As Earl and June lay in bed that night, they discussed the fight. They decided that, for Earl, boxing would be a means to an end, rather than an end in itself—or of his life. June prayed that some trained lethal weapon would not find the temporal portion of her husband's skull or the solar plexus of his stomach before he chose to retire.

The next morning, Earl was relaxed: he was determined not to let his fears of the night before keep him from fighting his way to the top. He loaded his car with an extra measure of silence, thinking, "I cannot let myself, or Canada down, and this is just another step in fulfilling June's goals, and mine." At this point, June leaned into the car to get her final goodbye kiss, but it was not to come. As Earl looked into his partner's eyes, he said, "Jump in the car, you're coming with me."

"But I don't have enough clothes."

"We'll buy some on the way," he said, but the words were unnecessary. She had already made up her mind.

Frank and Olive nodded their heads in appreciation of the carefree beauty of young lovers. "Earl, you win now, and don't give him a chance to hurt you," Olive said. She also felt compelled to follow with another statement, which had more motivational impact on Earl than the first. As he rolled up the car window, he heard her say, "Remember, you are the slave's descendant, just as good as anyone. You are Canada's champion."

Earl knew what he had to do.

MILE XLI

In the ring Tuesday night at the Salt Lake City fairgrounds, Rex Layne evidently forgot what he had to do. He led with his right and neglected to duck. To make matters worse, he made both mistakes at the same instant, right after the opening bell in the sixth round. Earl whipped his cobra-like right hand to Layne's jaw; the punch rocked Rex to his heels before he slumped to the floor.

> Layne staggered to his feet, but from then on until 1:42 of the sixth it was veritable murder, as Earl calmly measured Rex and powered in another, then another, then another terrific right.
>
> Rex was down twice more before he finally hit the deck, rolled over with his head resting on the lower rope, made an effort to get

up at the five count and then slumped back, battered, beaten and, while not unconscious, practically paralyzed.[15]

Layne's manager jumped to his feet in shock and disbelief, too confused to stay seated. His boy had pranced into the ring looking like the kid who had lasted six rounds with the champion of the world. He had trimmed down from some two hundred ten pounds to one hundred ninety, give or take a pound or two. He had entered the ring just eighteen minutes ago, as ready as he had ever been in his life. Sharp, smooth and set to go, he was ready to battle for one round or ten, however long it took him to wipe Earl's one-round KO off the books.

Had the second round been a figment of his imagination, the dejected manager thought. That terrific second round had been one of the best the State of Utah had ever seen. Layne had slowed Earl to a walk, slowed him so much he didn't even try to use his big right hand. During that whole round the manager was sure Rex was going to finish the Canadian off and send him back to the land of the Eskimos to be someone's sparring partner, but the combination of Earl's cover, when he was in trouble, and Layne's over-eagerness, allowed Earl to be saved by the bell.

"The third, yes, the third," the manager said out loud. "My boy knocked Walls down with a left hook in the third. Even from where I was sitting, I knew he couldn't get up. I could see the powerful black man's face as his chin hit the canvas. I could see the spit and I saw his mouthpiece, covered with blood, fall out of his mouth. I could hear him groan and mumble, yes, mumble. What on earth was he trying to say? Between the count of four and five, I heard him say, *Slave's descendant, just as good.* Then he stopped like he had found an inner strength, and got up from the canvas before the count of ten. What kind of man is this? Who was the slave he was mumbling about? Where does he get his strength?"

Layne's manager looked at his best hope for world heavyweight champion lying on the canvas. Then he finished his thought while looking at the back of Earl's kinky head. "This man could be the next heavyweight champion of the world if he wanted to. The champ better not make the same tactical error I made and underestimate Earl Walls."

"I was lucky again, just like in Edmonton," is how Earl Walls summed it up in his dressing room. "Everyone has one or two bad days and Layne just had them in a row, but he is a great fighter. He hurt me when he knocked me down with that left hook in the third and he sure was strong in the clinches."[16]

"The man is also a gentleman," Layne remarked to his manager, as he read these words in the morning *Tribune*.

His manager had been puzzling over Earl's character. He was still haunted by the words "slave's descendant," the words he had distinctly heard just before Earl's miraculous comeback in the third round.

"Do you hear me?" Layne continued, as he realized that his manager's mind was off somewhere else. "I thought I really had him in the third round. I hit him with everything but the kitchen sink! Didn't you think he would stay down? He was laying right by your corner—didn't his eyes seemed closed or anything?"

Layne's manager did not answer. He looked at his fading hope for world heavyweight champ and his head moved slowly back and forth, in disbelief. He couldn't believe Earl's physical or inner strength, an inner strength that seemed to have spiritual proportions.

The only two words the manager could utter were, "Slave's descendant."

To Layne, the words meant nothing and prompted him to ask, "What's wrong with you, coach? You all right? You look worse off than I do." Layne hoped this question would earn a smile or possibly even a change of topic.

"Oh, it's nothing, Rex, I was just thinking out loud."

The two men ended their conversation on a philosophical note. "What does it matter anyway? The fight is over, and we might as well bury it with other disappointments that men, during their lives, are forced to forget in order to survive."

They did not realize the true significance of what had taken place the previous night. Earl could not even finds words to explain what had happened. Only one other thing affected him as powerfully: standing among the graves of his ancestors. Earl reflected upon the unique course of events that had led him to this point in his life. His mind's eye could visualize the tapestry of black man, white woman, former slave, former slave master's wife, flight from North Carolina, fight with wolves, slave patrollers, the abolitionists. He could feel the peace of a home in Canada, clearing land, providing a church, making a living, raising children, praying on their knees, hands clutching side by side, each night in a tiny bedroom made of logs, in hope that their offspring would someday be great men and women. He could imagine them hoping that, through their children, they would be able to thank Canada, to thank the good people in the United States, and most of all through them be able to thank God for delivering them from the disease of slavery, into the healing arms of Canada.

Earl walked through the streets of Salt Lake, awed by the great American city and appreciative of the fact that he was there to fulfill a destiny, knowing, deep inside, that his feeling of greatness was the continuation of the courageous steps that those before him had taken along that long and winding road.

MILE XLII

The sports enthusiasts of Toronto, Canada, were beside themselves with excitement when they heard Earl Walls had returned. The whole country was proud of the champ.

However, Earl Walls didn't feel too proud as he walked

down Yonge Street. He was the Canadian Heavyweight Champ now, not the Windsor, Ontario champ he had been some eight years before. The psychological effects of possessing two lethal weapons, which were in his two front pockets as he walked, were almost too great a burden for a mind that had never known the killer instinct. Yet he had almost killed a man a few weeks before, in the Edmonton Arena in a post-Layne warm-up fight with Thurman.

"I can't continue in boxing—I don't have the heart for it. I am good, I know I am, but I almost killed." He remembered back to the minutes right after his fight with Thurman.

For a few tense moments an act of survival had taken place in Thurman's corner. The fight had further cemented Earl's determination to retire early from a profession that represented a means to an end, rather than the end itself. During that fight, Earl felt as though he were in a time capsule in which evolution was sent reeling backwards into time by the lightning strikes of his tawny, long-muscled arms. He felt as though he were in a jungle where man, if only to survive, felt compelled to prove his superiority. For ten minutes, Earl stood in the neutral corner with a look that brought sympathy from the four thousand fans at the Edmonton pavilion. His opponent's seconds worked over Thurman feverishly, afraid of the worst, as Earl lingered nearby with evident concern and compassion. The fans, even though they did not admit it the next day, thought they had seen a man kill his fellow man. They thought they had seen a man die by another's fist, a fist that had not travelled more than a foot, but had behind it all the power Earl could muster. The blow caught his over-confident opponent on the left cheek, spinning him into the ropes.

Thurman dropped, rolled over on his head and then out onto the apron of the ring. No one bothered to count. His handlers bounded into the ring. His manager groped frantically for the mouthpiece, because blood was welling up in his boxer's cheeks.[17]

They threw cold water on his face, and finally brought the beaten fighter around, but not before the fighting heart of Earl Walls had been cooled. The victim was carried to his dressing room where he sat, unmoving, for a quarter of an hour before he was able to shower. For fifteen unending minutes Earl had said a thousand times in his mind, "I have killed a man, I have killed a man, my God, my God."

That night, Earl slept in the home of his good friend in Edmonton, George Wharry. Before he retired to bed, he discussed his possible retirement from boxing with George, whose opinion he respected. The sight of happy children playing and jumping on his and their Dad's knees, contributed to Earl's final decision.

The walk down Yonge Street wasn't a pleasant one; neither was the gymnasium training, or the ten-mile run. Nothing except sleep and a resolution to return to Puce, Maidstone Township, could erase the tragic potential of his latest pugilistic accomplishment.

As Earl had done many times to collect his thoughts, he took June for a drive along the highway to Windsor. They discussed the possibility of his leaving the boxing profession. June, who had never seen Earl fight, was as objective as a wife who wished the best for her husband and family could be. Earl suggested that maybe they should wait on the decision until they had the financial security of car, home and business. June nodded; whatever Earl thought best about boxing she would help him do.

Earl appreciated June's understanding. She would never interfere with a decision he alone could make, but that he needed to share with the one who was closest. His wife was more objective than his managers; they would be more concerned about Earl the boxer than Earl the person. He was their best bet for glory and success in their lifetime.

243

Earl returned from his pensive journey to Windsor and continued his spartan existence. He remained dedicated chiefly because boxing meant money and a chance to save enough to start a business. Earl was like a machine with no heart. He rose in the morning, hitting the road for a long run through the Don Valley. Back to bed, breakfast at ten, rest till noon, work out at the gym, home for a glass of milk, relaxation till dinner—a steak and salad and green vegetables—and in bed by ten. If he was tired, then he would be asleep by eight.

His waning fighting heart was in need of more inspiration. Earl went frequently to visit young patients in the General Hospital. The boys were his enthusiastic fans. One young fellow, Clayton, a young polio victim in an iron lung, held a special place in Earl's heart. They would talk for an hour. Each time he left the boys, Earl would be aware of their need to idolize their Canadian heavyweight champion. He would regain extra strength from knowing he must represent his country not only for himself but also for those who were not capable of his physical prowess.[18]

Then one night, Harrison fought like Joshua at the battle of Jericho, and the Walls came tumbling down. That night Earl needed all the young fans in the hospital, a train-load of family and friends from Windsor and other Canadian hero-worshippers to give him the motivation to rise from the canvas in the fourth round. Everybody figured it was all over for the Canadian Champ, but he made a rousing battle out of the remaining six heats.

That knock-down was a dramatic moment in Earl's career. He had not lost a fight at all in three years, and not lost by a knock-out since his early days in New York. Harrison was scoring with short jabs; he flicked a left lead, then lifted Earl off his feet with a right upper cut. Earl landed on his trunks and was propped in a neutral corner with both arms dangling over the lower strand of ropes. He showed no sign of stirring until the last second or two of the nine count. But when he did get up, bleeding at the nose and from a cut over his left eye, he pounded Harrison with five successive lefts to the head. Harrison lost the fifth slightly and Walls was winning the sixth round easily; then Harrison delivered a wicked right to the side of Earl's jaw, which floored him for the second time.

The 12 April, 1955 upset of the Canadian favourite provided, according to veteran Toronto writers, the greatest fight in the history of Toronto Maple Leaf Gardens in twenty-five years. It came before the largest crowd to see a scrap in Canada, 14,737, and it poured a Dominion record of $45,261 into the coffers of the promoters. None of the fans thought the bout would go the limit. Walls's record was 27 wins in 34 fights, 25 by knockouts, 14 ko's coming in the last 15 fights. This was only the second time in his career the tenth bell was heard. The last time was in England in 1949. And if there were better ones before that, they must have been little less than sensational.[19]

Earl's fights with Layne and Harrison established that he did not possess a glass chin; instead, he was a proud man, determined that no opponent in any ring would keep him from fighting his way to the top.

MILE XLIII

"This next one," Earl Walls was saying. "I gotta win, I just gotta." The Canadian heavyweight boxing champion was dripping with sweat under his second-hand dressing gown.

Dan Florio, the trainer from New York, was bustling about while Jimmy Jones was getting ready to talk.

Jimmy was smoking a cigar, listening as his champ, whose pride had been wounded, vowed to avenge his loss to Harrison. Earl was not a vengeful man, but the damage to his prestige—and therefore his pocketbook and his ambitions—could not go unanswered.

He looked up from the couch in the hotel lobby, which was

full of press reporters, "You know, Jimmy," he said, breaking into Jimmy's conversation with a reporter, "I didn't think I was going to lose that last one. I had worked hard for it. Yes, I had a cold and I should not have fought—I'm not using it as a cop out, it's over now. I had my chances and I missed 'em. But you can bet your last money I'll win the next one. And win it good. John Freeman Walls's great grandson won't hit the canvas again. No, Lord!"

Another reporter had listened intently to Earl's words. "Who was John Freeman?" he asked. Before Earl could answer, Jimmy butted in.

"He had 'em, two, three, times, in the last bout. Blew it, that's what. He ain't gonna blow any this time. He'll murder the guy."

Florio, standing behind the couch, nodded at the reporter to indicate his agreement with Jones; he thought Earl was ready, too. He remarked, "Sparring with Earl is war." As he spoke, he thought of Earl's second last box session before the fight: it had only been an hour ago. One of his opponents had found an opening and hung a small bomb on Earl's face. The nervous assailant stopped.

"That," said Earl, "was carelessness. And what did you stop for?" he asked as saliva dripped from his mouthpiece. "You should have followed up. If I get any shot like that at Harrison, I'll follow, believe me, and I won't get careless. Bet your money on Earl."

Those who did bet their money got a chance to see the Walls revenge. "Look out, Rocky; Earl Walls is now after you."[20]

Overcome by excitement, Olive threw her arms around her son, almost losing her hat in the process. Earl didn't have to tell her he won; she had been right there to see it.

There were other important sport fans who saw the fight, which catapulted Earl into third contender for the World Championship.

The National Boxing Association vice-president, who was also chairman of the Wisconsin Boxing Commission, was eager to remark, "He's ready for them all, and that includes Rocky Marciano, from what I saw tonight. He doesn't have to take a back seat to anyone. Walls will climb right up in the high ratings. I imagine he'll be third or fourth contender. He's only showed six losses in 37 bouts, and he won 14 out of 15 in a row of them by KO's." The vice-president was interrupted by Joe Louis's manager. "He's in the big time now, he's got to be a headliner. He could easily be champ. What a hitter!"[21]

Less famous but equally enthusiastic fans saw Walls, their Canadian champ, become the number-one menace to the World champion.

As he battered Harrison, he was demonstrating that his losing fight in January had been a mistake. The uncertain, fumbling fighter of that bout had become the coldly calculating killer. At ring-side odds of seven to five on Harrison, he made the smart-money look ridiculous.

It was a brute of a fight. Walls threw the first and last punches and most of those in between.

The fans saw Earl come out of his corner fast, jab Harrison with three short lefts, rap him smartly with a left hook and then whittle across his high hard one.[22]

It was an overhand right that caught Harrison on the left temple. It shook him and his knees wobbled and bent. It was such a terrible blow that it damaged Earl's hand, swelling the knuckles of his index finger.

And Harrison, who had fought a letter-perfect, tailor-made fight in January, committed a fatal mistake. He tried to fight back. He was hurt, and he could have tried to cover up and weather the storm. Instead, he caught the full fury of a man earnestly trying to go somewhere.

The Los Angeles kid jabbed Earl lightly with a couple of lefts and threw a weak right that was so pitiful it made even Olive feel sympathetic. He started to move in, but Earl was set for him. The Walls lightning right came over straight and in upper cuts.

247

Harrison pulled away, but the ring had become a cage: Earl followed. Earl's left curled high and hard against Harrison's left eye and dropped him. He took five, got up and was still trying to protect his head after the mandatory eight count.

Walls chased him across the ring and into the corner, a right wracking him back against the turnbuckles. The crowd came roaring to its feet. The crowd knew. Earl knew. Harrison must have sensed what was coming.

A right buckled Harrison's knees and his head slipped outside the ropes. A left hook brought it inside again. Another drove it out again. Harrison's hands came lower as he soaked up each punch. He had been up set for the kill.

A half-dozen lefts and rights showered on his head. Then it came. It was a tremendous, full-sized left hook, with the awesome power of a fist, forearm and shoulder behind it, as Earl twisted to bring it home.

Harrison's head flopped, his legs sagged and he slithered sideways along the ropes. He fell backwards, his shoulders and neck draped over the lower rope.

The fans were startled out of their seats by the savage fury of Earl's attack; they screamed and watched with horrified fascination as the referee counted Harrison out.

The newspaper commentary the next day pointed out that there had only been three other heavyweight fights in the past thirty years that produced the same kind of unbridled fury in the ring.

There was the horrible beating Dempsey gave Willard at Toledo to win the title in 1919: there was the jungle brawl of Dempsey and Luis Firpo at the polo grounds in 1923 and there was the brutal, calculated slaughter of Max Schmeling by Joe Louis in one round in 1938. Only these were comparable to last night's one-man war.

Harrison threw only half a dozen punches; Walls hit with dozens. Harrison proved only that he was a game guy. Said his manager, "I wonder if Walls could have stood up to that kind of · hitting?" The thought occurs, can Marciano, the hard-rock champion, stand up to it?[23]

The look in Olive's eyes, and the grin on her face, made Earl postpone the announcement, the hand-raising and all the rest of the pomp, ceremony and excitement of winning one of his most significant fights. He kissed Olive on the cheek. Everthing else would have to wait. His brothers and sisters were outside the ropes, waiting for a chance to pat their brother's back, a gesture to convey thanks for making the pride of being a Walls even greater than they had already felt. The after-fight party at Jimmy Jones's Toronto home was unsurpassable in laughter, humour and downright fun. Earl held June around the waist. Even though she had not seen the fight, she could sense the huge appreciation everyone felt for what Earl had just done.

She could remember the long hours Earl had spent looking at a film of the first fight, to detect what errors he had made. On many occasions she had even found it necessary to call him to bed, as he would still be watching well past his self-imposed ten o'clock curfew.

She was not surprised that the husband whom she could hardly recognize after the first fight, as he stood in the door-way with closed eyes, hematoma in both cheeks and lips twice their size tattooed with black stitches, was this unmarked Sir Lancelot of the second. He had armed himself with, instead of steel armour, the cloak of weeks of serious training and study. His opponent had no idea that the ring of the first bell marked, not an opportunity to present his boxing skills, but the need to fight for surivival. Harrison had no idea that when Earl Walls sprang from his corner, he was fufulling his destiny. Harrison represented but a minor obstacle in the path of the fugitive slave's descendant.

MILE XLIV

Earl's rubber-clad feet, led on by thoughts of his fighting career, had carried him back to the original homestead of John Freeman Walls. The headstone in the cemetery was like a magnet to Earl's mind. He found himself looking down at the grave for the second time in as many days. He gently ran thick, black fingers under the name on the stone, just as he had done some twenty years ago.

It was October then, and he had driven with June to the homestead. It was his refuge, the place he went when things were troubling his fertile mind, and important decisions needed to be harvested.

As he had so many years ago, he left June at his parents' house to visit. With no conscious forethought, he interrupted his pensive walk to peer at the tombstone of a descendant he had never met but felt drawn to, because of his mother's oft-repeated words.

He remembered the decision he had made so long ago, standing among the stones as he stood now, and smiled.

As he smiled, he knelt down on the thin blanket of snow, which covered his ancestors, black man, white woman. How could it be?

Earl's head bent and a tear fell onto the smooth stone. His whole body shivered from a strange tingling, as it had that day so long ago.

He had felt fulfilled then, because he had made the decision to retire from boxing at the height of his career; he felt fulfilled now because he finally realized his decision had been right.

The words echoed triumphantly out now as they had then:

You are a black, be proud, and the slave's descendant, just as good as anyone.

Just as good as anyone, just as good as anyone. The words echoed in his mind. Olive's words intoxicated him; he realized, finally, that boxing had been only a means to an end, not the end itself.

The determination of the people buried under his knees had given the world eternal proof of racial harmony. In a climate free of racial bigotry, a corner of the world by an untroubled creek, peace and harmony could be reality. That reality had inspired the great grandson of John Freeman and Jane King Walls to fight until he fulfilled his destiny.

As an older and wiser Earl Walls rose from the ground, he spoke. His voice was charged with happiness and pride: "I am the slave's descendant, John Freeman Walls's descendant; twenty-three years ago I showed the world my worth as a boxer, now I feel my worth as a man."

With trembling lips he yelled, "Thank God, thank God." The words echoed throughout the agrarian community proudly, and those within hearing range nodded, not knowing why.

I am the slave's descendant, John Freeman Walls's descendant, Jane King Walls's descendant, just as good as anyone.

The pride manifest in Earl's words symbolized the pride of the entire Walls family, and all families of those courageous black fugitives who braved death to follow the side of the tree the moss grows on, and the light of the north star.

PART VI

1979

Freedom's Hope
Clearwater, Florida

MILE XLV

The Florida sun in early January was a welcome relief to Canadian snowbirds, who were used to much less comfortable weather. As Earl Walls half ran up the third hole of his luxurious Golf and Country Club in Clearwater, the southern sun held even greater significance.

Earl's companions, Dr. Tom Stevens, who was a long-time friend, Cliff and Brad Walls, his brother and nephew respectively, joked about the fact that they needed their carts to keep up to Earl's long stride. Brad, who was studying to be a chiropractor, was worried about Earl's back, due to his awkward swing. Which club to use was decided by Earl's clear, concise mind before he even reached the golf ball. In fact, club selection, stance and swing were certainties; the only uncertainty was where the ball would land, which Earl was reluctant to admit until it actually did turn traitorous in the air. On this peaceful, serene Florida day, Earl could not take solace in blaming the wind and, as his ball landed in the right sand trap, he could only mutter, "Damn."

The eighteen holes of golf that day brought their share of "Oh, damn" from Earl, and "It's just nice to be out here" from Cliff, his brother. At the end, all were in complete agreement that they had a great time. As Earl sat around the luxurious pool and recreation facilities of his condominium, he could not help but be happy. On his right was a glass of gin and tonic with a little touch of lime, and on his left Tom Stevens, his friend. "What more could I ask for?" Earl half muttered to himself. The conversation between Earl and Cliff was light, and touched on how happy they were to have bought this home away from home in Florida and, owing to inflation, how they were almost sorry they hadn't bought a bigger one.

Earl slapped Cliff on the back with thick, black hands, reminders of his great boxing career yet still tempered with gentleness. "Cliff," he said half laughingly, "why did our great grandfather have to leave this warm, southern sun and run north to cold Canada?"

Cliff looked at Earl, half puzzled what to say for a few seconds, and retorted, "Earl, if John Freeman Walls had not escaped along the road from slavery to Canada, you and I would certainly not be playing golf and owning land here in Florida. In fact, if they would have caught the African, he would not have had any descendants at all."

Earl was half startled by Cliff's seriousness, which set off a serious thought in his own mind, a thought that had been haunting him since his induction into the Canadian Boxing Hall of Fame in October 1978. *You are a black, be proud, and the slave's descendant, just as good as anyone.*

Earl sat down and picked up his glass of gin and tonic. As it reached his lips he stopped. "You know, Cliff, you're right."

Tom was lying on the cot beside Earl, his leopard skin bathing suit contrasting with his black body. He had placed a newspaper over his face, but was asked by one of their new white acquaintances and potential friends at the pool, "How are you going to get a tan like that?" Tom was not a patronizing black and certainly not of the Uncle Tom variety or stock, with connotations of servility. He looked at his friend who, for a brief second, thinking he had mistakenly made a racial slur, was labouring over whether or not he should apologize.

Tom recognized this look, which he and other blacks had seen countless times. It was a look that represented a meaningful step towards racial harmony, as it bespoke concern for humans' feelings; but at the same time it indicated a definite need for better understanding and communication between races. Tom jokingly remarked, "I have a year-round tan and do not need any help from the sun." Tom's remark relieved tension and brought laughter and a sense of camaraderie to whites and blacks at the pool. Deeper than this was Tom's concern that his fellow man's feelings, be he white or black, not be hurt over such a trivial comment. Trivial because it could not insult Tom, who was a contemporary American black man, secure, proud and confident about his black skin.

Tom left this thought and, his fertile mind overhearing conversation between his two contemporary Canadian friends, could not help but interject, "Thank God for 1979 in Canada and the United States." Tom stood up. His six-foot frame here in baseball training country was often sought after by autograph seekers. He would sometimes oblige, other times tell the truth. Tom was fanatic about keeping physically fit—once out of necessity, to survive the Ohio ghetto and now out of choice. He wanted to live, and enjoy the fruits of his and society's improvements.

Tom knew even better than Cliff and Earl the significance of being a free black, capable of free choice and movement. Tom was born in Youngstown and educated in podiatry in Cleveland. He had grown up during the civil rights movement, Martin Luther King, black Muslims, riots of 1967, assassinations, the march on Selma, Little Rock seven, civil rights reforms and so on. Further to this, and as a result of the great psychological impact all those events had on him, he had not forgotten his responsibility to help his black brothers and sisters and was still very active in recruiting and encouraging qualified blacks into his profession.

Thus when Tom spoke on this topic of social change, Cliff and Earl listened.

"You know there is much need for improvement in racial harmony in the United States and Canada still, but I certainly would not want to relive the 1960s."

"God, no!" Earl interjected, "and those in the 1960s certainly would not like to relive the 1840s."

Tom had moved to Canada for business reasons. His move had served to enhance his American black experience with a truer concept of Canadian blacks and their problems.

"We, gentlemen, are in a critical, exciting period of history where opportunities are unfolding and enlarging, but critical in the sense that we are not past the point of no return. A prime example of increased opportunities in the United States is OIC."

"Is that like NAACP [National Association for Advancement of Coloured People]?" someone asked.

Tom replied, "No, because OIC's philosophies and principles include the advancement of underprivileged black and white and other minorities and underprivileged groups world-wide, not just in the United States. Opportunities Industrialization Centers [OIC] is one of the most positive non-profit, minority founded organizations ever in the history of the United States. Founded in Philadelphia in 1964 by Reverend Leon Sullivan, it has mushroomed in the past fifteen years to include one hundred forty training and retraining centers in the United States, several in Africa and the Caribbean.

"Gentlemen, it is a minority help and self-help program, which is helping to make racial harmony a reality. But we are not past the point of no return, and programs like OIC must be helped to further its development."

Tom knew he had to elaborate on many programs to the two brothers. Although Cliff and Earl knew about OIC through their sister's involvement with it, they were representative of a lot of Canadian blacks in that their awareness of social changes in the United States was minimal. Earl, at this point, could not resist an emotional thought of international and very personal significance to himself and to Canadian and American black relations. As he poured another ounce of gin and was covering it with tonic, the warm Florida sun was glistening off his black face and masking the piercing stare he was directing at Tom. Tom, if he had not been absorbed in conversation with Cliff, would have jokingly queried Earl's stare. Earl, however, was looking into and through Tom's face. His mind's eye saw some of his good black friends in Canada, other former Americans like Tom: Richie Richardson, owner of Wayne

Distributors in Toronto, who had come here from Pittsburgh twenty years ago (and has not stopped yet); John Henry Jackson, owner of the Underground Railroad Restaurant in Toronto, an eatery of international repute; Hartiman Curitan, former all-American and Hamilton Tiger-cat football great were but a few of the people brought into immediate focus in his mind.

He continued to remember how, when they first moved to Canada, they were opinionated and would even, at times, feel superior to their black brothers in Canada. As time went on, however, he could almost sense them respecting the fact that Canadian blacks had been allowed to accept the Canadian white culture they found themselves in. They had been assimilated by that culture while still using it to their best advantage and without loss of dignity.

The precedent set by Governor Graves Simcoe in 1793, which abolished slavery in Canada and opened the road to the underground railroad and thousands of slaves, gave rise, in the next centuries, to no real need for radical social upheaval. In fact, Canadian black activism existed directly in proportion to Canadian white society pressures. These pressures, though present, were historically sporadic and much less organized than in the United States.

Nonetheless, Earl had to admit that his friends who had lived on both sides of the border had noticed a certain lack of industriousness in many Canadian blacks, caused by too easy a sociological road. The American black who could not, even though legally free, go into white establishments for his sustenance, had to take the initiative out of necessity. He provided his own businesses and staged his own reforms. This gave him an advantage not shared by many black Canadians. His American friends, however, were rewarded by the knowledge that black Canadians were very appreciative of and thankful for their American black brothers' hard-fought climb towards racial equality. As Earl saw the smile coming to Tom's American face, Tom realized he reflected the positive feelings of Rich, John, Hardi and countless others as he talked to his two Canadian friends. He was proud to know them, and they him.

The conversation continued, interrupted only by the need for more liquid refreshments or a swim. As Tom became more intense in his description of society past and present, Earl's thoughts lingered in the past: *You are a Walls, be proud, and the slave's descendant.*

While Earl was deep in thought and Tom in conversation, Billie, June and Laverda came down the elevator from their condominium anxious to visit with their husbands, and share with them their shopping extravagances. They knew only too well that their husbands would hope they had limited things to window shopping.

A small lizard ran over Laverda's foot and she let out an instinctual shriek; the laughter from the three girls was the only thing that broke up Earl's thought pattern. As he looked at his wife, June, coming towards him, he smiled and said, "She is another reason I am glad John Freeman escaped to Canada."

The plane ride back to Toronto took two hours. Packed into those two hours were reminisences of how warm and inviting Florida was, how comfortable the condominium was and how enjoyable it had been to play eighteen holes of golf each day with his friend and relatives. Earl's mind was refreshed and he felt pride welling up inside at the thought of returning to the Earl Walls Real Estate Company on Monday. The only thought that marred the trip was his remembering a poolside reading of the recent edition of a national magazine that depicted racial unrest in South Africa.

"Could it be starting all over again?" Earl thought. "One hundred thirty-three years later, to be pressured and harrassed to stay in Canada. Why, when Martin Luther King, John F. Kennedy and John Freeman Walls risked their lives for freedom, does racial bigotry and hatred creep in again, even to this haven of potential paradise and harmony in Clearwater, Florida? Is Tom right, is it really a critical time? Are we past the point of no return? We must move in harmony and not erase good."

Mankind must follow the Road to Somewhere as did John, of African descent, and Jane, of Irish and Scottish, who died in racial harmony and love, propagating new generations of proud people who were, as in the words of Olive, *just as good as anyone.*

Dr. Bryan E. Walls with Esther Gordy Edwards founder; chief executive officer of Motown Historical Museum, Inc. Hitsville U.S.A., Detroit, Michigan; Sister Museum of the John Freeman Walls Historic Site and Underground Railroad Museum, Windsor, Canada.

The epilogue to this book is in the form of a song. Fugitive slaves lived the lyrics and their descendants put them to music.

Stephen Bard – From the forth-coming album "The Road That Led To Somewhere"   CD Includes Digital Video

Mickey Yannich   Esther Gordy Edwards   Dr. Bryan E. Walls

"In 1989 when I first visited the John Freeman Walls Historic Site and Underground Railroad Museum in Ontario Canada, I said to Bryan and Allen Walls; you don't know what you have here. Your site is so unique from other Underground Railroad museums that I have visited. Visiting here is like travelling the nineteenth century Underground Railroad, you experience a journey that rekindles memories of past history.

The uniqueness, quality and action of the museum experience continues in these songs produced by Mickey Yannich and inspired by Bryan's book

The Road That Led To Somewhere."

*Since 1989 the Motown Historical Museum and the John Freeman Walls Historic Site and Underground Railroad Museum, although independent of each other, have evolved by mutual consent into sister museums.

Esther Gordy Edwards

Founder/Chief Executive Officer
Motown Historical Museum, Inc.
2648 West Grand Boulevard
Detroit, Michigan 48208-1237

Let's Go There
(Dr. Bryan E. Walls, Anna Davis
Christine Tripp, Mickey Yannich,
J. Mulrenan)
We will lift our hands up high
With respect for human kind
Let's go there (let's go there)

We will promote diversity
Peace and love and harmony
Let's go there (let's go there)

Love is the innocence of youth
We're in the candle lighted booth
Let's go there (let's go there)

Spirit tell us what to do
Our arms reach out to you
Let's go there (let's go there)

Love makes life and joy come true
Freedom all for me and you
Let's go there (let's go there)

Let's have fun along the way
Laugh and sing and dance and play
Let's go there (let's go there)

Hate destroys all that is kind
Yeah, it cuts the ties that bind
Don't go there (don't go there)

Peace and love and harmony
All respect diversity
Let's go there (let's go there)
Sax solo

Hate destroys all that is kind
Yeah, it cuts the ties that bind
Don't go there (don't go there)

Peace and love and harmony
All respect diversity
Let's go there (let's go there)

PUBLISHED BY CENPRO MUSIC / OLIVE PUBLISHING CO. LTD.

Ooo love is the innocence of youth
Us in the candle lighted booth
Let's go there (let's go there)

Spirit tell us what to do
Our arms reach out to you
Let's go there (let's go there)
Let's go there (let's go there)
Let's go there (let's go there)

Only The Rainbow
(Stephen Bard)

A black boy playing master
His white friend playing slave
Whipped within an inch of his life
This day for not behaving
Saved there by his best friend from a father's rage
Neither one could understand the violence of the age

Chorus   There is no black
                  There is no white
                  All the colors make up the light
                  If one is lost, the world is night
                  Only the rainbow

Their childhood years together
A bound of brotherhood
This hatred between color
Something neither ever understood
Hungry for escape he stayed a slave to save his
friend
A sacrifice he made on which a brother could
depend
Chorus (repeated)
A white man on his deathbed
A black man by his side
Entrusting wife and children to his friend
before he died
One man frees another
That he himself may die free
Open up our eyes with love that we may all
see Lord
Chorus (repeated)

PUBLISHED BY CENPRO MUSIC/OLIVE PUBLISHING CO. LTD.

FOOTNOTES

PART I

1 National Boxing Magazine Rating.

PART II

1 Research data of Floyd B. Walls II, Member of the Michigan Genealogical Society, 1976-1979.
2 Ibid.
3 Signed affidavit of 95-year-old Aunt Stella Butler, 94-year-old Mr. Glenn, 78-year-old Frank Walls, 80-year-old Mr. Johnson.
4 Research data of Floyd B. Walls II, Member of the Michigan Genealogical Society, 1976-1979.
5 Bible, Proverb 3; actually John's favourite passage, confirmed by Stella Butler.
6 Research data of Dr. Bryan E. Walls, 1976-1979.
7 Speech of Dr. Martin Luther King, Jr., "March on Washington".
8 George M. Allen, "Rare Song Collection", University of Michigan.
9 Research data of Dr. Bryan E. Walls, 1976-1979.

PART III, PART IV

1 Benjamin Drew, *The Narratives of Fugitive Slaves in Canada*, Toronto: Coles Publishing Company, 1972, p.349
2 Ibid., p. 348.
3 Ibid., p. 342.
4 Ibid., p. 347.
5 Ibid., p. 342.
6 Ibid., p. 321.
7 Ibid., p. 322.
8 Ibid., p. 326.

9   Ibid., p. 367.
10 Ibid., p. 368.
11 Benjamin Drew, *The Narratives of Fugitive Slaves in Canada*, Toronto: Coles Publishing Company, 1972, p. 369
12 Ibid., p. 291.
13 Ibid., p. 234.
14 Ibid., p. 308.
15 Ibid., p. 234.
16 Research data of Floyd B. Walls II, Member of the Michigan Genealogical Society, 1976-1979.
17 Refrain of song, written by Dr. Bryan E. Walls in consultation with Jerry R. Walls.
18 Benjamin Drew, *The Narratives of Fugitive Slaves in Canada*, Toronto: Coles Publishing Company, 1972, p. 236.

PART V

1   Newspaper clipping from the Sports Section of the *Vancouver Sun*, Vancouver, British Columbia, Canada.
2   Newspaper clipping from the Sports Section of the *Edmonton Tribune*, Edmonton, Alberta, Canada.
3   Excerpt from *The Canadian Heavyweight Boxing Championship Souvenir Program*, Friday, June 13, 1952.
4   Ibid.
5   Ibid.
6   Newspaper clipping from the Sports Section of the *Edmonton Journal*, Edmonton, Alberta, Canada.
7   Ibid.
8   Ibid.
9   Ibid.
10 Ibid.

11 Ibid.
12 Ibid.
13 Ibid.
14 Ibid.
15 Newspaper clipping from the Sports Section of the *Edmonton Tribune*, Edmonton, Alberta, Canada.
16 Ibid.
17 Newspaper clipping from the Sports Section of the *Edmonton Journal*, Edmonton, Alberta Canada.
18 Ibid.
19 Newspaper clipping from the Sports Section of the *Toronto Star*, Toronto, Ontario, Canada.
20 Newspaper clipping from the Sports Section of the *Toronto Telegram*, Toronto, Ontario, Canada.
21 Ibid.
22 Ibid.
23 Ibid.

This letter, which Jane received from Mary Stout in 1854, has been puzzling the Walls family since it was discovered more than twenty years ago. It has been analyzed as knitting instructions, the musical notes for a song or an abolitionist code of some kind. But the puzzle remains unsolved.

Puzzle buffs and amateur—or professional—decoders are invited to send their ideas to Olive Publishing Company.

About the Author

DR. BRYAN E. WALLS

Dr. Walls was born a proud Canadian on a farm near a little place called Puce, Ontario, outside of Windsor, in 1946. His ancestors before him, back to a time before the end of slavery in the United States, were also proud. He was first educated in the same one room schoolhouse as they were, until he moved to the seemingly big (compared to his humble beginnings) city of Windsor.

He proceeded to Assumption High School, and in his senior year became the first Baptist student council president in this Catholic School. In short, he was learning to successfully know and harmoniously enjoy the people he met, and the culture in which he found himself.

After high school, Dr. Walls enrolled in the University of Detroit where he received a first-hand foundation for understanding and insight into American society.

He transferred to the University of Windsor and graduated in 1969 with a Bachelor of Science degree before proceeding to the University of Toronto.

In Toronto he was rewarded again in terms of his awareness and understanding; he graduated with a Doctor of Dental Surgery Degree in 1973, and he learned what it meant to have a true feeling of being Canadian. Added to Dr. Walls' list of credentials are:

ACTIVITIES: founder and co-curator, of the John Freeman Walls Historic Site and Underground Railroad Museum in Puce, Ontario; a noted historian and lecturer on, how the Underground Railroad can teach Math and Science, anti-bullying and little-known African Diaspora history; a deacon of the historic First Baptist Church Puce, founded by his ancestors in 1846; author of The Road That Led To Somewhere (based on a true story), of the Underground Railroad; and has co-authored an educational study unit for teachers and students

AFFILIATIONS: Past President of the Essex County Dental Society; past board secretary of the Ontario Heritage Foundation; Past President of the Ontario Historical Society, founded in 1888; committee member of the Metropolitan Toronto Police Services Recruiting Unit

HONORS: several including: Chancellor's Award, Iona College University of Windsor 2002; Order of Ontario, in 1994; Ontario Government Outstanding Achievement for Volunteers, in 1992; Lamp of Learning Award, Ontario Secondary School Teachers Federation (OSSTF), in 1989; Hon. Doctor of Humanities, Urban Bible College, Detroit, in 1982

WORKS: The Road That Led To Somewhere, concept album 2002; The Road That Led To Somewhere, 1980;

EDUCATION: screenwriting, 1998 Ryerson; Dr. Dental Surgery, 1973 University of Toronto; BSc 1969, University of Windsor

Dr. Walls has been tireless in his efforts to advance education and in extolling the importance of the equal sisterhood and brotherhood of mankind. His novel The Road That Led To Somewhere picks up where Uncle Tom's Cabin leaves off and the book is a tool he uses to achieve his goals. He has gathered resource material for many years on the first great freedom movement of the Americas - THE UNDERGROUND RAILROAD, a virtually forgotten portion of Canadian and American history. This material is a source of information for his writing and lecturing. The resources are presently being used by Bryan and his brothers in writing a Unit of Study at the request of the Windsor Board of Education so this important history can be taught in the Canadian and American school system.

Bryan has also spearheaded the development and preservation of his family's homestead known as THE UNDERGROUND RAILROAD MUSEUM AND THE JOHN FREEMAN WALLS HISTORIC SITE. The property was purchased in 1846 by his great-great grandfather from the Refugee Home Society. This was an abolitionist organization who received tracts of land from the Canadian government to be resold to escaped fugitive slaves.

Dr. Walls intentions are to not only provide the vehicle for teaching this history in the schools with the use of his book, but he is also providing a creative and unique hands-on museum to bring alive the past for students.

BIBLIOGRAPHY

Drew, Benjamin. *The Narratives of Fugitive Slaves in Canada*. Toronto: Coles Publishing Company, 1972.
Newspaper clippings from: *Edmonton Journal, Edmonton Tribune,* Ford Local 200 Union *News* in Windsor, The *Toronto Star,* Toronto *Telegram,* The Canadian Heavyweight Boxing Championship Souvenir Program of Friday, June 13, 1952, *Vancouver Sun, Windsor Star.*

Typesetting: ATTIC TYPESETTING

Book assembly: Pam Davies
Cover art and design: Judy de Passio
This book is set in twelve-point Sabon.

F.B. Tedford Graphics salutes Dr. Bryan Walls' accomplishment with *The Road That Led To Somewhere.* We are proud to have been of assistance in this effort.

"This book is an inspired work that has a message for Christians and non-Christians."

Bishop F.A. Walls
Church of God in Christ
Ypsilanti, Michigan

"I am confident that your endeavour will have lasting value for students and adults in this area."

Walter P. Willms
Director of Education
Windsor, Canada

"In The Road That Led To Somewhere students can easily identify with John Freeman Walls and his family as they experienced homesteading and established a fine life. Dr. Walls' book makes these people "read" bringing to life their fears, strengths, love and tolerance of others."

Sue Zanin
President of District 1,
Ontario Secondary School Teachers Federation

"There are many good things about this book...the adventure of escape, discovering new land, and people."

Ernest J. Gaines
Author of the Autobiography of Miss Jane Pitman

"Others read history. The difference is that Dr. Walls decided to bring it alive, and he succeeded."

Jim Head
Ontario Secondary School
Teachers Federation Provincial President.

"From the book The Road That Led To Somewhere, I learned that if you truly believe in yourself and the good Lord you can be a somebody and accomplish any goal you want. This book I will treasure all my life."

James Salmons - Student

"In the name of the staff and students of William Hands Secondary School, I wish to express our heartfelt thanks to Dr. Walls for taking the time to come and talk to us about the history and the contribution to Canadian life of his family.

Andre Comeau
Social Science Teacher
Windsor Board of Education

"Dr. Walls commitment to Canada's multicultural heritage as a pillar of this country's identity has prevailed at all times."

Dr. Jamie L. Henderson
Ed. D. Co-ordinator of Social Sciences,
Windsor Board of Education, Canada.

"By documenting one family's journey on the Underground Railroad, the novel helps students understand their own heritage and that of others and appreciate the need for all people to live in peace and racial harmony."

David W. Lawson
Assistant Co-ordinator, Race Relations,
Windsor Board of Education, Canada

"Visiting the John Freeman Walls Historic Site and Underground Railroad Museum is like taking a journey...you get an action kind of story."

Esther Gordy Edwards
Senior Vice-President of Motown Productions
and Director of the Motown
Historical Museum in Detroit, Michigan

"Dr. Walls' book certainly gives the public and scholars a greater insight into and appreciation of the Walls family. You have made a significant contribution to Canadian black history--keep up the good work and continue to write."

Dr. Daniel G. Hill
Ombudsman of Ontario, Canada
and author of the acclaimed book "The Freedom Seekers"

"The Road That Led To Somewhere tells of an unique master-slave relationship that shows the multidimensional aspect of the 'Peculiar institution'. The novel leads us from North Carolina, U.S. to Maidstone Township, Canada, from slavery to freedom, and serfdom to citizenship."

Dr. Norman McCrae
Co-ordinator of Social Studies, Detroit Public Schools
Detroit, Michigan, U.S.A.

"I have found your book to be most interesting, inspiring, consoling and invigorating. It gives the reader a feel of hope that there is still a good chance for racial harmony. I would definitely recommend it to be used at all levels of the educational system. It is definitely an asset to the different sociological and historical schools of thought in North America."

E. Oscar Brathwaite
President of Canadian Alliance of Black Education

"Dr. Walls' novel reveals to all students a part of Canadian reality that has been neglected - a record of Black roots and achievement. The book also provides opportunities for all students to develop a sense of identity and a positive self concept by stimulating interest in their own heritage."

Spurgeon G. Montague
Consultant - Special Education Services
Windsor Board of Education, Canada.

Towards Multiculturalism

Dr. Bryan Walls received the 1989 Lamp of Learning Award from the Ontario Secondary School Teachers' Federation at a meeting of the Federation's Provincial Council in Toronto, Canada. The award is the highest honour which OSSTF can pay a non-teacher for his contributions to Secondary Education.

Dr. Walls was accompanied by his family who assisted him in turning a Maidstone Township cabin once used as an underground railway outlet into a Historical Museum. The site is named for their great-great grandfather, John Freeman Walls, who escaped slavery in North Carolina in 1846 and built the cabin that year.

The Award-winning documented novel - The Road That Led To Somewhere is suitable for grades 4-10. It's part of a dynamically important unit on the underground railroad in Canada.

> *— can be used for English, Social Studies, Theatre, Etc... This Novel Study:*
> *— follows ministry documents*
> *— offers a wide variety of styles: large and small group activities; learning centres; independent projects and open-ended materials*
> *— includes assessment strategies and answer keys where appropriate.*

From the office of the Chief of Police
Volume 17 Number 6
August 1997

Metro Comes Through Again

COMBATTING HATRED, VIOLENCE AND RACISM THROUGH EDUCATION

Using history and stories of personal family struggles is an effective way to teach children about racism. Stories surrounding the Underground Railroad provide insight into a period of Canada's history and the people who struggled to reach freedom.

Metro's Hate Crime Unit began working with the Walls family last fall. Officers may remember Earl Walls from the Sunshine Games at Variety Village. Dr. Bryan Walls, nephew of Canadian boxer Earl Walls, wrote the book, "The Road That Led To Somewhere." The book is the story of the Walls family's escape to Canada in the 1800's. The book and a lesson plan are used by teachers to combine a history and human rights lesson.

The Walls family has maintained the John Freeman Walls Historic Site and Underground Railroad Museum, the site of Earl Walls' great-grandfather's house.

In January, Dr. Walls presented the Chief with a picture depicting the theme of the site "Equal sisterhood and Brotherhood of humankind." Divisional Unit Commanders will also receive a copy of the picture, to show Metro Police's commitment to ending racial violence.